Fortunate Soul

Michael Cantwell

To Kristen & Dan, two souls joined forever.

Please enjoy more titles from Michael Cantwell

A Beautiful Song

Three Long Days

Soul Intentions

Soul Directive

www.ksmmike.com

1

*S*adness and euphoria are intertwined within the fabrics of our lives. I should know; they are the emotional landscape I've crossed back and forth for decades. I never wanted for material items, mine were more spiritual. Maybe I didn't care about the material things because I never had to think about them. They were always provided to me by my fellow disciples. The spiritual ones were developed over decades of following my instincts and intensive education. My entire life was dedicated to my craft, which led me to another dangerous exchange between sadness and euphoria.

My name is Caeles Novo. My grandfather believed I was sent from the heavens to change the ways of our disciples who have misplaced their values. This is why I was given my particular name. You won't know me. I work in the shadows. I look like any other human wandering the busy streets of large cities. I can also appear as a broken man on the side of a dusty country road. That's the idea.

My education and that of my fellow disciples was more extensive than most who travel the earth. My life expectancy was once more than three times longer than ordinary humans, so my structured learning lasted three times longer as well. Most would have you believe that more education could only be of value. Think again. Our superiority has destroyed our way of life. We are not ordinary humans.

Despite my superior intelligence, I was victimized by some who no longer found my way of leadership in compliance with their own way of life. Priorities changed for some, mine were more secure. My fellow disciples and I were trained for one mission in life. I followed my gut and continued our predetermined journey, others became wayward. I again crossed over from euphoria to sadness. I realized I lost the ability given to me from the heavens and was destined to do. In those mere seconds of self-realization, when you have once again crisscrossed back to the other side, you must decide who you are as an individual, leader, husband and father.

Some are designed to lead, while others follow. Some are dominant. Others live a more submissive way of life. Some live conservative lives while others want to change the structure of every institution they meet. Some are men, some are women. Some have dark skins, others the shade of cream. None of that mattered to me. I only cared about the next soul on my list. I could read souls like some read the daily newspaper. If yours was broken, I stole it. That was my mission in life. I make no apologies for who I am. If you couldn't appreciate all that life had bestowed upon you, welcome to my list.

I was trained to be an unseen shadow. You never found me. I found you. When I did, you would either fall to the ground or barely feel a scratch. Everyone has a soul. However, depending on how much one believes they own a soul, determines how much the loss affects them. Non-believers are fools. I know the truth. I stole your most prized possession if you made my list of being a dark soul. I've taken from some who laugh in my face, or cry for redemption within moments of my thievery. Either way, I was completing what I was born to do.

If I wasn't taking your soul, one of my fellow disciples would do so with as much passion as me. After all, we trained for fifty years to be experts in our decree sent from the Lord of Life. However, because of our extensive education, some of our disciples evolved past being mere soul stealers. For their sin in wandering away from our decree, I will destroy their perfect lives.

However, I am now the broken one.

I was so involved in restoring the number of soul stealers on earth, being the leader on our High Council, as well as a good husband and father, I never saw the fact that our disciples had become leaders in their communities across the globe. The less than thirty of us who did remain loyal to our goals on earth, were constantly on a mission attempting to steal souls. That's where our power resides. If we are no longer removing souls, we become mere mortals. Greed for power and money while abandoning our true task has become our collective downfall.

Because I no longer had my ability, to see into, and remove souls, I was replaced as leader of the High Council. Members of the Council had decided long before my appointment as leader, ruling the world's economy was a better option for our disciples than to remain loyal to our original decree. Before they removed me, I was driven to make sure no mistakes were made in taking souls not dark enough to be stolen. I became dangerous. I would on occasion, return a soul which was preposterous to our leaders. My own kind set out to destroy me. They succeeded.

The crossroads where sadness and euphoria intertwine had found me once again. Many days came and went where I wanted no responsibility to anyone but my family. But that day had arrived without my consent. My destiny was stolen from me. I had to ask myself, could being restricted to being only a good husband and father be the path to euphoria, or the conduit of sadness? I had to answer one important question. Did I still have a burning desire to be the ultimate soul stealer and follow my mission sent from the heavens?

Kalani had been my wife and confidant for decades. She was furious when she heard what our fellow disciples had done to me. It took all of my best powers of persuasion to calm her over the phone and not allow her to seek revenge. I didn't know what my response to my newly formed sworn enemies would be, but sending my wife on a suicide operation was not option one. She always wanted to protect me, as I did her, but we needed to think through our next move.

Kalani was on assignment the day we met in Hawaii where she was born and raised. I was on vacation from removing my first few souls when we met. Neither of us had any idea we were both soul stealers until days after our initial encounter. She found herself in some trouble with the local band of drug traffickers on Oahu, when we were both shoved off the road while bike riding. When the attacker stepped out of the car to finish his task, I instinctively removed the soul of her attacker. I caught grief with our Council for that mishap. It also exposed my identity as a soul stealer to my future wife. It wasn't until later that she admitted we shared more in common than our love.

We were married soon after and have been faithful companions ever since. She got herself into trouble with the Council protecting me, as I have her, more than once. We don't see each other as much as we would like because of our extensive travels, but we attempt to live as a normal family as much as possible.

Kalani and I wanted to grow our family. At the time of my removal as leader, we had one son, Nicon. He was training to be a soul stealer and already had what would be equivalent to a Master's Degree in Business. Because we aged slower than full blooded humans, our son looked to be a child of seven or eight but was already nearing his twenty- fourth birthday. Kalani and I didn't want to wait much longer to make a decision about having another child.

The tender ages were the toughest for our disciples. We are far more educated than others who look our age, until we appear to be in our late twenties. By the time we look to be twenty, we have traveled the world usually more than once, speak multiple languages, have read all the classic literature, explored many of the world's great museums, and lived with one or more ancient culture. We are immune to most earthly diseases but we're not super human. When attacked with common weapons such as a knife or bullet, we are wounded like an ordinary human. Those were the difficult years for our son, to look so young, yet still be so mature.

It wasn't easy for Nic to associate with others who appeared his age on a physical level. He played little league baseball, and other physical activities with children who looked his age, but weren't. He was forbidden to tell the other kids he went to the World Series at Yankee Stadium several years before they were even born. He had the mind of a student with an MBA degree, but he still struck out like an eight year old boy. That frustrated him to no end. But he needed the physical work as much as the mental side of life.

My dilemma was to decide if I had become one of those people who couldn't appreciate all that was given to him or her. My choice was to live a secure and peaceful life with my wife and son, or seek revenge on the people who removed my ability to do what I was destined to do. I was not put on this earth to live out my remaining years selling used cars but I was a broken man.

I needed to make a decision. One issue was that the one person who could assist me with regaining my power was not exactly my best friend. I was told by my former Council members that Doctor Grayson Winfield created the potion which blocks my ability to remove souls. It was possible he had created such an evil toxin, but I had been misled so many times. The truth was always complicated.

I returned home to California to Kalani with my wounded ego and damaged self to figure out what to do with my life. She looked as radiant as ever. Her dark olive skin and shiny black straight hair that reached an inch above her waistline hadn't altered since the day we met. Her jade colored eyes and Polynesian shape that curved in all the proper places still made me smile knowing she was my one and only. A few had tempted me to stray over the years, but Kalani would always be my one true love.

My wife knew my short comings. "So, Cale dear, since you plan to sit on the sofa watching the woman from New York tell fortunes and do your best to cook us all dinner, does this mean you aren't the best soul stealer now? I will admit maybe you were better at kicking ass and taking names than you are a cook, but hey, at least I know now I can buy you cook books for Christmas."

She looked directly into my eyes, and offered me her stare

she used when she wanted to challenge me. I wasn't biting. She continued.

"But then again, we really don't know if your numbers were legit since you liked to return half of souls you stole. At least when I take one, they stay taken. It can be official now that I'm the best. I still think while you were sitting on the Council, Bink gave you far too many easy assignments. I had to earn all of mine slinking down dark alleys, chasing violent criminals. Your targets were white collar professionals who have to take in a Stallone flick to see a gun."

Another stare, only this time longer.

"I'm sorry I introduced you to that Timmons woman, Cale. I might tease you, but I never tried to get the best of ya. It seems she did. I'm sorry."

That was the wound. Fireworks started to blast through my skull. A pain rushed from my head down to my gut and back up again. It was as if someone was playing a game of pong between my head and belly using a bottle rocket as the pong ball.

"That woman didn't get the best of me. And don't you ever, ever suggest she did. Just for that, I'm not making you any dinner tonight!"

I could see Kalani's ruby lips curl at each end, knowing she made me realize, I was the best ever. Not Tasha Timmons, not Charon Orcus, Peter Pascal, or any of the others who schemed to derail me, could keep me on that blasted sofa that sagged in the middle. I ordered take out for Kalani and mapped out how to proceed.

At my core, I was and always would be a collector of broken souls. There were occasions when I did find reason to return one, because deep inside I believed in redemption. I needed to come to grips with that.

Being a husband and father didn't have to be secondary to my work. I think my conscience had been getting the better of me since my father had always been in the house with me and didn't travel. I would spend time with Nic and Kalani but it never seemed to be enough. In that regard, I was like most humans.

It was imperative I board the first available flight to Texas to speak with Doctor Grayson Winfield. The desire to be the best soul stealer as well as to restore our disciples to prominence had returned. Kalani assured me, I had made the right decision. She kissed me as I made my way towards the front door of our modest home.

"I married you because of who you are, Cale, not because of something you're not. If I wanted someone at home cooking dinner and polishing the silver, I woulda married someone else. It's important to me that you are happy in who you are. Go be that person again."

Kalani knew how to motivate me in those rare times where I felt lost. My personal pity party had ended. It was now time to seek my destiny not because my grandfather assured me he knew what it was, or because I was told it was sent from the heavens.

For the first time in my life, I was one hundred percent certain of my chosen path. Life is not a simple choice of one direction or another. It's a long complicated one with peaks and valleys filled with every emotion one can imagine. I had long been on my journey. This slight detour wasn't about to alter my destiny and who I was as a person.

I never thought I would return to Winfield's office, but there I was. I walked in the door to find Nurse Simon sitting behind her desk.

"Good afternoon, Nurse Simon. I need to speak with Doctor Winfield. It's an emergency."

"Well hello, sugar, Rose sure has missed seeing you. How you been?"

"Rose? What are you doing here? Where is Doc Winfield?"

Rose stood up from behind the desk, walked over and put her arms around me. She offered a loving hug; then whispered in my ear.

"I told you, sugar, Rose would take care of everything and she has."

2

The only lights turned on in the office were in the main entrance. The long hallway to Winfield's office was dark and even creepier looking than I remembered. The phones were silent. No one was waiting to see the Doctor. I unlocked from Rose's hug and moved backwards to regain my personal space.

"Rose, what do you mean, you took care of everything? I need to see Doc Winfield and I need to see him now!"

The woman in front of me flashed a soft smile and retreated in the direction of her desk.

"Mr. Novo, I was fixin to call ya. I didn't know what ta do. This is the second day I've come ta work and the Doctor hasn't been here. Most times he lets me know if he's gonna be outta town for a conference or sumtin. But there's nuttin on the schedule. I tried calling his house a few times. I even drove by and knocked on the door this morning. I was picking through ma purse looking for that card ya gave me. You told me if I ever needed sumtin to ring ya. Like magic, ya always seem ta appear."

The tone in her voice had changed. Her demeanor was softer.

Rose had again become Nurse Taylor Simon. I didn't have time to play mental games with this disturbed woman. I needed to find Winfield. Winfield was my best option at becoming a soul stealer and leader of our disciples again. Unfortunately for me, this woman was my only real starting point.

"Nurse Simon, when was the last time you saw Doctor Winfield?"

She frowned at me then sat in her desk chair. She crossed her legs and shimmied her tight skirt down her perfectly shaped thigh. She then had a puzzled look on her face.

"It was the craziest thing, Mr. Novo. The Doctor and I were having a lovely dinner a couple of nights ago and the next thing I remember, I woke up in ma apartment. I haven't the slightest idea how that happened. But that night at dinner, well, that's the last time I saw him. I hope nuttin bad happened to em."

"I need you to think real hard. Did anyone come over and speak with the two of you, or did Doc seem nervous? Did he mention anything to you that seemed odd or out of place?"

"No, not really. He takes me there a couple times a month. He says we go there cause he likes the piano player who's there on the weekends, but I think its cause no one ever bugs him there. We've gone ta other places and sure enough as soon as we sit down, somebody always spots him and wants ta say howdy. I don't know if ya know this or not, but Grayson is not the most sociable critter."

I had to chuckle. That was possibly the sanest thought this deranged character ever had.

"So, you are out to dinner and you woke up home alone the next morning? You don't remember how you ended up there? Were you drinking?"

"Mr. Novo, I know you and I don't know each other all social like, but one thing I'm not is a drunkard. I have a one drink limit or I turn into a giggle monster."

"I'm sorry Nurse Simon. I didn't mean to insult you. I was only trying to figure out how you ended up home alone and what happened to Doc Winfield. Are you sure nothing seemed suspicious to you that night?"

Nurse Simon swiveled in her chair and bit her upper lip before replying.

"I don't reckon this would be considered suspicious, but he did keep trying to run his fingers up my skirt during dinner. I don't recall him ever doing that in pubic before."

I didn't want to draw conclusions too quickly but I was starting to think that Doc was too frisky with his nurse in public and Rose didn't take too kindly to his actions. She was the protector of the three trapped inside of one body.

"Ok, Nurse Simon, make sure you have my number. I am going to make a call and see if I can run down Doc Winfield."

I moved to the other section of the room, near the window and called my old buddy Special Agent Elliot Nesstor. I'd given him leads for some of his biggest busts of his career. In return, he helped me many times with investigative favors. I'd known him since he was a detective back in Chicago, where we were both started our careers.

"Novo, I don't know what you want now, but I have less than five hundred days till my retirement. Don't get me in any jackpots with your next request."

I never knew what to expect from Nesstor and his moods. But I knew him as well as he knew himself. My wife Kalani had removed his soul many years ago. I risked my own life returning it. So he was the only law enforcement officer I knew, who did believe in my abilities.

"It is nothing bad, Elliot. And why do you want to retire? There is no way that wife of yours wants you under her feet at home. Your kids must be old enough to have their own families. I never saw you as the retiring type."

"Ah, it's a forced retirement, Cale. Damn government cutbacks and all. Once you hit your early sixties round here, they're looking to shove you out. If I take early retirement before I hit sixty-five, I'm still going to have a nice pension. My back's been barking at me for years, so I think another year and a half and I'll hang up the badge. Who knows, maybe I'll move to Florida and play golf with your dad."

This was unsettling news. Without knowing who I could trust inside any of the government departments any longer, I needed Nesstor more than ever.

"Well, Elliot, I will miss you. But for now, I have a big problem. The one guy who can help me has gone missing. I have my suspicions as to who might know where he is, but she, well, let's just say it can be complicated."

Nesstor laughed and replied. "Is it ever not complicated with you? And what's the problem? Did that cute wife of yours get caught up with drug runners again, or maybe borrow someone's soul she shouldn't have?"

I debated for a moment before I told him the truth. He would believe me.

"Elliot, this is bad. I have lost my ability to steal souls. My former Council members set me up and the guy I'm looking for, he's the guy who created the potion that did it. I need to find him so hopefully he can reverse it."

The phone went silent for a moment before Nesstor responded. "Did I hear you right? You lost that special voodoo thing you do? What about Kalani? And why the hell did your people do that to you? I thought you were the leader of the band?"

"You heard me right, Elliot. Not only am I neutered; I was removed as the leader. It is a long story and maybe one day we can meet up and I will fill you in, but for now, I have to find a Doctor Grayson Winfield. He has an office here in Texas. I think I might have asked you to run a background check on him years ago. Yes, he's one of us soul stealers, but he's never practiced it. Doc Winfield is an internationally known blood specialist looking to cure cancer."

"Yea, I do remember you asking me to look into him before. Why do you think he's gone missing? Did you file a local missing persons report?"

"Elliot, like I said, it is complicated. Do me a favor and have your local boys keep an eye out for any floaters or maybe someone who shows up dead in a hotel with no identification. I would appreciate the head's up. I need to find this guy. And by the way, once I get my power back, I might have some of the best leads for you, I have ever had. You can retire with a big gold star across your chest."

"Soul Man, I'm not sure what you are up to now, but if he turns up, I'll give you a shout."

I hung up from Nesstor and turned from peering out the window and back towards the center of the room. Nurse Simon was within a body length of me. She was looking directly at me with a frown.

"Sugar, why would you call that nice man looking for that horrid doctor? I already told you that Rose took care of everything."

It wasn't Nurse Simon, but Rose. This was only the second time this person who I knew as three, switched so easily between personalities. Usually, only Nurse Simon made an appearance in the office. Rose would appear later in the evening and Isabella would work in the library on weekends. It was rare for her to be bouncing back and forth like this. Maybe I could use this to my advantage.

"Rose, please understand. I need to find Doc Winfield. If you know where he is, you need to tell me. I don't know who you think you were helping; or what you thought you were taking care of, but it's time you tell me where he is."

"That man called Izzy his baby girl. Then he slid his chilled boney fingers under her skirt while she was eating. That was unacceptable to Rose. He was molesting a child. Rose makes men like that pay."

"Rose, he wasn't molesting a child, he was seducing his lover. Maybe it wasn't the best timing but that's what was taking place."

Rose gave me a look of disgust before moving back into my personal space. She slowly ran her tongue up the side of my neck and bit the bottom of my earlobe. She then whispered in my ear at a level that was barely audible.

"Rose knows the difference between seduction and molestation. Now if you want me to tell you about your evil doctor, there is something you must promise Rose. She knows you are a man of honor who has special powers. You are going to forever use those powers when Rose calls for you. If not, your child molester will die."

She then reached down and squeezed between my legs.

"Ahhhh, what the hell was that for Rose? That frigging hurt!" I tried to break free.

After a couple of seconds she released her grip and kissed my cheek. Rose moved back far enough so I could focus on her face. I exploded with pain.

"Rose knows the difference between joy and pain. If you ever doubt her again, you will be reminded. Don't make Rose remind you. Now, do you want to hear Rose's offer or not?"

Of course I wanted to hear her offer. Before I could say anything she continued.

"Rose read the reports. She has listened to all of the conversations between the doctor and you in this office. Rose knows who you are. One night, Rose came back to this office and put your blood from the samples you left here into her arm. Rose tried to become you. So far this did not work. She will keep trying."

Stunned by her admissions, I interrupted her. "Rose, you cannot merely inject a few drops of blood into your arm and expect to become a soul stealer. Why do you even want to do that to yourself?"

"Izzy is a ferocious reader, sugar. She reads medical journals late at night. I heard the evil one tell you about your type's special DNA. Rose wants to become like you."

The situation was getting more bizarre by the moment; I needed Rose to speed it up.

"Rose, what is your offer?"

"Sugar, you do need to unwind. Rose doesn't like her men tense. But since you seem to be in a hurry, Rose will tell you. She wants you to steal the souls of all the child molesters in this world. I know you can do it if you try. If you won't do it, then teach Rose, so she can do it."

"Rose, you have to realize, it is not that simple. I will promise you that I will make child molesters a priority once I am back in control of the Council, but there is not much more I can do for you. Besides, until I can locate Winfield, I could not take a soul for you even if I wanted to. That is why I need to find him."

"Liar! I heard you talk with the doctor. I know you have the power! Rose is now upset."

"Rose, you must believe me. I was stripped of my powers by a potion that Doc Winfield made many years ago. He never wanted us to be able to remove souls, so he created a drink that over time removes our abilities. That is why it is imperative I find him. If you want me to take souls from child molesters, I need Doc Winfield to reverse what he did to me."

Rose sat on the waiting room sofa. Her head lowered to her chest. Her shoulders slumped. She rested her arms on her legs for several moments. She then started to tell me her story.

"After your doctor friend tried to molest Izzy in the restaurant, Rose grabbed his manhood harder than she did yours. He didn't enjoy it. He excused himself to the men's room. Rose decided to finish Izzy's steak dinner. Then she noticed two men escorting the child molesting doctor from the restaurant. No one escorts anyone of Rose's men away from her, even if they are evil. So, she followed the two men and the child molester."

I sat next to Rose as she continued her tale.

"Rose followed them to a motel way out of town. This was a place Rose would normally never be found, but she wanted to know where everyone was heading. Rose watched as one man went into the office then came back out and drove the car to the opposite side of the motel. The two men took the doctor inside room 12B. Rose sat for an hour until the two men, but not the doctor came out of the room. She watched as the two men entered the room next door, at 11B."

Rose raised her head and looked me in the eye.

"Rose stepped out of her car and knocked on the door at 11B. They let Rose enter. Rose told you she took care of everything and she has."

I never knew what to ask this persona because I was never

sure I wanted to know the answer.

"Who were the men? What did you do to them?"

"Those men said they knew the doctor. One was aggressive with an Italian accent. The other one was easy for Rose to have her way with. She taught them about the word pain. Then she went home to rest."

"Rose, did you go and see if Doc Winfield was still alive?"

"The child molesting doctor can rot there, but no one escorts a man from Rose."

"Where is the motel? Will you take me there?"

"Rose didn't like that place and won't return. But if you promise her, you will remove the souls of child molesters, she will draw you a map. But Rose is tired and needs to go home. She isn't well."

Rose drew a map of how to find the motel. I had no idea if Winfield was alive or what happened to the other two men. For all I knew, they could have escaped and moved Winfield to another location or have succumbed to Rose's garden of pain.

When I arrived, the motel was poorly lit. The road sign read, "Turn Here", with an arrow pointing towards the building. The arrow light was burned out. There were two cars in the parking lot, with one at the far end of the building, where Rose claimed Winfield was last seen. I was worried that if something had gone wrong inside one or both of those rooms and I was the first to enter, I would be a suspect. I also didn't want to walk in front of a loaded weapon. I wanted someone to verify I had recently arrived on the scene. I went inside to speak with the manager.

A short man, in his late fifties or early sixties, strolled out from a door behind the countertop. He was in need of a shave and as he moved closer, a shower as well. His buttoned down shirt with mustard stains was only buttoned half way up his chest. His tone was impatient and in need of a refresher course in customer service.

"You looking for a room? Dere sixty bucks a night, you get two towels, two, if you want more towels dere an extra five bucks for each one and if I hear any screaming or especially gun shots, I call the cops. I don't take personal checks. Now, you wanna room or don't cha?"

I didn't know how to react at first. I generally stayed at fine accommodations. His awkward tone was unexpected. "Well my good man, as enticing as your offer sounds, I am looking for three men who may have checked into rooms 11 and 12B, possibly two nights ago. One may have an accent and all were dressed in suits. Can you help me?"

Again, he offered me an unexpected reaction. "Look pal, I don't take notice of who stays here and who don't. If the credit card clears, or they got green stuff, I give em a key. If not, they leave. I don't look close at faces or what dey wear. Too many cops come here asking too many questions. The less I notice; the better fer me."

It was time to speak his language. "I will give you a hundred dollars right now if you look to see who checked into those rooms two nights ago."

The man, who looked one step from being homeless, scratched his nose and sorted through some papers on the other side of the countertop. He stuck out his hand until I placed a crisp one hundred dollar bill in it. He crumpled up the bill and shoved it into his dirty pants pocket.

"Here it is. Yeah, some guy took room 11B two nights ago. He paid widda credit card. Dere is a note here that says that no one is ta disturb him till he comes ta check out. But I don't know nuttin about 12B. Like I said, he paid, so I don't ask no questions."

"Is there a name on the credit card?"

The slightly balding man opened up his hand and put it back on the counter. I shoved a couple of twenties in it.

"Name says, Faustino, Dante Faustino. Now don't go round disturbing em and causing trouble. I try ta run a clean establishment here, I don't like no trouble."

I thanked the man for all his "troubles" and pulled my car in front of unit 11B.

3

My first inclination was to enter the room where Winfield might be but I felt naked without the ability to defend myself. I wasn't carrying a weapon. I would need to advance like a mere mortal.

I walked back to the office and disturbed Mr. Motel Manager of the Year. "Sir, I did not want to have to do this, but I am afraid someone's life might be in jeopardy in room 11B. I do believe it would be best if you call the police to investigate."

"I dun told ya once, that man asked not ta be disturbed and I don't like no trouble round here. We don't need no police snooping when I ain't heard no yelling or gunshots. Now I think it best you be on your way."

"Sir, I know this Faustino character. He tried to kill me in Mexico. I have a feeling he's going to do the same with one of the men he was with when they checked in. I don't want to open that door not knowing what I might find."

"I'll tell you what you'll find. You'll find paying customers dat don't wanna be disturbed. Look here, mister, I dun asked you nicely once ta not disturb nobody, if I find ya banging on dat door, you gonna find yourself staring down da barrel of my Winchester. Now git!"

Discouraged from the lack of understanding and effort from Mr. Congeniality, I moved my car around the corner and out of sight. I waited until the light was out in the office window and went to room 11B. I had been watching both rooms 11 and 12B. Noticing neither had a light on after dark, I put my ear to the door of 11B. Nothing. I went to 12B. Nothing. Not a sound from either room. I took out my lock picker and cracked open the door to 11B. As quietly as possible, I peaked my head around the door.

Someone was stretched out spread eagle, tied to the bed posts. I peered around the room with a small flashlight to see if anyone else was inside. No one. I took one last look around the room with my flashlight. Scanning the room, there was a dresser with an old television on it, a mirror, an ugly painting, a small nightstand, two chairs and one person lying across the bed. In the back of the room sat a sink and another door I assumed was the bathroom.

With caution, I entered the room. My heart was racing. I checked the door at the back of the room. It was indeed the bathroom. I pulled back the curtains in the shower. I then moved back to the front door, and locked it. The person tied to the bed was motionless.

The tiny flashlight came in handy as it illuminated the face of Doctor Grayson Winfield. A pulse was present, yet faint. I cut the ropes that bound his arms and legs. His eyes opened briefly as he tried to speak. His body was limp. Noticing his soiled trousers, he had not moved in days. I hustled into the bathroom to fill a glass of water. Winfield was offered a short sip as I cradled his head in my arms. Time was of the essence. We needed to get out of this seedy environment.

"Doctor, its Cale Novo. We need to find you a safe haven. I know you were kidnapped by Faustino and his incompetent counterpart. I don't know where they are or if they will be returning anytime soon. Do you think you can move enough to get you into my car?"

He tried to speak, but only raspy sounds emanated from his parched throat. The two of us struggled, allowing him to lean on me long enough to place Winfield into the car. We drove to another hotel at the opposite side of town, where I checked in using cash and fake identification that was not known to anyone, including my wife. After settling Winfield inside the room, I drove to a twenty-four hour store that carried first aid supplies, and vitamins. I spent the remainder of the early morning hours and half of the next day pumping water and vitamins back into Winfield's system. He was dehydrated.

Sleep deprivation caught up with me. After Winfield was stabilized, I fell asleep. Then the nightmare ensued. I was being chased by an unknown assailant trying to take a pouch that I was carrying. He was getting closer with every step. I must have screamed out loud because Winfield woke me up, bitching in my ear.

"Can't anyone get some rest round here? Wake up, cowboy. I never have met anyone else as annoying as you."

Sweat was seeping from every pore in my body. A minute or more passed before I could gain my bearings. By the time I did, Doctor Winfield was sitting upright on the side of his bed staring my way and flapping his gums.

"How the hell did I end up here, cowboy? And what day is it? The last thing I can remember, I was having a good ole steak dinner with my best filly and some asshole stuck a needle in my arm in the restaurant's men's room. Was that you, El-Dar Novo?"

This was not going to be easily explained. The man had no clue that he had been kidnapped by men likely sent from the Council.

"Doctor Winfield, I can assure you, I had nothing to do with your kidnapping. I am the one who found you and brought you here. I then pumped you with vitamins to heal you. Look at the rope burns on your arms and ankles. You were strapped to a bed for more than two days until I could find you."

"I dun thought I'd seen the last of you, Novo. But you gotta do better than that heap of cow dung of a story if you expect me to believe you."

"Oh please, Winfield. Think about it. What reason would I have to want to kidnap you? As painful as it was for each of us, when I wanted to see you, I would come to your office. I faced you man to man each time. Why the hell would I want to kidnap you? Sometimes I wish you had one ounce of common sense. You might have a wall filled with your fancy diplomas but sometimes you can be pretty stupid."

Winfield frowned. He then tried to stand but was unsteady. I helped him balance and assisted him to the window. He stood in better light for a few moments inspecting his abrasions. He gazed at me suspiciously, more than once, before carefully sitting the chair next to the window.

"What really happened, cowboy? I know it wasn't you in the men's room, so who was it? What did they want with me and better yet, why were you even looking for me?"

"It's a long story, Doc. But the short version is that while you were researching our bloodlines and discovered that many of our disciples can still take souls but chose not to, the Council knew it all along. I had been left in the dark. It turns out that many of our people wanted careers like you. They have abandoned our original decree sent from the heavens. The Council attempted to murder me. When that failed, they discovered a way to remove my ability to steal souls. They claim it was a concoction you created years ago."

"Stop right there, Novo. We made our peace after you put me in a room face ta face with my daddy. I don't reckon I have any more beefs with you. I didn't make any secret potion fer dem boys."

"Relax, Doc. I know you didn't intentionally do it. But think back, there must have been something you did when you worked in the compound that allowed them to create something to do what they did to me."

Winfield sat in the chair rubbing his damaged wrists. He sat near motionless for several minutes. At one point, I was going to make sure he was still awake, until I realized his foot would occasionally tap the floor. Winfield cleared his throat and asked.

"What's one gotta do ta git some chow, Novo?"

"I'll go get you something to eat but I want you to think about what they did to me. I need you to make me whole again."

Winfield chuckled. "Hell, Novo, I'd be willing to bet my prize steer all dem boys did was take sumtin I worked on decades ago that plays with your mind. I'll bet you ain't lost nuttin, you only think you have. They tricked your mind, cowboy."

I wasn't thrilled with his assessment. "First of all Doc, you don't even own a ranch, so stop with all the cattle talk. Second, you haven't checked me out yet. I saved you from those people. I can easily find them and offer you back. And by the way, the one who likely stuck you with that needle tried to leave me for dead in Mexico. So the Council must want you dead too. I highly suggest you do better than to offer some less than adequate response to what you think happened to me, or I'll turn you back over to the Council's henchmen."

Winfield gave me that evil stare he used since the first time we met. Only this time, it didn't have the same impact. I had much to fear, but a man who could barely stand without my help, wasn't one of them.

"One last thing before I get you something to eat, Doc. I saved your ass. One thank you would be nice." With that I slammed the door behind me.

After I arrived back, we gulped down a couple of burgers and then checked out of the hotel. Despite my objections, I dropped him off at his apartment, near his office. He swore to me several times his apartment was only a place he went to when he worked late. "My cattle ranch takes me close to an hour ta git to. I mostly go there on weekends and holidays. My ranch hands, take care of it fer me."

"Whatever you say, Doc. But you don't own a ranch."

Leaving him there without protection wasn't a good idea, but he claimed he was feeling much better and he had an "excellent alarm system and a Saturday night special."

The next morning I met him at his office. He still wasn't sure why he should aid me in regaining my ability. Reminding him that I possibly saved his life wasn't good enough. I tried a different approach.

"Doc, since we met, who has done everything he could to get you what you wanted and who has shunned you, including your own father? One thing you must have learned about me by now, I am relentless. Even if you don't agree with my removing souls, you must have noticed I am a principled being. I do as I say. Once I regain control of our disciples, you will have all the funding you desire for your research. I promised you that before, and it is still my pledge to you. But I need your help. Or, you can continue to look over your shoulder every time you leave the office. But make no mistake, I will destroy these people."

Winfield smirked. "Novo, I must admit I do enjoy watching you take yourself so seriously. And I'm not much of a fan of dem boys right now either. I have a perty good idea what they dun to ya. I knew the moment ya told me. But what I made had nuttin to do with stopping you boys from taking souls. It was sumtin I was researching back when I was still working in the compound. Gimme another blood sample. I gotta shoot it over to the lab, but I suspect I'll have sumtin fer ya in a few days."

He drew a vial of blood from me and tried to place it next to my older sample. "That's odd, cowboy, your blood is pretty much gone. Ya got any ideas why?"

I had to laugh. "Doc, I've tried telling you several times, your nurse is quite the character. You don't want to hear me, so I've given up. But she needs to see a psychiatrist in the worst way."

"I'm a trained physician. I've never seen one time where I would suspect anything like that from my nurse. Now drop the subject."

"That's fine. But you have never seen her outside this office, except as your lover. Your ignorance may get the best of you one day."

We spent a few more minutes discussing his nurse and where the blood sample went, but Winfield wasn't listening to me. He let me know he would come up with a solution and sent me on my way. As I was walking out the front door, Nurse Simon was coming up the walkway.

"The lights are on in the building, Mr. Novo, does that mean Doctor Winfield has returned?"

"Yes, he's in there and as testy as ever."

Her pace quickened as she approached the door with a huge smile on her face. She practically knocked me over to get through the door. As I was closing the door, she came back outside, ran her finger from my chin to my belt buckle and whispered in my ear. "Rose gave you what you wanted. Don't forget your promise, sugar."

She turned and went back through the door a second time, this time smiling back at me just before the door closed. "Rose is very fond of you, sugar. Don't make her inflict pain on you." With that, the door closed and I went home to California to prepare for my next move.

As I was sitting in the airport terminal, a strange thing started to occur. I started to see into others' souls again, but it was brief and faint. I focused hard on people. A pounding headache came over me, which stopped me from continuing to try. It was a rare occurrence for me to acquire a headache.

Once home, I called Nesstor. "Elliot, I need a computer hacker. Not any old hacker, I need the best. I'll pay."

"Soul Man, I might be able to offer you the name of a reliable programmer, but we don't associate with people you call, hackers."

"Yeah, I know, Elliot. You are counting the days till retirement. Have someone call me."

The next several days were spent anxiously waiting at home until Winfield asked me to return to Texas. I was on the next flight.

"It was as I suspected, cowboy. When I started my research concerning how to stop the spread of cancer in the human body, I found a way that slowed it down considerably. The problem was and still is; it won't last very long. I imagine Doc Chamoun used my notes and altered it enough to stop you from stealing souls. But it wears off, unless you take the drug on a daily basis or an extended period. Even then, eventually your body's immune system will override the drug's effects. You will eventually git back to your stealing ways."

All of this was great news but I needed more information. "How long before I get better, Doc?"

"Oh, I rekon bout a year or so based on the fact you told me you drank that water for three or four days when they dun tried to kill ya."

So much for the good news. "I can't wait a year, Doc. I have major plans. I need to able to remove souls and get my life back quicker than a year. Who knows, from what you are suggesting, it could be even longer."

"Could be, cowboy. Ya gonna have ta be patient and let it git all the way outta your system."

I kept pressing for a better solution. "What would it take for you to recreate the formula they gave me and the antidote, Doc?"

Winfield scoffed at the idea. "Ya gonna have ta be patient, Novo. I could do it. Hell I can do about anything, but I got no real incentive ta help ya. Don't come round here thinking we'ze friends or nuttin. I know ya helped me. Hell, I know I might even have been left fer dead back at that hotel. I am mighty obliged fer that, but I dun found out what happened to ya, so again, we're dun here."

We went back and forth with several exchanges on ideas I thought would get him to help me, but nothing was making the man budge. I was resigned to the idea I was going to have to wait it out until the toxins they gave me, were no longer affecting me. Then like an angel sent from heaven, she appeared.

"Doctor, I'm sorry, but I've been listening to this whole story outside the door. Mr. Novo has kindly helped me more than once, including returning my soul. He risked his life for me and now I want you to help him. Please Doctor, for me?"

Nurse Taylor Simon had come to my rescue. Her boss wasn't

happy with her request.

"Look here, darling. This man has created nuttin but trouble round here. I know you're hiding a soft spot fer him, but not me. Now you git your perty self back up front and answer them phones. We can talk about this over dinner."

Her voice had a different tone, one with defiance. "No we won't Doctor. If you don't help, Mr. Novo, there will be no more dinners, or lunches and especially no more breakfasts."

A week later, not only did he hand me a bottle with an elixir that cured me almost instantly, but Winfield also handed me a bottle with the same toxin that was used to poison me. He did mention however that his mixture was more potent and would act within minutes.

"Next time I see ya in these parts, it sure better be with a check showing your gratitude. It had better be enough ta support my research fer decades, cowboy.

"Thanks, Doc. I am a man of my word. You will get your money, once I settle the score with some old friends.

The following day, I set up a time and place to meet with my old assistant, Peter Pascal. He was a conniving little creep who betrayed me when I was the leader of the Council. I didn't trust him. He didn't trust me. But I had something he wanted, information.

We met a few days later at a small upscale, family run, Italian restaurant in the suburbs of Virginia. Peter was in town to meet with one of our disciples, who worked in Washington, D.C, and I wanted to drop by and see my old buddy, Elliot Nesstor.

The eatery was bustling with the lunch crowd when I arrived. My reserved table was waiting for me between the bar and the men's room. I had been a frequent patron of the restaurant. I knew the owners on a first name basis. Reserving a specific table was not an issue. I waited patiently ten minutes for Peter's arrival.

As Peter entered the front door, I noticed his appearance hadn't changed since the last I had seen him. He was thin, dark hair, smaller than your average man with skin so white you would think he was covered in baby powder. His boyish looks matched his immature mind. Despite being named to the Council, I suspected they would find a way to remove Peter quickly. In my opinion, he would be old news any day now. I think he suspected his fate as well. His insecurity with his new position of power was how I lured him into having lunch with me.

He sauntered over and we exchanged cautious pleasantries before ordering our drinks and meals. I removed myself to wash my hands before eating and any meaningful conversations began. I assumed Peter had no idea that I met with Winfield and was my old self. But then again, I needed to be careful. This was the crucial step in reclaiming my position as leader of our disciples.

Peter broke the ice first when it came to our real intentions for meeting. "I have to admit, Caeles, I was taken back when you asked to meet me. I'm quite sure you're still pissed at how I betrayed you. But I can assure you, if you think I'm going to help you regain your strength and position on the Council, forget it."

He sat back in his chair as if he was king of the world with his boney chest trying to flex itself through his expensive suit jacket. With his stare, I wasn't sure who he was trying to convince that he was in charge. I snickered under my breath, before moving forward in my chair. My goal was not to scoff at his weak attempt to intimidate me.

"Peter, only a fool would think I could every fully forgive you and the Council. I gave everything to our people, including you, but you all had another way of thinking. I am still working through your choices. Possibly my destiny was never what I assumed it was. I have decided to be a husband and dad and sit back and let the Council care for me now. I consider my fate an early forced retirement."

I took a sip of my drink and a bite of my meal before continuing with my response. "So, Peter, I saw how Tasha Timmons dismissed you, the day you all removed me as leader. Don't you think since you two are the youngest on the Council, there might be a power play once the others retire or die in their seats. I know you still have two positions to fill on the Council given the resignations of my grandfather and Elder Rex. I have heard whispers that Timmons and Elder Robus are hand selecting the new members without your knowledge."

Peter nearly choked on his chicken parm sandwich. "That's total bull, Novo, and you know it! I've been involved with each interview so far and we've narrowed it down to three candidates, for two positions. I suspect we will have them in place in another week or so."

With a hint of sarcasm in my tone, I offered a few words. "I am sure you are right, Peter. I mean the Council betrayed me, but I see no reason why they would do you wrong, right?"

"You're trying to start trouble, Novo. The Council would never harm me. I helped them get rid of you. Timmons though, you're right. Her I don't trust. So if you have any ideas on how I can eventually be the leader and not have to answer to her, I'm all ears."

Oh, the fear. I loved seeing Peter squirm in his seat. Now I knew he was ready to be brought to shore and gutted. "Well, Peter, here is my offer. You are going to get me the list of all of our disciples with information about their family bloodlines, home addresses and a list of the remaining soul stealers and what assignments they are currently working. You are also going to get me a list of all the companies we either partially or completely own. If you do that for me, Timmons will disappear. That clears the way for you to be the leader of the Council for many decades to come."

His reaction was expected. "Are you insane? I don't have access to all of that information and even if I did, it would be suicide to give it to you. No way. Besides, you think I trust that you won't go right to Timmons and make her the same offer."

"What do you know about what the Council did to me, Peter?"

"I know they took away your ability to see into others souls and remove them. Why?"

"How long does it last? Did anyone tell you that?"

"Why are you asking me these questions? I assumed it was forever."

He was as misinformed as he was out of his league against me. It was obvious that he would crumble, momentarily.

"Peter, please scan the room. What do you see?"

He scanned the room. He then scanned the room slower. He

turned to me with his best impression of a deer in headlights. He remained silent. I spoke.

"Let me tell you what I see, Peter. The guy over in the corner, he possesses a soul as black as coal. The woman who walked past us to the ladies room, she might not be on the list yet, but soon. Tell me what you see, Peter."

His eyes grew wider. Small beads of sweat were forming on his upper lip. Peter asked for the waiter to bring him another drink. He scanned the room over and over.

"Your secret is safe with me, Peter. That is, as long as you get me what I asked for. Did you actually think I would come here unprepared? When I left to wash my hands, I slipped the same thing into your drink that was put into mine when you all assumed you had ruined me. Only, yours is far more potent. Did you believe I would lick my wounds and never return?"

Peter lurched at me, grabbing my shirt collar. "What did you do asshole? I'll have you and your family killed if you don't reverse what you did. Do you hear me?"

My friend Angelo came over to the table to make sure everything was alright.

"Please, Mr. Caeles, this place is my home, my lively hood."

I assured him all was fine. Peter sat back in his chair now realizing he no longer could see or remove souls. If anyone on the Council found out, he would be instantly removed from power.

"Peter, your threats will only dig you a deeper hole. In case your feeble mind has yet to figure it out, I can remove your soul right here, right now. And we both know; if you tell anyone else about what happened to you, you will be run out of the compound in disgrace, same as me."

Peter bowed his head. His hands were shaking as he took a sip from his freshened drink. His voice now sounded resigned to the idea that he had little choice but to assist me. "I can't get all you need. But if I get what I can, what's in it for me? You must have an antidote, don't you?"

"I have no desire to sit on the Council ever again. So once you get me what I want, you will get what you deserve. I do have the antidote. And if you go ask Chamoun for help, he's going to question you. So don't be so foolish in seeking his or anyone else's help."

"What if I return home and not tell anyone and not do as you ask?"

"Please do, Peter. But my patience with you will only last so long. Then I'll have to let it leak to Timmons and the others that you are not only a sniveling twerp, but one with less authority to sit on the Council than my son. You have two weeks to deliver everything I want, or kiss your seat on the Council goodbye."

"I will kill you for this, Novo."

"No you won't, Peter. You had your chance once and failed. You won't get a second one. Now get your scraggly ass out of my face. You have a lot of work to do."

4

$\mathcal{A}$fter stripping Peter of what little manhood he possessed and enjoying every second of it, I was off to visit with Agent Nesstor. No one had contacted me for the computer work I requested. Elliot needed to be reminded in person that I needed assistance. We set up a time to meet on the steps of the Lincoln Memorial.

"Cale, seriously, you have to stay clear of Washington, at least until President Morrison's term has expired. When you silenced that blogger, who was pumping propaganda for his reelection, the President made it known through channels he wanted to know why the guy stopped writing. Don't forget, my boss knows you did your magic on the blogger. My boss doesn't want to arrest you, but you can't mess with Presidential elections."

"Elliot, what the President was doing was spreading lies about his opponent to win reelection. Wasn't that the true crime?"

"Not in this town. Do me a solid and stay clear of Washington until I'm retired, please? This town has enough scandals. We don't need to arrest a hundred year old guy who took the soul of a mysterious person spreading rumors for the President. That won't go over well with the voters. You have the rest of the world as your playground. Trust me. I know there are whack jobs all over the world. Go find some of them."

"Alright Elliot, I admit there is plenty to keep me busy. That brings me to why I am here to see you."

I stopped, took a deep breath and did what I did best. Then I continued speaking with Elliot.

"Let me check to make sure your soul is still clean. Yep, it is. Ok, did you get a name for me? I need a computer hacker in the worst way."

Nesstor shook his head at me. It made me smile each time he did.

"Soul Man, I wish I could check out criminals like you." He shook his head and snickered. "I told you over the phone, we at the Bureau don't associate with any hackers, other than ones behind bars. But should an, Iza Tappen, contact you, it had nothing to do with me. Will you please let me retire on the proper side of the law?"

This time I was the one shaking my head and laughing. Nesstor could only offer an exasperated sigh and shuffled into a crowd of tourists peering up at Mr. Lincoln. I disappeared back into the shadows. As much as our methods were different, I did want to believe that Agent Nesstor believed we were working to accomplish the same goals. His way removed evil from walking freely in society. Mine was to incarcerate evil before reaching a path to a higher existence.

Exhausted, home was calling me. The moment after walking

through the front door, Kalani was upset. "Cale, you look horrible. You're pale and you've lost a lot of weight."

I was run down. Part of it was from all my body had been through in recent times. I had been shot, left for dead in Mexico, lost my abilities, then regained them and nursed Winfield back to health with little rest for days. Days were spent working overtime putting my plan in action by destroying Peter and dealing with Nesstor. Watching a ball game on the tube would have been a perfect start to recharge my batteries.

My wife had other plans. "Excuse me, but you can read the box scores in the tomorrow's paper. If you think you're going to park your butt in that chair, forget it. How do we become stronger? We remove souls."

Didn't this woman realize Sunday Night Baseball was on television? "I've been traveling for weeks. One night to relax is not asking too much, Kalani. Please, go knit a sweater or do whatever it is you do to unwind. Plus, am I to assume a home cooked meal would be asking too much?"

That wasn't the response she wanted. At least my cell phone was close enough so I could order Chinese food without having to get up from my chair.

The next morning I awoke to the smell of bacon and eggs. My wife delivered a nice breakfast in bed. "I hope you enjoyed your game. Possibly I was a bit harsh last evening. I know you've been under pressure lately. I handled it poorly. I apologize, Cale."

My first reaction was happiness that Kalani acknowledged all I had been through. My next reaction was; what did she want? It didn't take long to find out.

She continued. "I overreacted last night partially because I think I'm being set up. My next assignment has been all over the media for weeks. I've never taken more than one soul at a time and this one has multiple thefts. Unless I get them all in the court house at one time, it might be difficult to find some of these characters again. I need your help on this one, my love.

I began munching on my bacon letting her continue to make her plea.

"We've never done a case together. If souls start getting removed that aren't scheduled, the Council might get suspicious about you, Cale. But if you help me take ones scheduled, then they are less likely to suspect anything. Plus you can regain more strength with every soul you remove. Come on, it's a win, win for both of us."

She batted her eye lids and refilled my glass of orange juice. Did I really have a choice? Before I could take another bite of eggs, the file was sitting on the bed next to me. "I guess this is your way of letting me know I should read the case file?" I said to my wife. After finishing breakfast I did.

Kalani was correct. This case was far too much for one soul stealer to handle alone. It made me curious if this was a way for the Council to send her on a suicide mission. There is no telling how her body would react to removing so many souls in such a short time span. Even with two of us, there would be danger. There were so many to blame in this case, I wasn't sure if the two of us would be enough.

The first person to review in the overstuffed file was the President of NOZY, a national cable news network. Maxwell Duper was first to lead the charge, claiming his network would offer twenty-four hour coverage of "The trial of the century." He followed it up by stating, "Even if we have to run the same ten second loop of this deranged person sitting in the courtroom over and over for hours to prove how non biased our reporting is, we're going to do it."

Mr. Duper had to defend accusations that despite the Arab world reeking of turmoil and the country of Sharona toppling its regime and ousting President Fieger, the trial in the sleepy town of Inocente, New Mexico, would take priority. "We at NOZY believe everyone has a right to a fair trial by a jury of their peers. Our network is in New Mexico to ensure our audience can receive a firsthand account of all the happenings around the trial. We have no desire to sway this case one way or the other. We are here purely to push our political and social agendas to boost our ratings and nothing more." I scratched my head a few times while reading about this guy to make sure I was reading it correctly.

The second person in the file was Reverend Malin Menteur. He was a self-proclaimed minister with a small nightly following on a nearly bankrupt cable network called, NUTS. Menteur was famous for showing up at every "trial of the century" or anytime he thought he could get television face time for sticking up for whomever the media claims to have been wronged. Facts of the case or the United States Constitution could never stand in his way. He stood on principle, his. When asked as a young man starting his career where he was ordained, his only response was, "Do you think you can buy these collars just anywhere? Next question."

As I was reading the report, I wanted to believe Kalani was pulling a prank on me. I looked her way shaking my head. She looked back and giggled. I kept reading.

Next in the report was the Attorney General of the United States, Elizabeth Holmes. She directed the Department of Justice to send government employees at taxpayer expense to New Mexico to teach the locals how to hold semi-peaceful rallies. "If the people of Inocente are going to march in the streets, we at the Department of Justice will make sure they have all the resources they need to do it properly."

In a White House briefing the day after the Attorney General's statement, Press Secretary Jason Kearns was questioned, "With budget cuts being a hot topic around Washington, how does it look to the voters when funding was eliminated for school children to tour the White House but there are funds to create signs and send hundreds of employees to aid the prosecution in a case that's not federal, but local?" Kearns was quick to respond. "Kids can't vote. Plus, the more shiny objects we can keep in front of our supporters, the less likely they will remember they're unemployed and broke." There were no follow up questions.

The next person in the file was the Governor of New Mexico. Scott Gramm ordered a special prosecutor to the case after the local sheriff refused to press charges against the defendant in the trial. When asked why he appointed a prosecutor when the local authorities found no evidence of a hate crime, Gramm responded, "I don't need NOZY reporters up my ass in an election year."

Again I looked at Kalani. She went in the other room hopefully to get me something to calm my nerves. I kept reading.

Next in the file was the special prosecutor selected by the governor. James Plant had been a state prosecutor for over two decades. He was known to be tough on criminals, especially involving crimes along racial divides. He was brought in specifically because he was an expert in hate. "If this woman thinks she can walk away from a crime involving so much racial tension, she has another thing coming."

When asked if he hid evidence from the defense, Plant said, "Why give them extra reading?"

While reading through page after page, I realized running a council of soul stealers was much easier than dealing with the media and politicians who only show their faces when they think it will help them garner a vote, or boost their sagging ratings.

If any group of people could no longer appreciate all that was given to them, it was this bunch. There was no chance Kalani and I would be able to remove enough souls to clean up this train wreck, but even a few would be better than standing on the sidelines. We packed our bags and headed for New Mexico.

When we arrived the next evening in Inocente, throngs of people were wandering the streets near the tiny court house. In speaking with the owner of the local hardware store, Arnie Hammer, he told me, "I ain't much recognizing many of these people. They're not our people. We don't get many city folk from back east visiting us, unless they took a wrong turn outta Santa Fe."

Kalani made her way through the crowd of reporters and city officials to the steps of the tiny courthouse. I went across the street to a quaint public park where all the major news networks had set up live remotes. The first group I came across was from NUTS. Carlin Masterson was reporting live with his show, "Talking Crazy." I stopped to listen for a few moments.

Carlin and his two guests were explaining to the audience how, without hearing any evidence in court, they were convinced only a guilty verdict could be rendered. "Carlin, this is an open and shut case of racial profiling. The woman knew exactly what she was doing. If the jury doesn't find her guilty, the Attorney General should file charges."

I stood there wondering what drugs these people were taking. I read the entire report and I didn't see where a hate crime had been committed.

Opening arguments were scheduled to begin in the morning. Jury selection had taken seven days. It was hard for both sides to agree upon six jurors because the case was so highly charged. The entire town of two hundred and seventeen had heard about it. Every local citizen was called for the jury pool. The prosecuting and defense teams finally selected six women for the jury who had returned from a trip to Alaska. They were the only six who hadn't heard anything about the unfortunate accident. They were immediately locked away from all the madness that was sweeping their town.

I walked around the park listening to all the live feeds commenting about how this was an obvious case of profiling.

"This is a hate crime, pure and simple. The woman had no right even be at the scene of the crime. She was told to stay away."

I could only question what was I missing?

Once all the cameras were shut off for the night and many of the talking heads had found their way to wherever they were staying for the evening, I saw Masterson leaving the park. Since he was on the list, I figured I would start with him.

"Good evening, Mr. Masterson. May I have a few moments of your time?

Carlin Masterson kept his slow pace towards his car but did offer, "I traveled eight hours to get here, then spent the better part of three hours on the air and now you want a moment of my time?"

I kept pace and stated, "Sir, really, I only wanted to shake your hand and thank you for opening my eyes to what really is destroying our country. You are a huge part in helping me see the light."

Masterson stopped his stride long enough for me to look deeply into his darkened soul and remove it. He looked at me and belched. "Damn southwest food, gets me every time." He started walking again as if he lost nothing valuable. I too felt little from removing it. Usually I start to shake soon after stealing a soul, but I too felt like I had a bad case of heartburn.

I found Kalani and we checked into a motel several miles away. The town was so small; it couldn't accommodate all the people that had barged in from across the nation. The room was clean and provided a place to rest with my wife.

Before daybreak, we made our way back to Inocente. The morning news crews were already beaming signals across the world from their tiny outposts. Kalani and I listened as reporters and talking heads used words almost demanding people riot in the streets as they were condemning the defendant for profiling. It was a confusing message indeed.

Since the tiny courtroom had seating for only a handful of people, the vast majority who couldn't get inside were left loitering the streets. The governor had ordered the National Guard to beef up security in the area. After all, the town of Inocente only employed three law enforcement officers.

Small monitors were set up inside the park so people could hear the trial. Judge Virgil Petty sat behind the bench promptly at ten o'clock. He spouted out a few instructions and reminded the extra people in the courtroom to behave or all cameras would be removed.

Kalani and I kept an eye out for anyone in the crowd who were on our list. She found one the previous evening. Between us we had taken two souls. But with so many expected in town on our list, this was a soul stealers delight. Still, we both kept one eye on the monitors because neither of us realized how politically correct, and at times misleading, the reporting had been concerning what should be a local trail, not national news.

The crowd of people ranging in ages from preteens to senior citizens huddled around the monitors scattered about the park. I watched as Carlin Masterson arrived in his Chevy Volt. He hopped out and walked over to his company's makeshift studio. Masterson bounced around like a little kid with a huge smile and full of energy. Despite his soul now resting in the Surrounding of Souls, he seemed invigorated. Whatever. I had much more to accomplish in a short time frame. The trial was not expected to last more than two days.

Both sides in the case offered up opening statements. The prosecution laid out its case proclaiming the defendant was warned to go back inside the store and wait. Yet, she didn't listen

Michael Cantwell

because she was so distraught. She knew she would create a struggle if she went back to her car.

The defense claimed she was an older lady not sure of her bearings. The people involved had nothing to do with why she didn't listen to warnings from others to sit and wait until help could arrive. Defense attorney Emily Placente pleaded to the six woman jury that her client may have been negligent returning to her car, but she wasn't a profiler or some wicked type of stalker. The judge allowed for a short lunch break after opening statements.

After lunch, the sheriff in the town, who was put on leave for his controversial decision not to press criminal charges in this case, took the stand. The prosecutor quizzed Sheriff Tull about what he saw when he arrived on the scene.

"When I arrived Mrs. Cass was standing next to both cars, visibly upset. She was disoriented as if maybe she had banged her head in the crash."

The prosecutor, James Plant, interrupted the testimony. "So you don't know positively if Mrs. Cass had banged her head in the crash? It is only speculation on your part?"

"I've been trained to recognize people who are disoriented, and in my opinion she was not herself."

The prosecutor looked at the jury then continued questioning the sheriff. "Is it true that Mrs. Cass lives two doors down from your parent's home? The same home where you were raised? In fact you have on many occasions called Mrs. Cass your second mother?

48

"Well I've never called her Mamma Cass, but I've known the Cass family since I was a young child."

More accusations in a terse tone from the prosecutor ensued. "So it would be safe to say, that it's possible your personal feelings for your admitted second mother, Mother Cass, could possibly cloud your judgment in this case?"

"I'm an objective and fair sheriff. I happen to know everyone in this town on a first name basis. If you used that as your guidelines, you could say I was just as concerned about the other party in this case, Mrs. Phillips."

The questioning went on for another thirty minutes with the sheriff describing the crime scene before being excused. The talking heads were in full throat explaining to the audience what they had heard. "Did you hear the explanation from the sheriff, Carlin? He called the defendant Mamma Cass but the victim Mrs. Phillips. Obviously, the sheriff's testimony is tainted. He didn't sound like he had any respect for Mrs. Phillips. Why couldn't she be Mamma Phillips? I'll bet he calls Mr. Cass, pappa too.

Kalani and I stood there motionless, not wanting to believe the lunacy coming from the mouths of people called journalists, or even worse, experts. We moved along the makeshift corridor of news organizations reporting on the case. We knew we had to grab as many souls on her list as we could find, and get home.

The afternoon had more witnesses called on behalf of the prosecution. There was the local insurance adjuster, a few witnesses, who partially noticed the accident. All testified though a terrible accident; none saw it as any type of racial crime. At day's end, the prosecution rested. Listening to the testimony, I didn't think the prosecution proved their case. Attempted murder using a moving vehicle would carry a heavy burden of proof. Adding the element of a hate crime was only adding to the burden. But after listening to the network news reports all day, spin their words; even I was starting to believe the case had merit. Newscasters could be very convincing.

Kalani removed the soul of a politician who arrived on the scene that evening making the rounds on every network. My wife swore he was on her list, but I think he ticked her off. He had a dark soul. No one was going to complain back at the compound. I don't think it affected the congressman. In listening to an interview he spewed after Kalani took his soul, he sounded exactly the same as before. He was as polished at not answering direct questions and making it sound like he did before his soul was removed. Didn't any of these people believe or care if they had a soul or not? If they were believers, they should be showing effects, not continuing to offer interviews and belch out excessive gas from rice and beans.

5

*D*ay two was the defense's turn to present its case. Friends of the defendant, Mrs. Murial Cass, entered into the witness chair one by one, speaking of all her kindness and virtues. The prosecution attempted to punch holes, but it wasn't working. Still, the defense team took the calculated risk of allowing Mrs. Cass to testify on her own behalf. She would take the stand after the morning recess.

Kalani and I walked through the public park past the reporters. Off in the distance, you could see the mountains, partially hidden from the clouds cascading the late morning sky. It was a relaxing moment until Reverend Malin Menteur showed up with his three vigilant supporters.

He started his sermon speaking of justice for all, except for Mrs. Cass. "We must rise up against discrimination", he shouted for all in earshot who cared to listen. "The disrespect she showed her victim with pure hatred that cannot and will not be tolerated. Rise up my people. March in the streets. Make your voices heard. People like Mrs. Cass believe they can knock us down, not allow our voices to rise above. But we will not stop till we knock down anyone who attempts to knock us down. But do it in a semi-peaceful and respectful way of course."

I double checked Kalani's list. Reverend Menteur was on it. I looked for his soul. I couldn't find it. I asked Kalani to look. She couldn't find it either. Did this guy ever possess a soul? He must have one, because he was on the list. I looked again. Finally, I saw it. It was the smallest soul I had ever run across. It had decayed so much that it was nearly impoosbile to find. After he finished his sermon about stamping out discrimination by destroying anyone who disagreed with his beliefs, I spoke with him.

"Reverend, you do realize this was a traffic accident, right? This wasn't a senior citizen on a crime spree. Must you see profiling and discrimination in even the smallest of incidents?"

Reverend Menteur shot back. "There is no such thing as a little discrimination. There is no such thing as a small amount of injustice. I will continue to shine a light on all evil!"

"Tell me Reverend. What happens when you shine your light on what you claim is an injustice and it turns out not to be? You have been known to do that in the past, then walk away with destruction in your wake. Where is the justice in that?"

Malin Menteur moved closer in his Armani suit and silk tie. Not a hair was out of place. He was taller than me and tried to use that to his advantage. He tilted his head down at me. "I accept certain destruction when it achieves my goals."

I reached out and shook his hand. "Funny thing, I feel the same way." I removed what was left of his soul. He moved back towards his followers and continued boasting his mixed message.

As court resumed, Mrs. Cass took the stand. She was a slight woman, in her late sixties, gray hair, well manicured. She was visibly shaking in her seat as her attorney, Miss Placente asked her to describe what happened the day the accident occurred. She spent the next several minutes slowly describing her version of the story. She would occasionally sip from the bottle of water provided and peek over at the jury. She stood up after answering the last question thrown out by her attorney. The judge struck and gavel asked Mrs. Cass to remain seated. "Mr. Plant, the prosecutor, now gets his opportunity to ask you a few questions."

Mr. Plant had blonde hair with a sprinkling of gray that reached his dress shirt collar. He wore a nice suit, but it was likely off the rack. One thing I did notice was his Jerry Garcia tie. I wore them myself. I could spot them anywhere. He had a firm tone about him, but not overpowering. Plant stood upright and moved towards the jury box. He stood within inches of the six ladies who would decide the fate of the elderly defendant.

"Mrs. Cass, your testimony was that you went to grocery store for breakfast items for the next morning and some ice cream for your husband. Did I hear you correctly?"

"Yes", she said, as her hand shook taking a sip from the bottled water.

"And you testified that you went to do your shopping soon after dinner, about seven in the evening. So it was still light out, is that correct?"

"Yes."

"You went into the store, bought your items and arrived back to your car at approximately seven thirty. Again, still light enough to see clearly, am I correct, mam?"

"Yes, I think that was about the time."

"Thank you, Mrs. Cass. So you stepped into your car after putting the bag of groceries in your back seat and then you realized you had lost your glasses, yes? They were your reading glasses, not your glasses worn for driving, is that correct, Mr. Cass?"

"I don't wear glasses for driving, but I didn't want to leave my others behind. They were brand new glasses."

Plant paused. He looked at the jury pool then moved closer to Mrs. Cass. "So when you realized you had lost your glasses, you went back into the store. Is that correct? And if so, how long were you back in the store?"

Mrs. Cass raised the water bottle to her mouth with her hand and arm shaking. "I knew I had ice cream melting in the back seat. I didn't stay long, I would say, five minutes."

"Thank you Mrs. Cass. In your initial hearing, you claimed to have called your husband. What did he tell you?"

"He told me to return to the car and wait for him. He would go and speak with the manager to make sure my glasses were found and returned."

Prosecutor Plant strolled back in front of the jury box. He looked right at the six women as he asked the next question. "Yet you disobeyed his instructions and you took matters into your own hands, didn't you, Mrs. Cass."

"Uhm, not really. For one thing, my husband doesn't' give me orders and for another, my ice cream was melting. If I waited for my husband to get there and search the store, my groceries would have been ruined. I wanted to get home."

Again, Plant looked directly at the jury pool as he continued the cross examine the witness. "That's a nice side story, Mrs. Cass. You had to get home and put away your groceries. We know what really happened. You watched as Beverly Phillips, the store manager and woman who previously told you she couldn't find your eyeglasses, make her way to her American made, black SUV. You waited, boiling with rage, until her car was behind you. Then you slammed your car into reverse and rammed her black car with your white imported car. Isn't that correct, Mrs. Cass?"

Miss Placente jumped from her chair objecting to the question being proposed, but as he had throughout the entire trial, the judge sided with the prosecution. "I'll allow the question."

"No, that's not what happened at all. My crème colored car, made in Tennessee, was blocked on both sides by larger cars. I couldn't see anything while I was pulling out. I started slowly then when I thought no one was coming, I pulled out farther. My car collided with Bev's, but I didn't do it on purpose. We're bridge partners for God's sakes!"

Plant looked again at the jury while speaking. "Oh please, Mrs. Cass, we have you on record of striking another black car when you were a teenager. You're a racist against anything black. Admit it!"

Emily Placente jumped up again. "Your honor, please, that last remark must be stricken from the record. She's being accused of being a racist against black cars? Really?"

This time the judge slowed down the rhetoric from Plant. "Mr. Plant, please keep to the facts of the case. Members of jury, attempt to strike from your memory that Mrs. Cass is biased against blacks."

Attention turned back towards Mr. Plant and his line of questioning. "Mrs. Cass, are we to believe that after you failed to murder Mrs. Phillips the first time, it wasn't your intent to finish the job when you rammed your imported car into her American made SUV?"

Murial Cass shook her head with her eyebrows raised. She then put both hands to her cheeks before responding. "After I hit Beverly's car by mistake, I was upset. I tried to pull back into the spot, but I missed the brake and hit the gas again. My car hit the pole that was in front of me. I hit my head on the steering wheel. I must have become disoriented from my head first banging on my head rest, then again when it hit the steering wheel. I didn't know what I was doing. I got all confused. I pulled out of the spot to go home. I turned my car towards the road not realizing Bev had parked her car to check on me. I hit the back end of her car with the front end of my car."

Plant jumped in. "No, Mrs. Cass. You were far from being disoriented. You had enough wits to then leap out of your car and attack your so called friend, Mrs. Phillips, yet a third time. You shoved her to the ground and beat her senseless. Even after you heard her scream, you refused to get off of her. Isn't that true Mrs. Cass? "

Again, Miss Placente jumped out of her chair. "Your Honor, please. I object to this entire line of attack by Mr. Plant."

The judge looked down at the witness. "Please answer the

question, Mrs. Cass."

"But I did, Judge, earlier when Miss Placente asked me what happened."

"Answer it again", the judge warned with a stern voice.

"I wouldn't attack anyone," a crying Mrs. Cass stated. "Bev and I have been friends for years. Why would I attack her? I was so confused after being in the wreck. I don't know why I tried to get out of the car, but I did. I was told later that I was stumbling all over and Bev tried to steady me. When she did, we both fell to the ground and she broke her hip. I feel terrible, just terrible. I've been making dinner for her husband every night since she's been in the hospital."

Mrs. Cass started to sob uncontrollably. The bailiff brought her a few tissues. That didn't stop Plant from his attacks.

"So, you admit in open court we can now add adultery to the list of your shortcomings? You have been taking care of your friend's husband while she's laid up in the hospital with a broken hip you gave her when you attacked her and attempted to murder her."

"My husband takes over the food, sir!"

Prosecutor Plant tried one last line of questioning. "Tell me Mrs. Cass, what nationality is Mrs. Phillips?"

"She's British. Her and her husband retired to our area about five years ago."

"So you know she's not an American citizen. Is that correct, Mrs. Cass?"

"I never thought about it in those terms, but I guess she's still a British citizen. I really don't know."

Plant went in for his last attempt. "So, we are to assume the fact that you know she's an illegal alien, she likely stole your glasses, she drives a big black fuel guzzling SUV, and you want to sleep with her husband. The woman who you threw out of your bridge club with no remorse for her happiness, was in the wrong place at the wrong time when you rammed your white car into her, before attacking her for a third time?"

The usually demure Mrs. Cass had enough. "You really are an asshole, Mr. Plant. My friend Beverly left the bridge group because her husband has early stages of Alzheimer's. She can no longer leave him for long periods of time. My husband John, and her husband, Bill, are close friends. I cook Bill dinner because even when he was feeling well, he didn't know where the kitchen was in his house. I feel so guilty over what happened in all this mess, it is the least I can do. As far as her car being black, give me a break. If you are insinuating I'm somehow a racist because I've hit one or two black cars in my life, stop right there. I've been in three accidents in my life. I'm not a particularly good driver, as my insurance premium will prove. But this whole trial proves our society and the media is constantly looking so hard to find some type of injustice or racism in places it doesn't exist, that when it does, it's like the boy who cried wolf. We are all so desensitized to it now; rarely do we take it seriously. Now, I have dinner to make."

The few in the courtroom, sans the media, started to applaud. The judge had to settle the semi- raucous crowd of ten. Mrs. Cass was excused from the witness stand. There was another recess before closing statements. The case was expected to be sent to the jury before day's end.

The crowd outside had a mixed reaction. Some cheered, others jeered. The media must have been watching a different trial than I was. Immediately the reports started with, "Cass covets her victim's husband." I needed to have my hearing checked. I never heard those words. Yet, it was being reported.

I wandered through the crowd and noticed, Maxwell Duper, president of NOSY network. It was time to remove his soul. Duper was exiting from the back of a stage being used by his network. He was heading in the direction of the coffee shop in the block down from the court house when I stopped him. He was with a few other people, but that wasn't going to curtail me.

I moved within a few feet when I belted out, "Mr. Duper why would your network imply that Mrs. Cass is having an affair when in open court she denied it."

Duper stopped in his tracks, smiled and remarked, "Because the audience feeds off drama. We are the younger generation's soap opera and as long as I remain at the helm, we won't disappoint."

I moved closer to Duper and extended my arm. "Sir, I would like to shake your hand, so you will know how much I appreciate you allowing me to feed from you." We clasped hands. His grip strengthened as I ripped out his soul.

Mr. Duper looked me square in the eyes and stated, "I would sell my soul to make this network number one in our key demographics. Thank you for being a part of it."

I released his grip. "I do believe you accomplished your goal,

Mr. Duper."

With that I walked over to the park and found Kalani. She had removed two more souls from her list. It was time for us to fade back into the shadows.

6

𝒦alani and I returned home to California feeling strong from removing multiple souls. It was the first time she had taken multiple souls on one assignment. She was still adjusting to having the excess energy. I wanted to relax and watch anything on television, other than the news.

Peter Pascal contacted me the following day. He assured me he had the list of anyone who shared our bloodlines, with their home addresses, phone numbers, emails, and any additional information in the Council's database. He also had the list of companies we either partially or fully owned. He didn't, however, have the list of where our soul stealers currently worked.

"Bink became suspicious when I asked," Peter moaned.

I arranged to meet Peter three days later at a hotel bar in Texas. I knew the place well. He didn't realize how well. He was told we should meet there because I had football tickets the following day in Dallas. Peter had never seen a professional game and assumed my extra ticket was for him.

I made a few calls before leaving and met him as scheduled.

Soon after arriving, Peter was anxious to hand off his end of the bargain, an external drive with the databases. He was expecting me to immediately give him the potion to cure his lost ability to steal souls. I was in no such hurry. I had my reasons.

"Come on, Caeles. You gave me your word you would make this right," Peter said in a timid, whiney tone.

"I have every intention of making it right, Peter. But how do I know these lists are real or even accurate? Do you really think I would trust you? You did try to kill me, at least once that I know about. Then you sat silent as the Council drugged me so I would lose my powers and removed me from my seat on the Council. The same seat you currently occupy. I am going to have to look up some of the addresses to see if they match the names. Then I will check the registered names of the stock holders against the companies you claim we own, to see if those are legitimate."

Peter twitched in his seat. "Do you think I would screw you twice?"

"I guess we will find out, wont we? But if these are accurate, I will give you what you deserve, including an extra bonus."

Right on cue, the bonus appeared. She was dressed in a skin tight black dress that scooped well below her neck line and ended well above her knees. The dress clung to every curve on her body like a fancy sports car to a mountain road. There was little left to the imagination. Rose collected several eyes as she sauntered over to our table.

"Hello, sugar. Rose was excited to receive your call. May Rose sit with you and your handsome friend?"

"Please do, my beauty. It is always my pleasure to see you."

I extended my hand towards Peter. "I would like to introduce you to Mr. Peter Pascal."

Rose batted her long lashes at Peter and smiled. "Rose has been looking forward to meeting you, sir. She has designed a special fragrance only for you."

Peter frowned. "What's this all about? I came here to exchange information for your antidote and now you offer me a two bit hooker? Are you crazy, Caeles?"

Rose took Peter's hand and stated, "Rose is not a two bit hooker, sir. No one has ever refused Rose and the pleasure she offers a young man like you. So don't make Rose upset by thinking she is something she isn't. Pain can be pleasurable; then again, pain can be otherwise."

Not wanting Rose to talk too much about pain, I jumped back into the conversation. "Peter, don't be an idiot and show some respect to the lady. Rose is only here to entertain you for short time, while I check your lists. Drink this. It will take a little time for you to fully recover, but it will get my desired results. While that is working, you and Rose can spend some quality time together. It's my way of repaying you for all you have done for me."

Peter was hesitant to pick up his drink. "What is it? Is this the antidote to fix me or not?"

I looked at Peter. "Would I screw you twice, Peter?"

"Yes, you would." He blurted.

Rose shifted her seat closer to Peter. She whispered in his ear while her hands disappeared under the table. His eyes became as large as water balloons as he looked at me. Then Peter smiled at Rose. He guzzled down what was inside the plastic vial I had placed in front of him. It was antacid mixed with sleeping medicine. Yes, I would screw him twice. Revenge was now my ally.

"Enjoy your time with Rose, Peter. I will head off and check on these lists and will meet you in the lobby in the morning. We can head over to the game after breakfast. All debts have been paid."

Rose offered a devilish smile. "Rose will take good care of Mr. Peter, sugar. She always does. Next time, Rose wants to spend more time with you. Rose always enjoys seeing you. Now run along and do your work, Rose will do hers."

It was time for me to take my leave. Peter would be left to the whims of the beautiful, but broken Rose. I didn't know for sure what she would do with him. I didn't know for sure what Rose did with anyone she met. I only knew I never saw them twice. I wanted revenge. But I still didn't want to think of myself as a killer, merely someone who was out to destroy all who attempted to destroy me. In hindsight, maybe I shouldn't have called Rose and lied about Peter being a child molester. She was now in charge of his body and soul. Was that wrong?

The next morning I sat in the hotel lobby waiting for Peter. He never arrived. I didn't want to call his cell phone in case he met with foul play. I didn't want to be associated with him. When he didn't arrive, I called Doc Winfield to see if he wanted to attend the football game with me. He declined in his usual condescending way. For a doctor, the guy had no bedside manner. I called Nurse Simon, who agreed to join me.

Since we were now running short on time, I met her at the stadium. In my younger days, when I was masquerading as a music executive to remove the soul of Johnny Joe Jackson, in Chicago, I would attend Cubs baseball games at Wrigley Field. In recent years, when I visited my parents in Florida, they would drag me to Marlins games. But it was a rare event for me to able to witness a football game in person. It was only my second Miami Dolphins game in person, and my first seeing the Dallas Cowboys.

The new stadium in Dallas was incredible. Nurse Simon was all decked out in her Cowboys jersey and pigtails. I was lucky enough to purchase the one Dolphins cap they had on sale inside the stadium. The entire game there was no sense that Rose was watching the game with me. It was the persona of Nurse Simon. As much as I enjoyed the bubbly nature of Taylor Simon, a little clue from Rose as the where Peter might be, would have been nice. But I had to take solace in the Dolphins winning on a last second field goal to win the game.

A couple of times during the game, I purposely called Taylor Simon, Rose. She noticed and wasn't thrilled. But I wanted Rose to appear and tell me about her evening.

"Mr. Novo, you've called my home asking for Rose a few times and now you call me Rose here. I'm starting to get jealous of this Rose person. I wish you would stop." I did.

As we muddled through the crowd towards our cars, I made sure Nurse Simon made it to her car safely. Without notice, before she slid into her car, she turned and kissed me. I was surprised and broke it off quickly. As attractive as she was, I was still very much married and in love with Kalani. The bubbly voice of Taylor Simon was no more. A seductive tone now resonated from the person standing close enough to me that I could feel the warmth of her body.

"Don't be alarmed, sugar. Rose wouldn't dream of hurting her man. She is not always kind to others, but you will always have a special place in Rose's heart. Now you go and save the world from those evil souls. Rose has everything here under control. Come back and take in the aroma that is The Rose anytime, sugar."

Rose got into her car and drove off among the throngs of cars leaving the stadium. She was gone. I did feel guilty about using her the way I did. After all, in my own way, I did care for her. However, in some warped way, I felt she was sent for a reason. Maybe it was my guilty conscience talking, but the woman did want to help me. I internally justified it, by deciding one day I would find her the mental health she desperately needed. Then again, who among us hasn't at one time or another wanted an alter ego? All I knew was that I needed to stop thinking about Rose, before it drove me to be mentally deranged too.

My flight home didn't leave until the following morning, so I went back to the hotel. After washing up and ordering room service, a text message arrived on my cell phone.

U looking 4 me?

I didn't know who was contacting me. I replied, *"Don't know. Who RU?"*

A mutual friend sent me.

After several cryptic text messages back and forth, it was agreed the mystery messenger would send me an email with more details.

We will never meet. If you seek me, I will be gone. I decide if I will work for you or not. We will not negotiate terms. You tell me the assignment, I tell you my fee. If that is agreeable, send me your assignment. IZA TAPPEN

I realized what was going on. This was the person Elliot Nesstor sent me for some "special" computer work. This person's attitude needed an adjustment. But being someone who lived in the shadows, I understood their concern about being secretive. Their terms for payment weren't as agreeable. I fired back.

Never to meet. Agreed. Never to seek. Agreed. Offer you an assignment, you may quote a fee. Fees are negotiable. If not, our mutual friend can find me another. Those are my terms. Many have tried to bully me. All have failed. Don't try it again.

It didn't take long to get a one word response.

Done

I sent Iza Tappen an email explaining that I wanted access to Brandon Bink's computer inside the compound. It was imperative to know who all the active soul stealers were and where they were. My guess was that many, if not all, would be just as committed to our real mission on earth as I was. I wasn't sure they even knew how few stealers remained and how corrupt the Council had become. My thought was that if I could warn them, I could control the strength of all the disciples, since their strength was still dependent on removing souls.

Iza responded with wanting to know a few things about Bink's computer and what internet provider was used inside the compound. Iza also demanded a fee of ten million dollars. I wrote back to let Iza know that was never going to happen. It didn't take long for another response.

Our mutual friend informed me that you are a person with many connections. You have great influence. Share the wealth. Looking to go legit. Need 10 million for start up.

I responded.

We invest in many companies. Send me a business plan and I will consider your asking price.

Again within seconds, Iza Tappen responded.

Won't share detailed plan. Will only admit to idea to make computer generated numbers into a world currency. Many countries are bankrupt or will be soon, will offer a new safe currency based on computer numbers. Call it BizCoins.

At first, I thought the guy was crazy. There was no way his idea could work. But then again years ago they sold pet rocks, so anything was possible. Plus, I knew we had hundreds of millions of dollars stashed away. I could pay his fee once I had access to the funds. Even still, there was no way I would write a check to some faceless person who would only email me. I wanted revenge, but I hadn't lost my mind. Any large sum of money was still beyond my reach. That's one reason I needed the mysterious Iza Tappen. I needed to use my leverage in knowing this person needed a large sum of cash and possibly advice. I fired off another email.

Get me access to Bink's computer. I will get you in touch with one of the world's best investment minds, Robert Rapio. I will also put you in contact with a congressman, George McAdams. Both are friends of mine and can help you with your plan by offering you feedback about your idea. I have other jobs for you. If you help me and are successful, you will be paid five million dollars.

Iza's response took less than ten seconds.

Deal on first part. Price is 10 million. Not negotiable.

I had him where I wanted him. Now only the price needed to be hammered out. I turned on the late night football game. I decided to let Iza sweat it out. Once the game was over, I sent off one last email before turning out the lights for the evening.

Everything is negotiable. Seven million and I get the first one hundred numbers generated. If not, have a nice life.

In our training we learned about negotiations. I knew all about finding common ground in any negotiation. First, settle those. Next, offer something you don't care about but make it sound like you do. When you give in, the other side believes they won something and are more likely to want to negotiate what is important to you. Yes, we were talking about a large sum of money. But what Iza didn't realize, I had no use for money. To regain power, money was a means to an end. I was a spiritual man. It's a big reason why when I was leader of the Council, I never bothered to look at our budget. I later paid a price for being so ignorant, but collecting money was never my mission on earth.

I wanted access to Bink's computer. Iza Tappen agreed to do that for me and all I had to do was place two calls to people who owed me favors. I would have eventually given in on the ten million dollar fee, but at that point, my ego wouldn't allow to give in to Iza's number. When I woke up, there was a text on my phone.

Eight million and fifty numbers.

I could have rubbed salt in the wound but I didn't. I agreed to the fee so that Iza was made to think they won something. Why start out a relationship with one side thinking they didn't get anything? Iza likely received millions more than they ever thought possible and I now had someone working for me who would be paid by others. What a deal. The best part was that if his crazy computer currency ever was a hit, I could tell my grandchildren I had the first number. Unless Iza Tappen was an unethical computer hacker? I so loved my job.

My grandfather, who still lived in the compound, researched through his old records to find me enough information to get Iza Tappen working. My grandfather knew bits and pieces of my plan but I didn't want to feed him too much information, and put him in jeopardy. Once I was closer to my ultimate goal, I would unveil the rest. It was possible he was being watched. As far as I knew, only my wife and Peter, who could easily have been planted in Rose's garden, knew I had regained my powers. I didn't want too many to know. There were spies everywhere.

I hustled back to California for Iza's report. I wasn't disappointed. Within three days, not only could I log onto Bink's computer, not leaving a trace I logged on, but I could access his cam. I could watch him working at his computer. Iza went well beyond my expectations. As promised, I made contact with Rapio and McAdams for Iza Tappen. Iza was informed there would be more work in the future.

In reading Bink's list of soul stealers, there were thirty four on active duty. I was no longer registered as an active soul stealer. The list to me appeared somewhat bogus, since Peter was also on the list. As far as I was aware, he rarely left the compound and didn't remove souls. If he did take souls, it wasn't often. I was curious how many other non-soul stealers were on the list. It also told me the Council still didn't suspect Peter was missing. Or was it possible Peter had left Dallas and was back at the compound? If I knew Rose at all, the odds weren't in his favor of ever returning home.

I started reading deeper into Bink's files. He had a list of thousands on the waiting list for soul removals. I needed a few specific people to assist me. After hours of scouring through all the names, I found my starting point. I would be on the next plane to London, England, to introduce myself to Dr. Craig Pickering.

7

*D*r. Craig Pickering was an aspiring tennis star and winner of several junior tournaments until multiple knee and ankle injuries made him a step too slow against the top players. Fortunately, Pickering was young enough that his injuries occurred young enough for him to devote his time back to academia. He chose chemistry as a career path. But the tennis racket was never permanently locked away in his closet.

Before leaving for England, I had done as much research as possible, but I wasn't finding much other than his tennis background. Dr. Pickering was working as a chemist for a leading drug manufacturer. From his limited social media footprint, he was listed as being married with two young children. The few photos I could find online, showed he was a man above average height, with brown hair and appeared to still be in shape for long tennis matches. There was no record of any trouble in his past, not even have a traffic ticket.

I was suspicious Dr. Pickering was a target of the Council for something other than being a dark soul. The Council had proven they would remove the souls of anyone who stood in their way of prosperity. I didn't know what a thirty-three year old chemist from the suburbs of London could have done to upset the Council. I needed to get a firsthand look at his soul.

Bink's file had Pickering's home and work addresses listed. Finding him was not as easy as I originally planned. On my way to his home before daybreak, I was pulled over for driving on the wrong side of the road. I had to take better notice of what country I was driving in. It was the second time in my years of driving, I had been pulled over for the same offense.

It was past seven in the morning before I made it to the Pickering home. After sitting outside for two hours and noticing his children leave for school with who I identified as his wife from the photos, there was still no sign of Dr. Pickering. I drove over to his office and snooped around. Security ushered me off the property.

I left peacefully, but returned several hours later, attempting to get a closer glimpse of Pickering. I parked in the lot across the road from his office. It was not an ideal spot but I didn't want security to notice me again. As the afternoon sky turned to early evening, several employees began to exit the facility. A few came out alone while others left in small clusters, making it more difficult to track my target. As I was about to give up for the evening, a man who I suspected was Pickering, walked toward his car. I decided to follow him in his car.

His car barely stopped at the end of the lot before pulling into oncoming traffic. Luckily, I had enough time to jump into mine and stay on the proper side of the road, while catching up to the rushed Pickering. He led me out of the city and into the country. His car pulled off the main road, down a smaller one and past a well landscaped entrance of a posh tennis club. I pulled my car into the lot a few cars down. By the time I could park and get my keys from the ignition, Pickering had snatched his tennis gear from his trunk and ran inside the front door. I waited hours for him to come back out. It was past ten in the evening before he ambled back toward his car.

I approached the doc cautiously, not wanting to startle him. "Doctor Pickering, may I have a moment or two of your time, please?"

Despite the floodlight on the front of the clubhouse, it was still near dark in the lot. At first, Pickering put his bag back into his trunk and acted as if he didn't hear me. His pace quickened toward his car door as I moved closer. I tried again.

"Please, Doctor, I am not here to harm you. I would like to ask you a few questions."

He juggled his keys before dropping them to the ground. He bent over to pick them up but fumbled them to the ground again as I stood next to him. He was forced to take notice of me.

"What can I help you with, mate? I've had a long day and my wife has a hot meal prepared for me at home."

I moved back a step. "I need your help, Doctor, and in return I will help you. If now is not a good time, we can speak tomorrow? I do believe we can help each other."

I peered through the dusky space between us and deep into his soul. It wasn't perfect, but who is? Pickering had some dark spots on his soul, but not close enough to be considered for removal. I knew he wasn't listed as a high priority to lose his soul, but still, by our normal standards he shouldn't have been a candidate at all.

Pickering began to ramble. "Look here my good man, if your wife is telling you those explicit photos of someone's private parts are mine and sent from me, it's all a horrible misunderstanding. I have already explained it to anyone who will listen. My phone was left for hours in my locker, unattended. For whatever reason, I'm sure some hooligan was attempting to get even with me."

"Relax, Doc. I am not here about any photos. But if you would like to run for political office in the States, you are now qualified."

We both started to laugh. He bent down and picked up his keys and leaned against his car door. "Well then, if not about the photos, what brings you out so late to disturb me?"

I looked Pickering square in the eyes. "I need your help in breaking down a chemical compound of a liquid I have, and I need you to make more of it. Much more, or tell me where I can get it made."

Pickering unlocked his car door. He looked over at me and said, "You have the wrong chap. I work for a private firm. They don't allow me to work for others. Sorry old man, but I have to pass."

I refused to allow him to leave so easily. "Doctor Pickering, it is not that simple. You are who I am looking for, and there is a reason why I traveled thousands of miles to find you. You will do this for me, or there will be consequences. There are people who want to harm you, but I am not quite sure why."

Pickering raised his voice. "Bugger off. The only people who are pissed off at me are the bloody husbands who received that wretched text and photograph of someone's naughty bits. So, if you're not here for that, I suggest you go find another chemist. I'm not for hire!"

As Pickering opened the door of his sports car, someone was leaving the entrance of the clubhouse. "Do you know who that is, Doc?" I asked.

He smirked. "Anyone who has ever listened to the blasted radio knows who that is, mate. That's Van Richards, the lead singer and guitarist for Ten Years from Yesterday. He's a member of the club. Why do you ask?"

"Do you believe you have a soul, Doc?"

"I'm going home, you loony bastard. My wife gets impatient when I'm late."

I needed to act quickly. "Watch this, Doc. This is why you need my protection."

I scampered over to Mr. Richards, knowing his soul was as black as the ace of spades. He had been on our list for years, but too many of our disciples enjoyed his music and didn't want him harmed. But his music would play no more. I introduced myself to Mr. Richards. I shook his hand and removed his soul. He immediately puked all over my brand new shoes. He doubled over for a few moments. He stood up and said, "Bitchin" and walked to his car. It wasn't the exact scenario I had wanted, but I never was a fan.

Pickering was now in his car with the engine running and the car window rolled down. I walked back over to him and calmly let him know what I had done to Richards. "That's what someone is planning for you, Doc. You must hear me out and understand there is a group of people who want to remove your soul, possibly worse."

Pickering smirked. He put his car in gear and quipped, "The only thing you did was have a rock and roll singer ruin your shoes. I can't imagine those were the first pair he's ruined in that manner, nor will it be the last." Pickering disappeared into the night.

A new approach would be needed with this guy. After seeing his soul up close and knowing he wasn't a legitimate candidate to lose his soul, I did more research. I contacted Iza Tappen to see what Iza could uncover about the company that employed Pickering.

Tappen dug into some correspondence between the executives within Pickering's company. Tappen discovered Pickering was working on a drug to lower blood pressure.

I did my more homework on Pickering and realized his doctorate was in computer sciences and not a medical doctor. Pickering was a computer geek, who created drugs using the computer, not an old school chemist with a lab coat playing with liquids.

After becoming better informed, I cross referenced the databases of companies our disciples owned and found a company that was the rival competitor of Pickering's company. The Council must have put Pickering on the list so that he wouldn't create a competing product. The drug on the market by the company owned by our disciples was a low priced alternative. I could only assume the drug Pickering was developing would compete in that low cost market.

It was time to approach Pickering with my new found information. This time I made sure I caught him before leaving for work. He dashed down the front steps of his home toward his car parked on the street when I caught him.

I yelled from a few feet away. "Doctor Pickering, I now understand why you will never be allowed to complete your project. It is imperative you give me a few moments of your time."

He kept walking towards his car attempting to ignore me. I spoke up again.

"Doctor, do you know about a company called Hayward Drugs?"

This time he stopped and with an impatient tone muttered, "Yes, so what. Do you think you're going to blackmail me and tell my boss I interviewed with them a few months back? Don't bother, he already knows."

"Actually, no, I had no idea you interviewed with them. It makes perfect sense though. They tried to hire you away to stop you from completing your work on the competing blood pressure medicine."

Pickering moved several steps in my direction. He got close enough to shove his forefinger into my chest. With a now angry tone he declared, "You really are a bloody fool. No one cares about another drug to lower blood pressure. My drug will alter history. Now don't let me see you around here ever again, or I'll contact the authorities."

I grabbed his wrist below the finger he stuck in my chest.

"You listen to me now you arrogant jackass, you are in danger. A powerful group of people, who must somehow know what you are developing, wants your knowledge. They are the same people who own Hayward Drugs. I am willing to bet since you turned down their offer to work there, they will try a different approach to get your research. If that doesn't work, trust me, you will never finish your research until Hayward Drugs owns the patent."

Pickering shook loose of my grip and stood tall. "And what does any of this have to do with you, mate?"

"I plan on destroying the people who own Hayward Drugs. You will be able to continue your research in peace, but I need your help."

Pickering gave me a disgusted look and turned away. He moved about half way to his car door before I shouted. "Johanna Callaghan has videos of the two of you stored on her computer. It shows you playing a doubles match in her bed. Plus, I have every email you sent to her and several other women who belong to your tennis club. If they reach President Callaghan's desk, I don't think he and the other husbands will be too thrilled. If you are not smart enough to let me help you continue with your research, at least be smart enough to save your marriage and your tennis club membership."

With two large strides, Doc Pickering was standing nose to nose with me. "Don't you dare distribute what are obvious lies and filth, you bloody bastard! Mrs. Callaghan is a fine woman, who would never sleep around with me or anyone but her husband. And any emails you have are pure fiction. I have never and would never send such filth."

"Maybe not Doc, but you do have a reputation now. And I

have employed someone who is a whiz on a computer, even better than you. So I suggest you tone down your testosterone and start to listen to me. One way or another, you will do as I ask."

Pickering with shoulders slumped and squinted eyes replied, "Are you the one who sent that trash from my phone last week?"

"No you idiot! I'm not trying to hurt you. Will you take two minutes and hear me out?"

With that Pickering bit his upper lip before asking, "How do you know people are even after me or my work?"

I crossed my arms and slowly stated, "For one thing, I am willing to bet you upset them when you turned down the job offer from Hayward and for another, I was once their leader."

We agreed to meet for lunch at the restaurant in the shopping center across from his office.

Trying to explain to humans what I do and why isn't easy. It's why most times I don't bother to even try. I rip out their soul and move on to my next target. This time I had to take it to a whole new level with Doctor Pickering. Not only did I have to try to convince the guy I could remove anyone's soul, I had to explain to him about the Council and the fact our disciples were powerful men and women across the globe. In scouring my database, I realized not only did our disciples completely own Hayward Drugs, but the president of the company was one of us.

Pickering was skeptical at best. I couldn't blame him. But I couldn't remove another soul to try to prove my story. I was contacted by Kalani the day after I took the soul of the rock and roll singer. She said the Council was furious and was looking for who did it. I couldn't draw any more attention by stealing souls from people not on the removal list. But I couldn't allow him to walk away again.

"Doc, think of it this way. If I am lying to you, all you did was put a few drops of liquid through your analyzer for me. If I am telling you the truth, you will be free to finish your project in peace. Either way, once you analyze what I ask, you will never see me again. What is the real risk here?"

Doc took a sip of tea then leaned back in his chair. "My company makes drugs to help you with your delusions, mate. But, I will admit the woman who interviewed me at Hayward was shocked when I turned them down. She also said it wouldn't be the last I heard from her. I assumed that meant they would make me a higher offer, but never did. So maybe there is a thread of truth in what you say."

Pickering agreed to analyze the last remaining vile that Winfield had given me. I wouldn't have needed Pickering except Winfield refused to give me the chemical breakdown so I could manufacture more. Winfield also refused to offer me any more assistance in my struggle with the Council.

True to his word, three days later Pickering gave me a print out of the chemical breakdown. I assured him I would do my best to keep him safe from the Council. I had been peeking at Bink's computer on an almost daily basis, so I would be alerted if Pickering moved up the list. With the compound in hand, I was off to my next stop.

8

John Corbin's birth certificate records his birth in San Francisco,

California. His mother is listed as an immigrant from Japan and his father of Irish born decent. No one has ever questioned when and where John was born. They should have. The truth was recorded in the Council files many years ago.

I met John, or as I knew him, Hisao, in the compound during my training. He was listed in the Council database as Hisao Jonathan Corbin. His parents met while his father, Liam, was sent by the Council to Japan to learn about their country's culture in the early 1800's. Liam was wounded while learning how to defend himself with a sword. He was nursed back to health by his future wife, Aika.

After months of courting, Aika's father refused permission for Liam to marry his daughter. Liam wasn't born in accepted country. Unknown to everyone but Aika and Liam, she was pregnant with their first child when he asked for her hand in marriage. Despite being shunned by Aika's family, Liam refused to leave her behind. He escaped with his pregnant girlfriend and married her following their long trek back to his native land of Ireland. Five months later,

Hisao Jonathan Corbin was brought into the world. He was named after the man who aided Liam and Aika in leaving Japan and Liam's father.

Liam and Aika had another child, a daughter and for many years resided in Ireland. Liam went on to become a successful soul stealer. However like many, his time away from his family began to wear on the entire family. Aika was pure human. As she aged, Liam and his family immigrated to the United States. In Akia's later years, Liam insisted with the Council he spend more time at home with his wife and children. His wish was temporarily granted.

I met Liam and Hisao soon after they moved to Kansas. They occasionally attended training sessions in the compound. Twice our times coincided and Hisao and I became friendly rivals in training. Soon after meeting Hisao and his father, the Japanese bombed Pearl Harbor. For safety reasons, he would forever be known as John H. Corbin. A new birth certificate was made appearing as if John H. Corbin was born in California. I was too young at the time to understand the influence and reach the Council enjoyed.

There is a conflicting story as to what happened to the Corbin family soon after the last time I trained with John in the compound. The locals tell the story that Akia passed away of natural causes and her husband's guilt drove him to drink, and later suicide. My father told me that Liam lost his soul.

My father went on to explain that after the death of Akia, Liam was ordered back to full time soul duty. He refused. Liam was guilt stricken over leaving his wife and children so much over the years that he refused to leave them for any length of time after his wife passed away. My father claims he was in the Council room the day Liam was ordered to resume his duties or suffer the consequences. My father believes that Charon Orcus removed Liam Corbin's soul for disobeying the Council's orders.

A week later, Liam was found dead in his barn with a gunshot wound to the head. My father told me that John was the one who found his father's body. No one knows what happened to John's sister, but rumor among the disciples has long been held that Orcus raised the girl in secrecy. John remained in Kansas and never finished his training. The Council reached out to assist John in paying off the mortgage on the farm and other living expenses, but he refused help of any kind.

John received a scholarship to law school and graduated near the top of his class. He also received a large insurance settlement after his mother's death. He had been unaware his mother was covered with life insurance. It was enough to pay for all his living expenses for years. John went on to law school and became a successful lawyer in Kansas City, for a top law firm. I lost touch with him after his parents died. I never met his sister.

My father and grandfather both told me that the Council and in particular, Elder Orcus, made it clear that John would be welcomed back to finish his training at any time. The Council made several attempts to assist John with his career path, but John wanted nothing to do with the Council or soul stealing. Looking back, I now question how much assistance John received either knowingly or not. His rise in politics from state senator to United States Congressman came swiftly, many times with no opposition. The time had come for me to either make or break the future of John H. Corbin.

It took several attempts of reaching out to John's office before anyone returned my call. Eventually someone from his staff did and a meeting was arranged. I would meet with Speaker John Corbin back in his home state of Kansas, rather than in Washington. Elliot Nesstor had advised me to stay away from the District of Columbia. The President was still upset over the journalist, who was his administration's main source of planted leaks, losing his soul. Despite my constant leads assisting the FBI; I was a marked man. I didn't think Corbin drew any connections between me and the journalist, until I met with Corbin.

We met at a steak house in his home district. The restaurant was filled with young looking professionals of both sexes all decked out in their best office attire. The establishment was across the street from the largest office buildings downtown, the courthouse only three blocks away. The ambiance was a put your bib on, eat quickly, and get out to make room for the next wave of hungry people. Corbin had called ahead for reservations. As usual, I arrived early to scan the room to find an escape route. Old habits die hard.

At first, I didn't recognize either of the two people heading towards the table. The first person to introduce himself was the younger looking of the two. He was dressed in a dark suit, with perfectly coiffed jet black hair, a slender body, carrying a computer tablet and three cell phones. "Good afternoon, Mr. Novo, I am Jeff Lanigan, Speaker Corbin's aide."

Following behind Lanigan was a frumpy looking fellow with a brown suit that was one size too big, a crooked tie, grey hair and shoes that needed a good polish. Corbin had put on a lot of weight since he was younger and even some since I last saw him in the news. He looked nothing like I was expecting being one of our disciples. I realize he didn't consider himself one of us any longer, but our group were normally health conscience. One look at this man and it was obvious he quit our training before our nutrition classes began.

Corbin reached out and offered a handshake. "Hello, Caeles, it's been a long time. I apologize for my delay in setting up this meeting but we have been debating a health care bill in the House for months. Darn bill has kept us all quite busy."

"It is fine, Mr. Speaker. I am pleased you could find time in your busy schedule." I said as I offered the two men their seats.

The three of us ordered drinks and made small talk about what was going on around Washington, the weather, and sports, until Speaker Corbin asked Jeff Lanigan to step outside and make a call on the Speakers behalf. Corbin then gave me a dirty look and started in with his lecture. "I'm going to tell you the same thing I told Orcus and all the other goons he sent looking for me. I'm never going back to your world, and I'm not doing you guys any more favors. Period. So, you can report back to your grand poobah and tell him to take a hike. I refuse to be bought like someone else we know."

"I don't think you understand, Mr. Speaker. I don't want you to go back to the compound or deal with Elder Orcus. Trust me, he and I have had our differences over the years. I will never be his errand boy. In fact, I am no longer associated with them. That's why I am here."

Corbin didn't take long before he asked in a slow quizzical tone, "So then, if not to bribe me, what do you want from me?"

I wasn't slow in my response. "I don't bribe, Mr. Speaker. I am more of a blackmail person."

It took Corbin about fifteen seconds before breaking a smile. "Be careful, Novo, blackmailing a government official can land you in jail for a very long time."

"I am here for two reasons. One, I think you know the truth behind my friend, Congressman McAdams. I know he was annoying you with all his questions about the budget, but the guy is as honest as they make them. His heart is in the right place. I am asking you to help him, once he's exonerated."

Corbin jumped in. "Hold on, if you are inferring I had anything to do with his arrest, you're mistaken. That had nothing to do with me."

I motioned the waitress for another round of drinks to calm the tension in the air. Once she was gone, I continued. "John, you forget, I can see into your soul. I do believe you. That's not why I am here. I can disrupt American politics for many years to come. I don't expect you to come clean with what went on with McAdams. But we both know the President had something to do with the arrest of McAdams. I can't prove it yet, but I will. I also know a former CIA operative who was ordered by the Vice President to kill a businessman in order to profit from a competing company in which he owns stock."

Corbin squirmed in his chair then grabbed the end of the table with both hands. His body became instantly rigid. "Novo, if you expect me to sit here and listen to this nonsense, you're sadly mistaken. I support my President and the Vice President."

"Really, John? Do you support them enough to turn down being the next President of the United States? Because I can make that happen. After all, as you are well aware, you are currently third in line for the Presidency."

Corbin raised an eyebrow and smiled. "If I am ever to become President, I'll do it the old fashioned way. I'll buy votes and rig voting machines."

I assumed he was joking but it took me a few moments to respond, "That's not the way they do it any longer Mr. Speaker. They promise everything is going to change. They register everyone they can, illegal or not, flood the internet with endless ads, then scream discrimination if you don't allow everyone to vote more than once, weeks before Election Day."

We both laughed knowing how close to the truth each of us hit.

Corbin started the conversation again. "Why are you here? It can't be over a two bit congressman who thinks cutting a million dollars from our budget will make a difference."

I shook my head and smirked. "That is part of it, Mr. Speaker. McAdams is an honest guy. You all could use a few more like him. In fact, if you spurn my offer, once I prove conspiracy against the President attempting to frame McAdams for murder, I have money people who could push George right into the White House. His story is compelling."

Corbin rubbed his hand across his now red face. I could tell he was growing impatient with me. I needed to get to the real point of our meeting. "Mr. Speaker, our disciples are dying. Too many have abandoned our mission of soul stealing to make their mark on the world. Look at you. You are one of the most powerful men on earth, but how long can you stay in power?"

Corbin blurted out, "I'll stay in power for as long as people keep electing me!"

"No you won't, Mr. Speaker. People are going to get suspicious when you are in office for fifty years and your appearance barely changes."

Corbin asked again with an angry tone. "Again Novo, what do you want from me?"

It was time to reel in my next catch. "Mr. Speaker, on occasion, I will come to you ask for you to use your influence to make life a bit easier for a corporation or individual around Washington. I will keep my requests at a minimum. However, you will do as I ask.

With a beet red face and curled upper lip, Corbin responded with an even angrier tone. "There is no way I am going to do anything for you, Novo. You have wasted my time and yours!" Corbin began to stand.

I started to speak before he could leave the area. "Mr. Speaker, with all due respect, I do know your true identity. I know the birth certificate from California isn't real. I know many things about you that I am sure you don't want the public to know. I can make it look like you set up a congressman for murder. Or, I can place the blame where it belongs, with President Morrison."

Corbin moved next to me as I remained seated and said, "First of all, only the crazies in the world will believe your fake birth certificate story. For another, I had nothing to do with McAdams being on trial for murder. And lastly, blackmail is a dangerous game, even for soul people."

I sat back in my chair shifting away from Corbin and firmly replied. "If I do nothing, our people will become extinct. Do you think twisting the arm of one congressman is going to stop me from trying to save my disciples, including you? John, the few of us left can't possibly steal enough souls to keep you and all the others from dying out much sooner than expected. The current Council has become short sighted with their greed. Others like you, who have abandoned our cause for personal gain, cannot expect us to keep working our asses off to support you. Please, sit back down and talk this out with me."

We both took a moment and looked around the room then back at each other before Corbin sat back down. We both took sips of our drinks before I continued.

"Look at what you do in Washington, Mr. Speaker. You make laws that takes money from people who earn it and give it some who are less fortunate no doubt, but you also allow too many to slip into the cracks and live off the hard work of others. We have become like your constituents. Too many who can provide for themselves don't, because they know with one vote you will provide for them. Our disciples have fallen into the same pit. I won't provide for you or others any longer to live three hundred years if you won't help me, John. It's that simple. I'll become one of the people on the sidelines who live off of others. And once we all are on the sidelines, we can all die much sooner than necessary."

Corbin looked at me and this time with a somber tone stated, "I have my own reasons for not stealing souls. I believe Orcus either killed my father or ordered the attack. I believe he stole my sister and still has her in hiding. As far as working for you, and risk upsetting the most powerful man in the world, there is no chance.

I've seen what destruction he can do."

"Who, Morrison?" I replied.

"No, you fool, Charon Orcus. Morrison's a pawn for Orcus. I've seen his goons at big donor fund raisers, at state dinners, and inside the White House. I'm not blind to it."

"But don't you see, John? This is exactly why I need you. I need to end this type of corruption that has taken over the Council. And as far as Orcus, you need to get caught up with the times, my friend. For a short time, I had ruined Orcus. I was the leader of the Council. But I didn't see how far off track they had become and they attempted to ruin me. I have already started to destroy all the members of the Council. Orcus is no longer the threat you think he is. Right now, they are in disarray. It is why I need to strike soon. Please, I only need to use your influence on a limited basis and I promise, your birth certificate will remain a secret. I will prove McAdams was set up by President Morrison. I don't know how the President did it, but when I find out, he's going to pay for what he did to my friend George McAdams."

Corbin took a deep sigh. "Caeles, when you were young, you did always have a brass set on ya. But going after a sitting American President, you should be old enough now to understand your balls aren't that tough."

"I don't want to bring him down, John. But I do intend to weaken him to the point where he is no longer any use to the Council. Your father was one of the best soul stealers who ever lived. Help me restore our disciples. Please"

Corbin took another deep sigh then shrugged his shoulders. "My father was one of the best and your Council murdered him when he wanted out. I owe them nothing. But I'll tell you what, Caeles. You find my sister and bring her back to me and I will give you three opportunities to attempt to use my influence. Mind you, I'm not promising you results, only that I'll do what I can, once my sister is returned to me."

I snickered under my breathe knowing I doubted I would need even three favors. I tried to finalize our deal. "I'll tell you what, Mr. Speaker. For your three favors, I will make sure your name is nowhere to be found when it comes to the dirty work surrounding McAdams, only those who set him up. I'll lose your birth certificate, because I am a nice guy. And I will find your sister as soon as possible. But, you will grant me one of your favors in advance of your sister being returned. Should I be successful you will not hear from any of our disciples ever again. Deal?"

One last giant sigh from Speaker John Corbin, then a handshake. He rose from the table and left. I finished my drink with the satisfaction of knowing I was one step closer to destroying all who attempted to destroy me.

9

"*H*ello, Mr. Novo. It sure is always so nice to see you. I can't thank you enough for taking little ole' me to that Cowboys game. Doc Winfield sure was grumpy when I told him we went, but like you said, he had his chance."

Nurse Simon always knew how to make me smile. I had to admit her zest for life always balanced out the usually miserable character who sat at the other end of the hallway. But unfortunately, I would have to make that trek down the hallway.

"Is he around today, Nurse Simon?"

She lit up like a tree on Christmas Eve. "Why Mr. Novo, I keep thinking one of these trips you're going to tell me you came here to see me, and not Doctor Winfield." Nurse Simon giggled with a devilish looking smile. "Yes, he's in the back complaining about the landlord raising the rent. Follow me please."

Yet again, I found myself wandering down the hallway to see a man I had grown to enjoy antagonizing. He would never admit to me, but I would bet he enjoyed seeing me every now and again as well. As we reached the end of the hallway, Nurse Simon announced my presence, then made her way back to her work area. Winfield knew he didn't have all of my attention as long as Nurse Simon could be seen wiggling her way back to her desk.

"When are you finally gonna forget my address, cowboy? You promised me after I helped ya the last time ya wouldn't be back buggin me. I'm startin ta think ya come just ta see my nurse. And from one man to another, that's not sitting well with me, Novo. So git on with what ya gotta say and mosey on outta here."

I didn't bother to wait for Winfield to ask me to sit. Being in a bratty mood, I sat in the chair across the desk from him, resting comfortably. "I never took you as the jealous type, Doc. But then again, if you lost Nurse Simon, you would be losing three lovely ladies, not just one. So, I guess I could see why you might be a bit upset she would go to football games with me and not you."

Seeing Winfield's face turn red made my trip worth it. This guy had rattled me so many times in the past. It felt great to turn the tables for once. Even if I knew it wouldn't last long.

"I swear, cowboy, ya love pokin me with that dumbass theory of yours about my perty filly out there being some kinda crazy three-headed monster. She's as sweet as the bee honey they git off my ranch. Now stop with all that talk or this conversation is dun."

I needed help from Winfield, but it sure was nice to poke his weak spot.

"Ok, Doc, let's get to it then. I will try to put the image of your girlfriend enjoying herself with me out of my mind and get to my point. What can you tell me about your dad possibly sheltering a young girl? Did you have an adopted sister when you were younger?"

Winfield leaned back in his chair, then put his feet up on his desk and said, "So I can add ya ta the list of people searching fer the girl, eh Novo? Well, guess what, ya dun told me ya would get enough cash ta fund my entire operation round here for many years and I reckon I've yet ta see one dime of it. Plus, you come prancing in my office like you own it and watch my perty girl wander down that hallway like you own her too, and now ya want me ta answer your question. Git your ass outta my office, Novo. Even if I did know sumtin, till I see some appreciation from ya for all my past help in the way of filling my checkbook, don't come back round here asking any more questions. Ya hearing me, El-Dar Novo?"

I knew I'd pressed Winfield harder than usual. I didn't think he would tell me the truth if his father was hiding what now should be a grown woman. But I did want to see his reaction to the question. He wasn't telling all he knew. So I had to twist the soft spot in his brain one more time before I left.

"Ok, Doc. You are right. I have not lived up to my side of the deal and pumped some money into your account, but it is coming. I thought maybe you would help me with one question for saving your life, but hey, I see now you have short term memory issues. It will be good enough for me for now that we both know I saved your life. I will be on my way."

I could feel the heat emanating from Winfield as he put his feet back on the floor and jumped up. "Git outta my office, Novo, and don't ya dare return till you bringing sumtin fer me. And don't ya say nutin ta my nurse on your way out neither, asshole."

I took my sweet time strolling down the hallway. I started

whistling the latest number one hit from Dylan James and the Overture, "Beautiful Girl", loud enough so Winfield could hear me. It was hard not to turn on any radio station and not know the song. The song was about a stranger walking into town and walking out with the most beautiful girl.

Nurse Simon was smiling as I walked past her work area, "Oh, I love that song, Mr. Novo."

"Dylan is a personal friend of mine," I told Nurse Simon. "Next time his band tours Texas, I will get us some back stage passes, and I will introduce you."

I'm sure Winfield heard the screech from Nurse Simon all the way from his office. I could hear him yelling, "Git, Novo. Stop talking with her, or I'll ban ya from this office forever."

Nurse Simon and I both stood there laughing for a moment. "Don't you worry about him, Mr. Novo, he's been cranky lately. I'm not sure why, but he's not been himself ever since you rescued him. But don't you worry. You come on back here anytime. I think secretly he likes it when you come around."

I made my way to the front door with Nurse Simon following me. She grabbed my arm as I reached for the door handle. She pulled me to her and wrapped her arms around me.

"Rose doesn't like it when you invite others to go on dates, sugar. Despite that, Rose will still watch over things here and let you save the world. But the next time you come to town, it better be to see The Rose."

Rose then pulled me even tighter, whispered something in my ear and bit my ear lobe. Rose was like a giant bag of Halloween candy. It tastes so good eating it, yet there is always a price to pay later. I knew she would never hurt me. Well, I hoped not. I gave Rose a soft kiss on the cheek and made my exit.

After leaving Texas, I added to my vast collection of frequent flyer miles and headed over to Northern Italy. I had made arrangements to meet with Brandon Bink. He not only handed out all the assignments for the remaining soul stealers, but prepared the financial statements for the Council meetings.

We met at a small café within a short drive of the compound. The café sat on the south west corner of the main section in town along a street built over three hundred years ago. The cobblestone street was littered with people going about their business. The white stone buildings, some with columns and some with a modern feel were all perfectly manicured. Many had flower boxes with fall blooming flowers while other boxes were now vacant and waiting for winter's chill. The sky was a pastel blue, people were smiling, and I was about to put my next step into action.

Bink was on time for our meeting but he didn't look well. His dark hair now showed touches of grey around the temples and his tall slender body had a slight tilt to it. He had traces of lines on his face showing either stress or his advancing age. He sat in a wooden chair across from me with only a small round wooden table between us. He looked tired.

"You don't look good Bink, what's going on?"

Bink let out a long yawn before responding. "Oh, you know why, Novo. Especially now that you're not working, we are so short handed. I have the Council screaming in my ear to keep all the soul stealers working as often as possible to keep us all healthy. But, hell there's only so many hours in the day, ya know?"

I felt bad for the guy, but I was about to add to his misery. "I feel for you, Bink. I do. But there is not much I can do about that. I have been banned from the compound and all duties."

Bink cut in. "Plus, you couldn't take souls, even if I assigned them to you, right? I mean they did take away your ability to remove souls, right?"

I couldn't figure out why this line of questioning, but I thought I would play along. "Well let me come clean, Bink. I refuse to allow the Council, and all the disciples to give up and become power players around the world. I plan on shifting the emphasis back onto soul removals and less on power grabs."

Bink looked at me with a raised brow. "Uhm, like you said, Novo, you are banned from the compound and without your power, how do you propose to do all this, big guy?"

"Let me worry about all that, Mr. Bink. For now, I have an assignment for you. I want you transfer one million dollars to the account of Dr. Grayson Winfield. I will get the account number for you. After that, you are to transfer two million dollars to the account of an Iza Tappen. I will have whoever this Tappen person is, contact you with the information."

Bink rubbed his fingers under his chin. He frowned before saying, "Why on earth would I do something like that for you?"

"Because, Mr. Bink. I want you to think about it. Unless things have changed recently, the Council has four members and two open seats. Two current members are so old they might not wake up on any given morning. Peter is a conniving little twit, who couldn't defeat me no matter how hard he tried. Timmons will get hers. Who do you want to bet is going to win in the end? Either you can be loyal to me, or you can take your chance with who is left for leadership in the compound."

Bink smirked. "Nice one, Novo. But Peter already defeated you. You can't take souls, right? I mean he already beat you. Last I checked you aren't running the Council any longer."

A cool breeze kicked up. Cooler weather was approaching. "Tell me Mr. Bink, how is our dear friend, Peter doing these days?"

Bink shuttered. I wasn't sure if it was because of his thin jacket attempting to ward off the cold blasts of air rushing down the street or my question. "Peter has been out on assignment for weeks. We are expecting his return any day now. Why do you ask?"

"Since when did Peter ever go out on assignments?"

Bink looked surprised by my question. "All of the elders go out an occasional assignment. You of all people should be aware of that, Novo."

"Bink, that's crap and you know it. There was a law passed not long ago that I instituted called the Soul Directive, and you are well aware of it. Council leaders no longer went out on missions unless it was approved by the Council leader."

"Things have changed since you left us, Novo."

I stared at Bink with my best poker face. "What's it going to take, Bink? Tell me. I want the money transferred and you have the ability to do it."

What Bink didn't know was that I could reach into his computer and make the transfer anytime I wanted. The problem would be that people would be asking questions if I did it. But if Bink did it, there wouldn't be questions.

"What I want Novo, is some respect, from you and all the others. Every one of you waltzes into my office and demands this and demands that. Even now, you demand I come here and meet you and demand I ship money to two people I know shouldn't be getting anything from us. Yet you insist I kneel and kiss your ring. Screw you, Novo. You wanna know what I want. I want respect! I want a seat on the Council. I've earned it, long before you ever did and especially that twerp, Peter Pascal."

"Fine, Bink. You want a seat on the Council, done."

Bink glared back at me. "No, you don't get it. I don't want a seat because you gave it to me, you jackass, I want a seat because I've frigging earned it."

Bink had a point. All the elders had treated him poorly over the years, including me. I wasn't sure he had the abilities to sit on the Council, but so many before him didn't either, including me. I needed to soothe his fragile ego.

I apologize, Mr. Bink. Possibly we have all underestimated your contributions to our disciples. After I clean up this mess, I will see to it that you are recognized for all your past work. Now, what else can I do for you to ensure you make the money transfers?"

Bink sat back in his chair and smiled. "There is a hockey star in Europe. He is on the list to have his soul removed, but not for months. His team is playing against my home country in the Olympics qualifier final this weekend. It sure would be a shame if he lost his soul and wasn't at full capacity. But of course, you couldn't possibly remove his soul for me, now could you? But, if somehow Nikolas Larsson didn't play in the event, I would think two money transfers could be arranged. I won't forget your promise of making sure I get a seat on the Council too."

I enjoyed Bink thinking he got the best of me. Everyone was now underestimating me. How hard could it be to take the soul of one hockey player? I only had to find his house and zap him on the way out the door.

"Get me the information on your hockey star, Bink. I will see what I can do. But you must promise me that no one knows of our arrangement. You will have to hide the transfers on the financials to the Council."

Bink offered a crooked smile. "Sure, Novo, of course. It stays between us."

10

$\mathcal{N}$ikolas Larsson was born in Kalmar, Sweden. Kalmar is an ancient town on the Baltic Sea situated on the south east side of Sweden. The town over time has become more of an industrial town building steam engines, trains and large machinery. Nikolas grew up watching his father work long hours in the automobile factory and later building steam engines. This was not going to be the fate of Nikolas.

At an early age, he was quicker on ice skates than most his age and older, including his brother, Albert. Despite being two years younger, Nikolas was bigger and stronger than his older brother. His parents didn't want either son to continue in the tradition of being local factory workers and encouraged Nikolas to develop his hockey skills, Albert his scholastic ability.

By the time Nikolas reached his seventeenth birthday, his maturity and mind matched his age, but his body was advanced. He stood taller than six feet and a tick over two hundred pounds. His bushy long blonde hair and piercing blue eyes might have made him appear as other Swedes, but his temper as not typical. Because he could push and shove others around on skates he assumed he could continue his advantage outside the rink. It was a fairly common occurrence for Nikolas to return home with scrapes across his body from his latest brawl.

It wasn't entirely his fault. Tough guys, who would marvel at Nikolas's ability on skates, would question if Nikolas was as physical off the ice. It led to many skirmishes after games.

While playing junior hockey in Stockholm, several scouts from the National Hockey League would be in attendance to observe Nikolas. One particular scout from the Boston Bruins was impressed enough to convince the team to make him their number one pick in the upcoming draft.

After Nikolas was drafted by the Boston Bruins, he stayed put in Sweden to finish his junior hockey career. However, not only was he a big bruiser on and off the ice, he was now a bruiser with money in his pocket. No one could tell him no.

Nikolas's dream was always to skate with the best, and he took little advice from anyone. His father, Erik, would always tell him, "Put away some money, you can't play forever." But his plea was mostly ignored. The agent for Nikolas did make sure some of his money stayed in his account. However, his agent couldn't keep a constant eye on Nikolas since the agent's office was in New York City.

As the following summer came to a close, Nikolas moved to Boston to start working out with his future teammates and become adjusted to living in another country. It was different for him since back home in Kalmar, Nikolas was a burgeoning star. In Boston, he was merely a big, strong, good looking blonde walking the streets without anyone offering more than a forced smile. No one in Boston knew the real Nikolas. Then again, few knew the real Nikolas, even in his home town.

A few weeks later, training camp officially opened for the Bruins. The first week of practice was uneventful for Nikolas and the team. Much of the work being done was conditioning and non contact skating drills. The second week was a different matter.

Dimtri Petrov, a Russian, who was a veteran with the Bruins, knocked Nikolas off his skates during one of the early morning scrimmages. Nikolas returned to his skating and smiled at Dimitri. Moments later, Bruins team captain, Gale Wild, was overheard telling Dimitri, "Wipe the smirk off of that kid's face."

Moments later, the two teammates were pummeling each other in the corner of the rink. It wasn't much of a fight. Dimitri understood the art of a good hockey fight. He pulled up Nikolas's oversized jersey so that he couldn't see his opponent. Nikolas was also caught off guard in having a teammate attack him on the ice, for no apparent reason. The unexpected assault only hardened Nikolas.

By most standards, Nikolas had a successful rookie season netting eleven goals from the checking line. He had won respect from his team and the league. He finished second in the rookie of the year voting. He was seen as a hero back home in Sweden. After the season concluded, he ventured home to see his family back in Kalmar. His brother, Albert was not in the best of health. Nikolas felt responsible for his brother.

Nikolas spent the month of July back in Sweden with his family. He stayed away from many of his old stomping grounds and friends. He was reminded of a provision in his contract with the Bruins, that if he was injured in a fight away from the hockey rink, his contract would no longer be in effect.

There was the occasional day and night Nikolas would

disappear, but he spent much of his time staying close to his brother. For the next five seasons, it became routine for Nikolas to spend July in Kalmar with his brother. As Albert became weaker, Nikolas grew stronger.

During those five seasons, Nikolas became a full fledged star. His fights away from the ice were rare. He was scheduled to be married to a fashion model he met on a trip the previous year, while playing against the Rangers in New York. Life was good for Nikolas.

After reading Bink's report, I was now curious why the soul of Nikolas Larsson was on the list. It was reported that the Swedish National team would be playing the heavily favored Canadian team in Montreal. Nikolas was granted a waiver in his contract so that he could play for his country's team in the Olympics or any qualifiers. Since the Bruins had three nights off in a row, Nikolas decided to play for his home team.

I waited in the dark shadows of the Montreal Forum, where team practice was held. After practice was over, I scrutinized the situation to ensure Nikolas boarded the team bus. I knew him from several photographs from the team web site. It also didn't hurt that he was on a recent cover of "A Man's Man" a famous men's magazine. There were a few security lights illuminating the bus. But even with my binoculars, I was too distant to see into his soul. I was however able to view Larsson as he hopped on the team bus.

I followed the team bus back to the hotel. By the time I parked the car, the team had unloaded into the hotel. I wandered into the hotel lobby and sat down as if I belonged. After pretending to be reading a newspaper left behind in my seat, some of the players started to emerge from elevators off the main lobby. Several cars pulled out front of the hotel entrance. Beautiful women instantly appeared from thin air. They swarmed the young hockey stars. They all jumped into the waiting cars and rode off into the night. Nikolas Larsson was unseen.

After waiting over two hours, I grew weary. It was now past one in the morning. I walked through the hotel parking lot and started my car. But then I noticed what looked like Larsson leaving the front of the building. I drove my car into a better position and watched as he ambled down the street, away from the hotel. He was alone. I couldn't imagine where he would be going at that hour. It was too dark and he was too distant to get a good look into his soul.

Larsson was now three blocks from the hotel. He jumped into the front passenger side of a waiting dark blue SUV that was parked under a street post. I followed the vehicle within a safe distance. I had been to Montreal a few times, but I had never been in the direction they were heading. The SUV drove slowly past several street corners, till it stopped, and Larsson jumped out of the vehicle. From my less than perfect line of sight, it appeared that Larsson was holding a gun to a smaller man's chest. Larsson then shoved the guy into the back seat of the SUV. They proceeded to drive outside of the city limits. I followed at a discrete distance, which was not easy since few cars dotted the roads.

The vehicle led me to an industrial section well outside the city limits. It made a turn down a narrow road with no lights. I knew I couldn't follow the SUV that close without drawing suspicion. I watched from the intersection as the SUV made another right off the darkened road not far from the intersection where I sat. With caution, I drove past the area where the truck made the right turn. The SUV had pulled into a junk yard.

I parked my car a hundred yards from the junk yards entrance and walked towards where I thought the SUV had parked. Inside the entrance of the yard were piles of rusting metal and old tires. With only the moonlight to assist me, it wasn't easy to see down the entrance road unless I stayed in the middle of the road. That wouldn't be prudent since I wasn't aware of where the SUV had parked. I walked as close to the side of the road as I could, without stumbling into piles of decay.

The crooked road strewn with metal, eventually led to a tiny shack of a building with one small yellow light above the door. There sat the SUV, parked horizontal to the building with the headlights streaming the high beams against a large stack of half rotted cars. I could see one man sitting behind the driver's wheel and two men walking in front of the high beams.

Nikolas Larsson was shoving a smaller man wearing jeans and tee shirt to the ground while holding a hand gun pointed towards his head. The smaller man then fell to his knees with hands folded and reaching towards the night sky. I moved quietly over and around piles of rubbish to possibly hear what was going on between them.

In between large sobs and loud screams, the man on his knees pleaded for divine intervention and his life. None came. Nikolas Larsson emptied six rounds into the pleading man's skull and chest. I was shocked. None of my extensive training had prepared me to witness an execution. My body stiffened in fear and horror.

Larsson wiped his brow then looked high into the night sky,

extending both arms straight out from his body and let out a menacing scream. He stopped screaming before kicking the dead man and rolling him onto his back. Larsson then reached into the backseat of the vehicle and pulled out a bag with fresh clothes packed inside. He changed clothes including shoes and tossed the gun and previously worn clothes into the same bag. I watched in stunned silence as they drove off leaving the corpse.

My body shook as if I had just stolen a soul. For one of the rare times in my life, I wept for a total stranger. After the sound of the car engine faded into the distance, I ran over to the bloodied body. This was no man. This was a kid, likely not even twenty years of age. His life was over. What could he have done to justify such a horrific ending to his young life?

My trembling body stumbled like a drunkard back to my car. Thankfully, the SUV went in the same direction it came and the murderers never saw my parked car up the road.

Not by design but within a few minutes, I had caught up to the dark blue SUV at a traffic light. It was two cars in front of me. I followed it until it pulled into a small designated parking area along the St. Lawrence River. I kept driving along the road until I could find a safe spot to pull over. I jumped out with my binoculars and with enough spare time, I witnessed Larsson toss a large bag into the river. He hopped back into the SUV and drove off. I had seen enough for one night.

Early the following morning, I contacted Special Agent Elliot Nesstor and filled him in on all the gory details. He was less than thrilled I didn't contact the Canadian authorities immediately after witnessing the crime.

"You know I couldn't do that, Elliot. The police would start asking me my name and why I was following the SUV in the first place. There is no way I will testify in any court of law."

"Cale, you witnessed a murder on Canadian soil, by a Swedish citizen and another who you couldn't identify in a crowd of two. What the hell do you expect me to do with this information? Should I call the Montreal police and let them know that my one and hundred year old informant, who steals souls for a living, called me to let me know that a world renowned hockey star went on a joy ride with a faceless person in a dark blue SUV and murdered a teenager who was standing on a street corner? Does that sound rationale to you, Cale?"

I knew Nesstor had a point, but I couldn't allow this vicious crime to go unsolved. I would handle Larsson in my own way, but he would also pay through the criminal justice system.

"Elliot, this could be a big case for you. The way Larsson executed that kid; it sure didn't appear to me like this was his first murder. Look in your files for unsolved murders of teenagers, or people in hockey towns. I don't know. I only know people don't act as calm as Larsson did after taking a life."

Nesstor didn't let me complete my thought. "You told me it was the first time you saw someone executed. How the hell would you know how they act? Look, Cale, there isn't anything I can do. I have no jurisdiction in Canada. This one's on you to make it right."

I was upset Nesstor wouldn't make any effort. But I couldn't let it go. The image of that poor kid's head being blown off was still too fresh in my mind.

"Elliot, please have someone run a search of unsolved murders in Boston, or even where Larsson is from in Sweden."

"Soul Man, I have a few unresolved cases of my own I'm trying to clean up before I retire. I don't want to add to the list. Besides, the list you are asking about is too long. Many crimes go unsolved. But when I get a chance, I'll make a few calls to some people down in Boston and see what I can come up with. But after that, I don't wanna hear any more about this Larsson kid. And do us all a big favor next time. Write down the damn license plate number."

Seeing an execution affected me. I had met and stolen souls from many a murderer. But it was either after the fact or not proven in court. I could only peer into dark spots on a soul, never witness what made it so dark. Seeing something first hand, so violent, changed me.

I drove back to the hotel where the Swedish National team was staying and perched myself in the lobby, seeking Larsson. Later in the evening was the game against the Canadian team. I needed to stop Larsson from playing, or at least have him not play his best so Bink would make my money transfers.

It was three hours before game time and the team started to assemble in the lobby. A bus pulled in front. I knew the time had to be near for Larsson to make his way through the lobby.

Players were already starting to board the bus when I noticed Larsson. I had to dodge a few autograph seekers to get close enough for him to hear me. "I saw you in the SUV last night, Larsson. I know what you did."

Larsson signed one last autograph before brushing a blonde curl from his steely blue eyes. "I dun know what you talk about. I was asleep in room all night after practice. Now, I go and beat Canadian team. Excuse me please."

"No, you weren't, you sick son of a bitch. You murdered that kid!"

I reached out and grabbed Larsson's arm. I could hear someone call for security as I refused to let go until I was sure my mission was complete. He shook free of my grip but it was too late. I now owned his soul. He glared at me. "You have me mistaken for someone else. I am hockey player, not killer."

Two of his teammates shoved me aside and escorted Nikolas Larsson to the entrance of the team bus. He stumbled up the first step. He looked back to glare at me. I stared back until someone assisted him to his seat on the bus.

The hotel manager was now in my face asking if I was a guest, and if not, to leave the premises. I did so peacefully and entered back into the shadows. Larsson played in the game but was ineffective. His team was on the wrong side of a lopsided score.

I contacted Bink the next day and asked him to live up to his end of the bargain. At first, he tried to disappoint me.

"I asked for the guy not to play at all, Novo. He played. You didn't do as I asked."

Bink wasn't going to deter me. He needed a reminder why I was the best soul stealer in the world. "You said you didn't want him to play at full strength. His team lost. You either do as you promised or one day you might not make it home. Don't ever cross me, Bink."

Hours later, the transfers were completed. I could now continue with my plan to regain control of the disciples and destroy the current Council members.

11

Skip Stanton had the potential to be an excellent soul stealer many decades ago. He was born in the shadows of the Liberty Bell in Philadelphia, Pennsylvania. Like many of us disciples, he and his family traveled the world as he grew up. He completed our extensive training and was enlisted in our ranks. I never met Skip during his training. He completed it before I started visiting the compound.

During one of his early thefts, he was stabbed several times by the man he was stalking. He lost so much blood; his ability to remove souls was eliminated. Elder Charon Orcus, who was the leader of the Council at the time, was furious when he learned an inexperienced Stanton was sent on such a dangerous trip. From what my father tells me, in those days, there were too many being injured on the job. Orcus removed the disciple in charge of assignments and placed Brandon Bink in that position.

Stanton was given money to start up a regional water company with headquarters in North Carolina, as settlement for his injuries. After years of stagnant revenues, Skip wanted to expand his sphere of influence. I wanted him to help me with my quest. I called Skip Stanton and arranged a meeting in his office.

I arrived a few days later for our initial encounter. After looking at photos of his grandchildren and him looking at my family photos, it was time to get down to business.

"Mr. Stanton, I have connections that will allow you to sell your water products to all the government agencies inside the District of Columbia for the next five years. You will have to submit a bid, but yours will be accepted as long as it's at your standard rates."

"Mr. Novo, let's not play games here. I know exactly who you are and that you were removed as our leader. I don't know why, but I do know they aced you out. That leads me to believe that you are only here attempting to use me for revenge. If not, why come with your desires to help me? You never bothered to visit me when you were our leader, so why now?"

I appreciated his candor and due diligence. Stanton was a straight shooter. "Mr. Stanton, maybe then you were unaware, and this is not a complaint, but a fact. While having the privilege of leading our disciples, I was learning on the go. Plus, Orcus put a spell on my family, for which I was I was finding a cure, all the while I also remained the top soul stealer. I would assume you were unaware of my side of the story, sir."

Stanton tossed out a skeptical frown. "So, I should feel sorry for you?"

"No, you should understand that my term was short, I was quiet busy, and I apologize if you feel slighted. But I am here now with an opportunity to grow your business. Think of all the networking you can do while having a lucrative government contract. Has anyone on the current Council done anything this for you?"

Stanton raised his voice. "The Council has been good to me and they ask for nothing in return but a few cases of bottled water each month. My guess is whatever you are offering, comes with a steep price."

I smiled at Stanton. "Not a steep price, but a fair one. The contract will be yours and all you have to do is add a few drops of chemicals to the bottles of water you send to the compound."

Stanton scratched the top of his head before responding. "So all I have to do is poison the Council members and others living inside the compound and I can grow my company. Is that right?"

Stanton paused before continuing with a snarky tone. "They are my people. They have given me all I have. I am not a traitor, Mr. Novo."

I was expecting his skepticism, but I moved forward. I parked myself for the next thirty minutes and recounted to Skip Stanton my side of the story. How the members of the Council removed me from power and why and how I would regain authority. I told him all I had gone through with Doc Winfield and what Orcus had done to my family. I divulged to him that I had a solution, that when put in the water, would temporality remove their ability to remove souls. I even related that I could get Winfield to inject him with fresh blood that might restore his powers.

"I realize we only met for the first time today. Mr. Stanton. But I am relentless. If you stand with me, I will see to it that your company will grow to the point where your children will be left with financial stability."

He nodded. I proceeded to outline how two gallons of what will look; taste and smell exactly like water will be delivered to him from a chemist in England. He is to add a few drops into each bottle of water headed to the compound until the bottles are empty. In return, his company would grow exponentially in the coming months.

"Why should I trust you, Mr. Novo?" Stanton asked.

"Because you once believed in our cause and I am confident that people like yourself, will do exactly what I expect them to do."

I left Skip Stanton and went home for a few days with the family. My respite didn't last long. Iza Tappen responded to my earlier texts.

Gratitude for cash. Your thoughts on Larsson appear accurate. Sending report. One question. Why release so much money in advance?

That was simple to answer. *"Because you are smart enough to know you can get much more from me and seem willing to work for it."*

I immediately buzzed Nesstor without realizing the time and woke him up. "Elliot, I have evidence to help you connect the dots with Larsson. I am emailing you the report."

Nesstor didn't appreciate me calling him well past his bedtime. Because I traveled so much, I didn't always pay close attention to time zones. It was ten in the evening for me in California. "Novo, next time I see you, I'm personally gonna put a slug in your ass. Couldn't this have waited till morning?"

"Elliot, this guy could be a huge case for you. Don't you understand the magnitude of the lead I am trying to hand to you? I have practically solved the case for you. Would you please read the report I'm going to send? This guy is a huge star. It's a big profile case. You can retire with a big attaboy."

Nesstor seemed less enthusiastic. "Soul Man, I have learned to tolerate many of your ways because you have handed me several cases, but they were usually when I was wide awake. Besides, I told ya more than once now, I have a few cases left to clear up and I'm not taking on any new ones. I'm gonna retire. But send me the file and I'll pass it along to a new guy in our office. He's from New York, Jim Groden. He was the commissioner of a small town for a while, but wanted a different challenge, so he joined us at the Bureau."

"You are kidding me, right? You plan on turning down a great case and giving it to Commissioner Groden?"

"Go to sleep, Novo. Or at least go hang upside down in a closet, or do whatever it is you do to rest. Jim will call you if he finds a connection."

I tried to impress on Nesstor how much each of these unsolved crimes appeared to be linked. "Elliot, look at the notes in the morning. Each murder was done in an execution style with the victim's hands tied behind his back. Each victim was between the ages of seventeen and twenty with blonde hair and were suspected low level drug dealers. There are five in the file and each time, Larsson was in the town at the time of the murder. Do your job and convict this monster."

Nesstor yawned into the phone. "Solving murders of low level drug dealers are not a priority for us. Jim Groden will call you if he's interested. Now good night!"

This didn't sit well with me. There was a bad man flying from city to city, known for wearing a hockey helmet, and it would be left up to former commissioner Jim Groden to ensure justice. After sitting home for two days with my calls being ignored, I decided to find proof to put Larsson away for life.

The Bruins were playing at home for three straight games. I had Iza Tappen break into the Bruins database and obtain Larsson's home address. Stalking people who no longer owned a soul wasn't something I had ever done in the past. It seemed Larsson was providing me with many firsts. For several days, Larsson only left his home for either practice or games.

The final night of the Bruins home stand was a Saturday night in March. The air still had a hint of winter. I sat in my car near the player's parking lot at the Boston Garden. I was half asleep to the sounds of Dylan James and the Overture playing when someone tapped on the car window where my head was leaning.

He was a tattered looking man in a coat two sizes too large and a dark ski cap pulled down over his ears. I could barely hear him with the music playing. "Can you spare a dollar for a hot cup a joe, mister?" I wasn't one to usually turn down someone for help, so I lowered the window to offer him a few dollars. I didn't need distractions, the game was over and the players were soon to leave.

As I reached my arm out the window, the man grabbed it and pulled me to the door's edge. He shoved a pistol in my ear. "It ain't nice to follow others. Now open your door slowly and git out!" I did. He frisked me, then flipped me around and stuck a gun against my body.

I could feel the cold barrel pressing on my neck behind my earlobe as the stranger marched me twenty paces to another car, where I was ordered to get into the trunk. My body was curled into a ball before the trunk lid slammed down with a decisive thud.

The car remained idle for several minutes. The moron who tossed me into the trunk didn't bother to frisk me other than for guns. He failed to remove my cell phone. I had an application on my phone, created by one of our disciples that would track me using the phone's GPS function. The application was given to me in beta months earlier but I hadn't activated it.

Being balled up in the trunk of a stranger's car, with shivering cold hands and an anxious mind was no way to start using a new application, but I didn't have any other option. I could now hear Larsson speaking with someone else in the car. I texted Nesstor several times asking for assistance with no response.

The car began to move. I was able to follow my location after getting the application to work. We drove more than an hour to a spot along the Charles River. I could hear the two men talking after the car came to a stop. I heard the car doors open. Then I watched as the lid of the trunk opened. I was grabbed by both arms and yanked from the trunk to the ground by both men. My hands were then tied behind my back.

The men picked my rigid body from the ground and shoved me in the back every few feet until we reached the edge of a boat dock along the river. I could see houses in the distance. I was told to turn and face the two men. The man, who I failed to recognize, pulled a revolver from his coat pocket and jammed it under my nose.

"Git on your knees," he insisted.

With my hands tied, there wasn't a way of taking his soul. I lowered myself to my knees. I felt my cell phone vibrating in my pants pocket as I studied every line on the strange man's face. I wanted to make sure I would be able to recognize him in the future. From the little I saw of the man in Canada who was with Larsson in the SUV, he didn't seem to be the same man. Larsson was standing next to him, studying me as much as I was studying the stranger. No one spoke for several minutes until Larsson took control.

"Are you that man I had seen in the hotel in Canada? I don't know what you do to me, but I'm not same since you grabbed my arm. I score no more goals. I get hit hard on ice and fall off my skates. Doctors tell me that there is nothing wrong. But I know there is something wrong. Now you follow me. What you do to me?"

I hesitated, not wanting to flame his temper or give his associate a reason to pull the trigger on the weapon now brushing my temple. "I did what I was born to do, Nikolas, same as you."

Maybe not my best choice of words as Larsson became even more agitated. "Don't talk in riddles. You tell the truth or Manny pulls the trigger."

I leaned backwards, resting my backside on my heels. I did my best to give off a whiff of sincerity before answering Larsson with my long sigh. "Ok, but it's difficult for most to believe. I stole your soul after you killed that boy in Canada. I was mortified watching you pull that trigger."

Larsson spoke again. "That boy delivered poison to others.

That boy and many like him do not deserve to walk on earth. They take lives with the shit they sell to good people. I make them pay. Now you think you be judge of me. No, let your maker judge you in hell, and mine will judge me in heaven."

In all my years of stealing souls, I learned things are rarely simple. There was no way I could be persuaded into thinking Larsson was justified in his brutal execution, but he did stir my curiosity. I bet he wouldn't allow me to die before I told him more, or his associate would have killed me already.

"Explain to me then, Nikolas. Tell me how you are justified in picking a total stranger off a street corner and executing him?"

"You think these people are strangers to me? I know these people. They destroy lives. They make my brother shove that shit in his veins. Turn him into someone no one knows. My brother was smart, could been king of the world. Now, he can't even write his own name. No more brains left in him. Now they pay for making my brother junkie."

"You can't justify murdering that boy for your brother. I am sure he's not the one who sold drugs to your brother."

Larsson raised his chin and thumped his chest a few times with his fist. "You think the man who stick my brother with heroin is still is alive? If you think that, you know nothing about Nikolas Larsson. Now you fix me, or you be as dead as the others."

I sat back up on my knees and peered up at Larsson. "How many others, Nikolas?"

"Only number that matters to me, is how many goals I make. And I haven't scored one since you touch me. If you drugged me, like my brother was drugged, you must fix me or you will die."

"I was telling you the truth, Nikolas. I removed your soul. There were no drugs, no magic, it was me taking from you because you took from others."

Larsson sneered at me. "I don't care what you say you did. You make me feel good again, or a bullet will be in your brain. This I promise you."

I had been in dangerous positions before but there always seemed to be someone around who could help me. I had stared down gun barrels once or twice in the past, but this time I was alone. I called for help from Nesstor earlier, but to no avail. This was the first time I was staring at death with my hands tied. I felt helpless. For the first time ever, I feared death. My mind rushed with thoughts of my wife and child. I worried for them and the survival of our disciples. I decided my best option was to restore Larsson's soul, convincing him I needed my hands free to do it.

Returning a soul was a dangerous task. Everything had to go perfect in order for it to succeed. There had to be total silence and I couldn't be touched during the process. Trusting these two would abide by my request was a long shot. Attempting to escape was a longer one. Returning his soul and walking away was the longest shot on the board. However, I assumed the odds of that were slightly better than kneeling in defiance. I wasn't ready to die.

"If I return your soul, what do I get, Nikolas?"

"You get to live one more day, maybe. I make no promises to you."

I may not have been in the best bargaining position, but I did have some leverage. I also knew since he knew nothing about returning a soul, I could use that to my advantage.

"Here's how it's going to work, Nikolas. First thing, your friend Manny is going to take that gun away from my skull. He will remove the ropes from my wrists. Then the two of you won't utter a sound or touch me until I speak to you and return your soul. You will both then return to your car and leave me behind, unharmed. If you or Manny make any moves against me after I return your soul, I'll steal yours again, Nikolas, and Manny's as well. You will never score another goal. You will never score again."

This time Manny spoke up. "Yo, dipshit, you don't get ta make any rules here."

He was quickly scolded by Nikolas Larsson. "Put the gun down. Make no sound and take off the rope."

I still wanted to hear Larsson say it. "We have a deal then, Nikolas?"

Larsson stared at me, as I twisted my free wrists. "If I don't feel better when you are done, I will shoot you myself."

I closed my eyes and began to focus all my thoughts on returning to the Surrounding of Souls. I could hear a clap of thunder despite the night sky filled with stars. Waves started to slam against the boat dock. The spirits lifted my soul once again so I could ask the gatekeeper to return a soul to its earthly body.

My soul was delivered to a large frozen pond. There were young adults on skates dressed in clothes from a time long passed. An older man was offering instructions to the younger men on skates. After barking out a few last words to the small group, he turned his attention to me.

"Unless you have a new rule for our game, I suggest you move. The game is about to begin."

"Who are you?" I asked.

"My name is James Creighton and we are forming new rules for the game called hockey. Do you play?"

"No, Mr. Creighton. I am here to take one of your players back with me. His time to play on this pond will have to wait."

Creighton shrugged. "That won't be possible. I only have fourteen players. It's in the new rules. We play with seven on each team."

Time is always short when attempting to return a soul. Gatekeepers like Creighton never want to release a soul they are responsible for, but if I went back without Larsson's, I was a dead man.

"Mr. Creighton, change your rules. Play with six on each side and have one player for when someone gets hurt or needs a break. The one I seek is not worthy to play in your game. Please release his soul to me."

I was out of time. The spirits lifted my soul back to earth. I could hear sirens. My body was shivering with cold and carrying an extra soul. As I opened my eyes, I was flat on my back looking up at the stars. The sirens were growing louder. I could now see the two men hovering over me.

"Help me to my feet. We need to do this quickly." I said to the two men. Each grabbed one arm and returned me to a standing position. The sirens were growing louder. "Hurry, we need to return your soul before the police locate us."

I grabbed Larsson's arm and released his soul into his body. He started to shake violently. Manny moved several steps away from the two of us. The sirens went silent. I realized all along Larsson would have been a fool to allow me to walk free. I knew too much. Escape was my only chance at survival. Suddenly, my prayers had been answered.

In the yard between the house and boat dock stood the silhouette of a man. He slowly crept towards us in silence. At first, neither Larsson nor Manny noticed the man.

"Help me please." I pleaded, looking in the direction of the oncoming man. Larsson was now on his hands and knees rocking back and forth. Manny turned and looked in the direction of the stranger. I dove into the frigid waters of the Charles River.

Thrashing through the river wearing a jacket, long pants and boots was a more than a subtle reminder while on active duty as soul stealers we kept our bodies in top form. If not, I would have drowned.

I made it to shore several hundred yards downstream. Looking back towards the dock it was too dark to be sure if anyone was still there. I was cold and tired. The fear of death was gone. Struggling to walk with my saturated clothes and tired body, I noticed a boat house along the river. Inside were towels and some fresh clothes. Emotionally and physically worn out, I spent the remainder of the evening sleeping in the boat house.

12

I spent several days recovering in a Boston hotel. The third night after returning Larsson's soul, my dreams were filled with a message from Mikael, my guardian angel. He explained it was he who was standing in the yard the night I was taken captive. After I dove into the river, his figure was no longer visible by anyone. He lectured on how I should never feel alone and ended my dream stating, "A thank you now and again wouldn't hurt either."

I awoke to the sports highlights showing Larsson scoring a hat trick and leading the Bruins to a win over the Florida Panthers. It turned my stomach to watch.

Returning a soul had a strange effect on me, the handful of times I was successful. After returning one, I would be lethargic, the second time I did it, I was near death. But days after, I would be at my peek. I would feel full of energy and ready to continue my journey in life. It was the same way after returning the soul of Nikolas Larsson. Only this time, I returned one against my will, so this time despite physically feeling better, I was still mentally on tilt.

Later in the morning, I contacted Elliott Nesstor about being taken against my will and held at gunpoint. "Thanks for sending the troops to save me, Elliot. Why didn't you respond to my text messages? I was close to being killed and almost froze in the Charles River."

"Caeles, you do realize I have a job, right? I mean more than answering your messages and following up your leads. I was on assignment and we were informed to turn off all devices. Besides, I don't have the authority to send Boston's finest on patrol."

"Alright, Elliot, I get your point. But Larsson confessed to me. He admitted he's going around killing drug dealers off street corners because years ago his brother became a junkie. He's going all Rambo around the world."

There was a long uncomfortable pause on the other end of the phone. "Let me tell you some simple realities, Soul Man. Every now and again, the bad guy wins. He remains free because there aren't enough hours in a day to catch em all. Unfortunately, the world is filled with guys like Larsson. We have zero evidence against the guy, zero. It's your word against his at this point."

"Let me tell you my realities, Agent Nesstor. In my world, the bad guys are all eventually made to pay for their sins."

"I don't live in your world, Caeles."

The phone clicked on the other end. I was frustrated with Nesstor's unwillingness to help. Maybe when people have lived their lives and given all they have, they lose some of that passion and desire they had on the way to the top. Or, maybe Nesstor was tired of me.

I had been sidetracked from my main mission for weeks dealing with Nikolas Larsson. It was time to get back to my goals and hope one day Larsson would pay for his sins. It wasn't a good way to think about it, but maybe he would save one of us soul stealers work in the future by eliminating a bad guy from our list. He might have believed he was stopping drug addicts from scoring, but in time, so would Nikolas Larsson. I wasn't going to forget about him.

Back home, I contacted Iza Tappen. I asked Iza to find a way to alert me when real estate that fit my criteria was going into foreclosure in the Northern California market. I would be looking to move in the coming year. One thing about Iza was that we had an understanding, neither pried into the other's business.

One person who did like to pry was my wife. It wasn't that I didn't trust her or want her input at times, but she was still an active soul stealer. I couldn't risk her saying something inadvertently to a family member or someone around the compound about my goals.

"Cale, you do realize that women can keep secrets, right?"

"It's not that. Think about it. The Council has removed me from power and yet you are still allowed to come and go freely around the compound. Why is that? You are still given assignments and no one treats you as an outcast despite being my wife."

"Oh, so now I'm a spy for the Council? For the record, I'm damn good at what I do. Did it ever occur to you that maybe they need me? Let me remind you, without you we are one less now."

I could see Kalani was visibly upset. I wasn't trying to accuse her or make her feel small, but it was odd that she was still treated as if the Council didn't try to assassinate me. Plus after a brief time of being upset, she slid back into her old life. Maybe she was right. The Council couldn't afford to lose any more soul stealers. However, they didn't seem to be in a hurry to maintain or develop more soul stealers from the younger generation. I was puzzled at everyone's motives.

"I am sorry, my love. I was not trying to imply you aren't good at what you do, or aren't valuable to our disciples. But if you do not know my plans, there is no danger of you having to lie. It is better if I tell you nothing. All they have to do is ask you a question and, if you are lying, they can see your soul. I am trying to protect you. Do you think it is easy for me knowing you could be in danger in allowing you to keep doing what you do?"

Kalani's jade colored eyes grew as large as marsh mellows. Her tone oozed with sarcasm.

"Allow me? You allow me to do what I do? Why let me get on bended knee and kiss your ring, Master. I was damn good at my job long before I ever met you, and I'm still damn good at it today. The moment you think you allow me to do anything, pack up your crap and don't return."

"That's enough! You know exactly what I meant. I have always been incredibly proud of the work you do. Right now, I feel all the weight of our existence on my shoulders. There are days I feel like I'm the only one left who cares if we continue on or not. The Council and too many of our disciples no longer seem to care. You of all people should see this. If everyone capable of stealing souls would remove one or two a year, you and I and the few of us remaining who work, wouldn't have to be on the road over three hundred days a year. We could be a normal family, like the others who take and take from our hard work."

After a brief pause, Kalani continued, only this time with a softer tone. "Explain to me one thing, Cale. What is normal? I was born and raised to do what I do. So were you. Yet ever since I've known you, nothing has ever been good enough. You can't save the world. But you can try to save yourself."

"You don't get it, Kalani. Saving our kind and doing all I can to remove evil where it lurks, is saving myself."

Hanging around the house wasn't doing me or Kalani any good. For one of the few times in our marriage, there was tension beyond a few hours. She was insistent I tell her my plans of how I would remove the current Council. I felt it too dangerous to allow anyone to know the entire plan.

I did want to tell her about the missing book but even that was dicey. It had been in the possession of Bastian "Doc" Duvaliar's family for hundreds of years. They were the keepers of our past. Most of our disciples didn't believe it existed, including my grandfather. I had seen and read from it. It was in my hands.

When I went to Jamaica seeking help from Doc, he was accidently stabbed and killed by his former caregiver, Raeini Clinkard. She was attempting to kill me, but Doc stepped in the middle of the battle and Doc died in his own home. Raeini and her daughter Carroline, whose soul I had restored a few days before the accident, slipped out before the police arrived. I was a suspect and ordered to stay on the island until Nesstor intervened and gained my release.

Doc's last words to me were, Grayson Winfield, which led me

to meet him in the first place. When I questioned Winfield about the book's existence, he acted as if he knew it was real and knew I would be searching for it, but denied he knew where it was. No one on the Council would admit it was real, or even acted as if they ever heard of it. I was informed about it in a dream from Mikael.

The last time I searched for it back in Jamaica, Tasha Timmons was vacationing in a hotel close to Doc's former home, the last place the book was seen. When I questioned her about it, she too acted as if she never heard of it. With so many telling me so many lies over the years, I had lost trust in everyone. Everyone in my family had lied to me about something.

It was another reason why I loved my wife, but there was always a little twinge of doubt she too wasn't being honest with me. I wanted to desperately tell her I was off to Jamaica in search of the missing book. I wanted to end our tension, but in the end, I scribbled a note that I would return in a few days and left it on the kitchen counter. Despite my scolding from Mikael, I felt totally alone as I boarded the flight.

Using my alias, John Latens, an FBI agent, I made it past the customs agents. I had skipped off the island after Doc's tragic accident despite being commanded to stick around. So I had to be careful not to be identified while staying in Jamaica.

I was in search of Carroline and Raeini Clinkard. Since Raeini had been Doc's nurse in his home, she knew the value of the book about our people's history. She was in the room when Doc took it from his safe and asked me to read the chapters about redemption and returning souls. It was a safe bet, that mother and daughter Clinkard would know what happened to it. I had gone back to Doc's house after the police released me but the book was nowhere to be found. I assumed the mother or daughter had removed it.

Locating them proved more difficult than I first imagined. The beauty shop where Carroline had been closed because it was discovered through Nesstor's investigations, and my tip, that indeed Raeini had been putting poison in the bottles used in the salon. It was seeping into the scalps of the tourists and winter visitors and the effects were not felt until months later when they were all back in the home land. It couldn't be proven either mother or daughter was responsible, but traces of poisons were found.

I found the former shop owner, but she wasn't in any hurry to keep in touch with Carroline. She had put great faith that Carroline would be a partner in the future. I had to inform the shop owner that Carroline didn't know her mother was poisoning her water bottles. The shop owner only heard rumors the Carroline and her mother had moved to the Black River area.

This turned out to be an expensive mission. I had to pay off several of the locals to give me clues where I might find a mother and daughter who were new to the area. It led me to a small wooden home, some might consider it a shack, down a dirt road that was lined with a dense jungle one each side.

I crept around the outside of the house before eventually knocking on the front door. Carroline answered the door. She had lost weight since the last I had see her. Her hair, though clean, didn't have the shine it had in the past. Her shirt had a few rips running down the side. Carroline had always prided herself on looking her best. This was a stark change. She seemed resigned in her voice.

"I'm surprised eet took you dis long to find us. Please dun't hurt me mudda. She ees upset over what she did ta Doc."

"I am not here to hurt anyone, Carroline. I am here looking for a special book that I think possibly you or your mother removed from Doc's house after he died."

Carroline came out from behind the creeky screen door and invited me over to a couple of rocking chairs at the edge of the yard. We sat. She rocked back and forth looking to the sky before planting both feet on the ground and staring at me.

"I know da book. I know where eet ees. You geeve me monies to move me and my mudda to United States. I geeve you book."

All I could think about was why does everyone want to negotiate something before I get what I want? Why couldn't someone help me because I asked?

"Do you actually have the book here, Carroline?"

"You geeve me monies and help wid passports and you get your book. Yes, or no?"

"How much money and do you physically have the book here, Carroline?"

"Fifty tousand dollars. I know where book ees. Eets not here. Friend of Doc found us. He tells me dat book has bad voodoo and eef eet stay in de house, we have curse. I geeve da book to da man. Mudda says da book eets evil. We only took eet because we taught you would want eet and pay us. But you were slow ta find us. So now, you pay, I tell you where eet ees.

I rocked in the chair for a bit listening to the breeze filter through the trees surrounding the make shift home. I didn't know why everyone thought I had this endless supply of cash and connections.

"I'll tell you what, Carroline. I will get you a passport for you and your mother and two plane tickets to Miami, Florida. After I deliver them to you, you will tell me where I can find the book you stole from Doc. And yes, the book is evil. Anyone who reads it from beginning to end will die. So if you do still have it, don't read it. It is pure evil inside the pages."

"And da monies? We need da monies too. We want ta visit New York, den we come home."

"After the book is in my possession, you get your money, not before."

I called my contact who made fake passports for both women. They would be ready two days later. I had Iza tap into the airline ticket center our disciples owned and I downloaded the plane tickets. I changed their itinerary to land at Kennedy Airport in New York, not Miami.

After delivering her the passports and tickets, she described a man known as a spiritual leader. She heard Doc speak about Josef Infante, but Carroline never met him till he showed up at her door step.

"I only know where he told me he live. Eets up in da mountains. You have ta take scooter, roads not good for car."

So there I was riding a small motor bike up a muddy mountain path. The locals told me where to find Josef. They spoke in reverence of the man. I had to admit it had me more than a bit nervous. The locals spoke about Josef's special powers and they were quite sure I would not be a welcome visitor.

As I drove closer to where the spiritual leader was supposed to be, I could hear faint drum beats. The road came to a wide bend. After motoring another few hundred yards, there was a clearing in the dense brush.

In front of me were roughly fifty men dressed in only small swaths of cloth tied around their mid sections. A few were carrying spears. As I pulled my motor bike further into the clearing, the drum beats stopped. Everyone turned to look my way. I glanced at a small wooden stage. One man stood staring at me, mouth wide open, holding a machete to a goat's throat.

A few of the men started to walk my way. I was about to turn and drive off when the man at the podium starting speaking in a language I couldn't distinguish. The men stopped in their tracks. I stared at them. They had painted faces of a deep blood red color with traces of white. The bright sun along with the humidity made their dark skins glisten. I sat motionless on my motor bike.

I quickly realized I had stumbled into an offering using the goat. I thought that if the men did rush me, I would stand my ground and remove a few souls. If they wanted to believe in dark magic, I was going to give them my brand. Thankfully, they didn't. They rejoined the remaining group and turned their attention back to the ritual on stage. The drums once again started to beat as the helpless goat uttered its last sounds. Where was PETA when you needed them?

Led by a tall thin black man, who looked to be in his mid thirties, he chanted and beat multiple drums long after the death of their sacrifice. Their ceremony reminded me of my time spent in the outback of Australia. Though each ritual seemed primitive, I knew there was a story being told in their chant and occasional dance.

The sunny sky gave way to dark rain clouds as the leader raised his arms to the sky one last time, before placing his hands on the dead sacrifice. The ceremony had come to an end. The men began leaving the clearing. Some disappeared into the surrounding jungle while others paraded past me and down the path I had used moments earlier. One man stopped. He informed me that if I ever invaded their private home again, he would kill me. The leader of the group began skinning the goat as I moved closer to the stage. He kept working as if I wasn't present.

His painted face oozed with sweat. The sky began to drop light rain drops on our heads as he hurried to finish his chore. Once the goat was skinned and gutted he put what was left in a pouch and slung it over his shoulder. He then started to speak to me in the same unrecognizable tongue he used in the ceremony. I had no fear of him. Something seemed familiar about this fellow.

"Do you speak any English?" I asked.

He clapped both hands together and a puff of smoke was released. No words were spoken. I inched closer to get a better look at his face. He looked even more familiar to me up close. I asked again if he spoke English, as he started to walk past me. Remembering where I had seen him before, I started to laugh out load. He turned back.

"Otis Buffet, I should have known from the start it was you."

He shook his head. "Dang it. I was hoping you woulda

forgotten bout me and left me alone. How the hell did ya find me way up here in dees mountains?"

I laughed even harder. "I don't think I want to know what scam you are trying to pull on these people. I had no clue I was looking for you. Carroline Clinkard told me about a man of great spiritual ability named Josef that came to her and took something valuable of mine. I want it returned. It does not belong in the hands of a con artist from Philadelphia."

"Hold on jack. You got da balls to call me a con artist? You were da one talking trash bout taking my soul if I didn't change my ways. Well guess what, mines still intact. I be thinking. You'ze the one who's jamming people up with all dis soul stealing talk."

Otis and his partner ran a church in Philadelphia where they promised eternal salvation to anyone who would listen to their sermons and drop a few dollars into the basket. They became friends with many of the older congregation and convinced some members to leave all their assets to the church. I was assigned to remove the soul of his partner and did. I took mercy on Otis.

"You can believe all you like about what I can and cannot do, Otis. But if you remember, your partner did lose his soul."

"No man, dat's not what happened. Da FBI man came charging in and locked him up, saying we was ripping off old ladies. I don't never remember nuttin bout him losing no soul. Den you told me ta find a new place ta preach. The city people took away our occupational license and I had ta close down my church."

"Otis, I am not here to rewrite history. I want my book back."

Otis flung his pouch of goat meat to the ground and shrugged.

"De ways I see it, you dun cost me a whole lot of monies closing down my church. Plus I'ze bet you da one who tipped off dat FBI man bout me and Richard. I'ze figuring you owe me bout a million. You get me sum a dat jingle and maybe I can find dat book a yours. Damn thing don't make no sense to me no how."

"So you read the book, Otis?"

"Course I did, fool. Being da spiritual man I am, I heard Doc talk about some book he had telling all da stories of da universe. Why wouldn't I wanna read a book like dat?"

"So then, Otis, tell me what did you discover about the universe? Did you read the part where I can remove your soul? Did you read the part where once I lose my patience, I can turn your brain to mush?"

He smirked. "I didn't read nuttin much I could understand. All I read was some hundert people from long ago and then some jibberish about numbers and blood and stuff that made no sense to me. And me being a spiritual man that I am, you'd think I'd be understanding it."

I winked directly at Otis. "Yes, I have a full understanding of the true spiritual leader you are, Otis. Since the book has no value to you, why not release it to me, you know, one spiritual leader to another."

Otis scratched his head and scrunched up his face. "The way I'ze seeing it is that maybe dat book don't talk to me in some spiritual kinda way, but must be important ta you. I mean fer you to come all dis way. So I'ze thinking maybe my million asking price is too low."

"Otis, I'm about thirty seconds away from losing all patience with you. I want that book and I want it now. There will be no ransom paid to you. Give me the damn book before I drop you here and now."

The guy had the nerve to laugh at me. "Awe dude, you can't con no con man. Stop with all dis bullshit bout dropping peoples and taking souls. You think you da only man on dis island dat talks about taking souls. Jamaica be full of peoples preaching bout dis shit. You don't scare me with your jive. Now you gonna pay da man if you wanna see dat book."

13

*C*learly my approach wasn't working with Otis. I asked him if he wanted a ride back to his home. He agreed and hopped on the back of my bike. We ended up at a small house near the bottom of the road. The place was clean despite needing a paint job and a few nails to fix the steps leading up to the porch and front door. He invited me inside.

"Ya know I forget your name. Guess I shoulda remembered beings you're a big reason why I ended up on dis island.

"My name is Cale, and why am I the reason you ended up here? Maybe you should be thanking me. It looks to me like you have a larger congregation in Jamaica than you ever did back in Philly."

Otis was tending to his goat meat and loading it into a standalone freezer in the only other room of the house. I scanned the room where I was standing. There were two windows in the room, placed opposite each other, offering a nice cross breeze. I sat in one of his two chairs. The entire house was only seven short steps across and I was estimating not more than fifteen steps in length. The place was decorated with little furniture and no sign of my treasured manuscript.

"Very funny, Mista Cale. Know dis, before you and dat FBI man took away ma preaching place, we had over two hundert strong on a good day. Bet you couldn't draw a crowd dat big to ever hear you preaching da good word."

Otis finished his chore and sat in the chair two steps to my left. He continued his tale.

"Dis was ma daddy's place before he moved us ta Alabama. Weren't till later we moved on up ta Philadelphia. Daddy tells me dis was his daddy's place before him. When things got hot fer me back in Philly, ma daddy told me dis here house was bout the only thing gonna be passed down ta me. So here I be."

"Speaking as someone who has seen the world many times over, this is a pretty nice location. You have the sea only a few steps down the road. It looks like you have all the goat meat one man could eat. You should be thanking me."

"You'ze a funny man, Mista Cale. But mocking me ain't gonna git ya dat book back."

"I wasn't mocking you, Otis. You have no idea how many days I would enjoy to be in a place like this where no one could find me. I would love no responsibilities, just be able run away to an island where I didn't have to see evil in the world. No more souls that needed to be taken, nah, you live in paradise. You don't appreciate what you have been given."

"Oh, maybe you right. But I'ze still not happy it ended like it did back in da states. I hear ma ex-partner Richard gonna be sitting in jail fer a few more years. I kinda feel bad since I lived on some of da money, but all he earned was the time. Never did sit right with me. But maybe you right, I should be more grateful. Maybe you did do me some good. Might only had been a matter a time before some relative of dem old ladies put a cap in us. Some did think we stole their inheritance and all. But I swear, Mr. Cale, we was saving some souls with our preachin. Dem womens wanted to donate ta our church. Not like we had a gun ta nobody's head or nuttin."

I shook my head at Otis. "Funny thing is I actually do believe you. I can see by looking into your soul that you are a decent man. So how did you learn that magic trick back in the clearing? The one where you clapped your hands and how did you ever end up leading a sacrificial ritual?"

Otis swiveled in his chair while looking out the window. A smile crossed his face.

"Ma daddy was a magician. He taught me a few tricks when I wassa boy. I still remember a few a dem. Ma granddaddy, well he was da spiritual king in dis here town. His preachin name was Josef Infante. I'm guessing ma daddy had ta leave dis place being a bit of a sinner and ma granddaddy beings da spiritual man he was."

He stopped and peered out at the trees bowing in the wind. The clouds had given way to stars. The late afternoon had turned into a beautiful tropical evening. I knew enough to sit still and wait for Otis to pick up where he left off.

"Well, when I turned back up here in town, some of da old men tells me I looked like ma granddaddy when he began his preachin dayz. I dunno how it happened, but maybe da spirit moved me ta pick up where ma granddaddy left off. I started up rememberin when he taught me his words. He taught me all dem stories you heard earlier. Not that you understand dem."

Otis chuckled before continuing. "I found some papers here in da house dat had all his preachin stories. I started readin dem and rememberin all ma lessons. Before you could yell Halleluiah, I was saying da words here in town. Da men cleared dat place up in da hills. It's why they didn't take too kindly ta you showing up. Ain't no white faces allowed." He peered at me.

"You can apologize to the men for me. I did not mean any disrespect. I was told by some men in town where I could find the holy man. I did not realize I would be interrupting your service."

Otis pointed to his freezer and smiled. "Well truth be told, some of da reason I was doin preachin in da hills is cause it do seem ta keep ma freezer full a meat. One week it's goat, da next maybe a pig or a chicken. Nice not havin ta pay much for groceries."

We both laughed before silence took over the room. Otis went back to swiveling in his chair staring out the window. He took a deep breath of the salty island air and exhaled closing his eyes. He was still wearing the same painted face from earlier.

"I don't have access to large sums of cash, my friend. I realize you are upset that you think I ruined your lifestyle back in Philly. But from what I was told, the FBI would have soon found enough evidence to bring charges against you as well."

Otis answered back in an angry tone. "We was only saving souls, dem peoples offered those houses ta us. Dat trial musta been fixed against Richard fer him being a black man. We didn't force nobody ta gives us nuttin."

"I realize this is hard for you to believe, Otis. But I am one of only a handful of people on this earth who can truly save souls. I can see into your soul right now. I can tell when you are lying and when not. I can own your soul in seconds. I did remove Richards. This is who I am."

"I hate my father," Otis said.

"That was a lie."

"I hid a million dollars in a Swiss bank account."

"Another lie. You have to try harder."

"I want a woman in my life."

"Another lie."

Otis laughed hard. "Well I kinda would like a woman now and again."

I laughed along with Otis.

"Alright Mista Cale, my turn ta ask da questions. Did you tell da FBI bout what me and Richard was doing in da church?"

"What I did was inform Agent Nesstor that Richard was a bad guy. I was going to take Richard's soul and maybe the FBI should take a look into why Richard needed to have his soul removed. Nesstor interviewed several people in your congregation, who informed him that Richard made a lot of promises he couldn't keep, in exchange for money. I had nothing to do with the investigation."

Otis sighed and looked out at the stars. A cool breeze came wafting through the window from the north. "You thinkin bout Richard all wrong. He was saving dem peoples."

"Otis, I do not want to debate why Richard went to trial and not you. From what Agent Nesstor told me, Richard seemed to be the one who was in it for the money and you were the preacher. Maybe you don't even know how much or where all the money is that Richard stole from your congregation. I am not here to investigate that, nor do I care. The FBI did their work and they did not find enough evidence to bring charges against you, only Richard."

"I never claimed ta be a perfect man, Mista Cale. We needed money fer da church. We needed money ta eat. Oh, maybe I got a few dollars stashed somewheres. But ever since I returned here on dis island again, I really am just a preachin."

"Now that was the truth."

We both stared out at the night sky. I was telling Otis the truth when I declared how a place like Jamaica could easily sway me to stay one day. But not on that night, it was time to get my book.

"Here is my offer to you, Otis. I will set up a bank account in the name of Josef Infante that only you control. There will be one hundred and ninety thousand dollars placed in the account tomorrow. It will be so you can build a proper church for your services. Or, you can keep the money and I won't ever ask you what you did with it. Also, I won't have my computer guy discover whatever money you have hidden and tip off Nesstor. I would be willing to bet you have it under the name Josef Infante, maybe even here in Jamaica. I will also call in a favor and have Richard transferred to a minimum security prison. That is if you give me my book."

"Dat book ain't here, Mista Cale."

"That was another lie. Now I'm positive it's here somewhere and you are about out of time. I will remove your soul and rip this place to shreds until I find it, or we can strike a deal. I enjoyed our evening together, but I will get my book, one way or another."

"I still not admitting ta believing inta da mind games you been trying ta play all night. But I told da FBI man as ta where some of da money was being hidden. That's da real reason why I wasn't charged." Otis looked at me with a gentle smile.

"Once again, you speak the truth."

Otis lowered his head. "Yep. Still feeling guilty too."

"Hand over the book, Otis. You'll get your money to build a church or retire for all I care. Plus I'll make sure Richard has better surroundings to finish serving his time."

Otis walked into the other room, opened the freezer and took out a package carefully surrounded in bubble wrap. He took a knife off the shelf and ran it over the wrappings, removing the book. He walked back into the room and dropped the cold manuscript into my lap.

He stared at me, then said, "From one spiritual man ta another, I hope you can find your congregation now."

I contacted Iza Tappen and had Iza loan me two hundred thousand dollars from the money sent previously, with the promise it would come back three fold. Iza was not thrilled at first but after I reminded Iza I had sent much more in advance than expected, Iza released the money to a bank in Kingston.

The following day, Otis and I drove to Kingston and set up his account. He must have been waiting for me to demand something else. He later informed me he was surprised when only he could move money from the account with no strings attached.

After dropping Otis back at his home, I went back to find Carroline Clinkard. I gave her ten thousand dollars for her and her mother's trip to New York City. She was told that after her stay in New York was complete, someone would meet them at the airport and they would get the remainder of what was owed. Carroline and her mother were both thrilled they would finally get a chance to visit the United States.

Jamaican authorities didn't come to the same conclusions as Nesstor did that Raeini Clinkard poisoned the tourists in Carroline's salon. Since neither Clinkard was charged with any crimes, the calls for them to be extradited to the Unites States went ignored. This was one of the cases that Nesstor wanted off his desk up before retiring.

I gave my old buddy Nesstor a call. "Elliot, I have a present for you. I will tell you where Raeini Clinkard will be in New York next week as long as you give me your word that you will allow Carroline to return to Jamaica."

"What? How do you know they're coming to New York?"

"I plan on putting both of them on a plane, but I want them to have a few days of vacation before you pick up Raieni."

"You never cease to amaze me, Soul Man. The old lady tried to kill you and now you want to treat her to a vacation in New York

City? Why aren't you doing your voodoo thing on the old lady?"

"I want Carroline to have some fun in New York. I owe her one. She's been through a lot and if I removed her mother's soul, I don't think she would be well enough to travel. Besides, you can clear up one more case which will give you ample time to look at the evidence against Larrson."

"You are a relentless son of a bitch, Novo. I'll give you that much," Nesstor claimed in an exasperated tone.

Possessing my prized book and with the Clinkards in tow, we made our way to the airport in Kingston. I made sure both mother and daughter boarded the direct flight to New York, before I caught my flight to California. Twice the stewardess attempted to put the book in the overhang compartment. There was no chance it was getting out of my line of sight. The centuries old manuscript would remain with me at all times from my flight to Atlanta and later to San Francisco.

Despite being anxious to read the book from cover to cover, the guy next to me had his prying eyes examining the pages. I didn't want any questions. The book was written in Latin, so I assumed he didn't understand. But I had been trained to never assume.

Too many times on flights, the people sitting next to me wanted to exchange in small talk. When asked what I did for a living, I usually said that I was a spiritual leader. One time after making my claim, I was sitting next to a church bishop who wanted to discuss his philosophy on spirituality. I finally broke down and told him my true occupation. He instantly requested his seat to be moved. I enjoyed a quiet ride once the bishop moved diagonally across the plane.

Back home, tension still filled the air. Kalani became upset when I wouldn't tell her what the book was about, and why I locked the book in the safe that only I knew the combination. She didn't understand that I was only attempting to protect her. The less she knew about my plans, the less she could divulge to the Council, even by mistake. Kalani still didn't see my point of view. I suggested a family vacation, but since we each traveled so much, neither of us were excited to go on another cramped airplane ride.

After three days of cold shoulders and colder dinners, I offered Kalani a few hints about the book. I had to trust her and relieve some tension. I told her what I had learned about the history of the book, and how it had been cared for by Doc's family for several generations. Most of our disciples didn't know it existed. She didn't even know until that afternoon. Kalani was better at translating Latin than I was, so I needed her superior linguistics to help with a few paragraphs. She reluctantly accepted my challenge.

"Uhm, Cale, this section explains that this book of yours is only to be held and read by the leader of the Council. No one else is to lay eyes upon it. The book is then to be passed down from leader to leader. Did you know that?"

"That's odd. Doc swore to me his ancestors had this stored away for over five hundred years. How could the book have been passed down from leader to leader?"

Kalani rubbed her fingers against the paper as she cautiously flipped through several more pages. "My dear husband, did it ever occur to you that this type of paper wasn't invented when this book is said to have been passed down? It's impossible for this book to have been created at the time the Lord of Life gave us our abilities. Each leader of the Council must have passed down our history by word of mouth or possibly something was written using papyrus, but this book was not written when we were given our powers."

She was right. The leather coverings could have been made from that era, but not the paper. But then again, I assumed it came from the heavens, so anything was possible.

"Take a look here." Kalani pointed to darker letters at the bottom corner of the right page. "See if you can decipher this section. If I am correct, someone with the surname of Orcus wrote down our history by hand in the early 1400's. These writings would go on to become the book that was to be passed down from leader to leader. My Latin was better years ago, but I believe this states that these writings became a book made on the first Gutenberg press in 1436. This isn't the original book. This is a copy." We looked at each other with a puzzled face.

I then attempted with Kalani to translate the remaining handwritten scribbles on the page. I read it the same way she did. "So where's the other one?" I asked.

"Who knows," Kalani giggled. "But I have a sneaky suspicion you'll be racking up more frequent flyer miles to find out."

Kalani wandered into the kitchen to make my first hot meal in days as I struggled reading the handwritten script, while lounging in my favorite comfy leather chair. There were a few chapters that appeared to have been added later since the handwriting was not consistent. The pages unveiled the history of the original one hundred disciples and their powers granted from the heavens. The story was told about the Surrounding of Souls and the gatekeeper. However, the following chapter was what I had been wondering about my entire adult life. My heart was now beating as fast as the night I watched Larsson execute that kid.

After reading the pages carefully three times, I called Kalani back into the room. "Read this paragraph right here and tell me what it says."

Kalani gave me her best skeptical frown and glanced down at the page. "Oh my, you've been right all along. If my translation is correct, it reads, any person void of a soul seeking redemption, is to have their soul returned for a second opportunity, to prove to the world they are worthy of such a chance. Should they fail a second time and the soul enters the Surrounding of Souls again, only the disciple who removed the soul the second time can return their most prized possession."

In that moment, I felt I was the one who had been offered redemption. "I knew it! We were always intended to return souls."

Kalani quickly corrected me. "That isn't exactly the way I interpret the paragraph. To me the translation reads that only people seeking redemption will be offered back their soul."

"Ok, whatever, but the bottom line is that we were always supposed to return souls. That means the original one hundred must have had the power to do so. I would imagine that many of our disciples still have the same abilities. I can't be the only one. Plus, since your old pal Paulo Kopono had his soul restored and it wasn't me who returned it, someone else knows too."

"Maybe so, but I don't know how to restore souls," Kalani proclaimed.

"Are you sure? You have never tried."

"Yeah well, this girl has no intention of ever trying. I've heard all your creepy stories of what happens when you meet the gatekeeper. Plus you get sick for a few days afterwards. I want no part of that nonsense."

"You also are forgetting that after I recover, I feel stronger than ever. Besides, where else would I get a chance to meet the likes of Jimi Hendrix, George Washington and Ansel Adams all in one place?"

Kalani gave me that frown of hers that I so detested. "There are enough interesting people who still have a heartbeat here on earth, Cale. I don't need to brush up on my Vulcan mind meld techniques to feel like I'm doing my job."

Not wanting to eat a cold meal alone, I stuck my nose back into the pages and read on. After dinner and some family time playing a board game with Nic and Kalani, I picked up where I had left off in the book.

The manuscript explained that should a person not seek redemption before their earthly body died, their soul would remain in the Surrounding of Souls for all eternity. The book went on to describe that if a soul was lost for a second time and disciple who removed the soul died before returning it, again the soul would remain in the Surrounding of Souls for all eternity. A soul would never be stolen a third time. The translation read, "Any soul not succeeding after a soul was returned twice would deserve the fate evident at death."

I called Kalani back into the room and asked her opinion as well. She read it over a few times. "The way I'm reading this Cale, is that let's say you take the soul of John Whoever and it's the second time the soul was stolen, you would be the only disciple capable of returning said soul a second time. If John Whoever screws it up for a third time, they discover their fate for all eternity at death. Three strikes and you are on the eternal bench."

"That's the way I read the passage as well."

Kalani slid the leather bound volume from my lap. The home cooked meal or even having my beliefs vindicated weren't the best part of my evening. Seeing her eyes sparkle as she flipped her silky dark hair and offered me her soft hand leading me to bed was the best prize of the day. Reading another chapter could wait until morning.

14

*T*he dawn broke on a glorious late winter morning. Kalani was snug in bed as I crept downstairs and cracked open the kitchen window along with a few eggs. My son Nic wandered downstairs grumbling about how lame school was as he gobbled down a couple of eggs and some juice before heading off to the bus stop. I filled a tray of fruit, eggs and toast and delivered them to my wife in bed. Tension wasn't going to return to our home.

After delivering breakfast to my sleepy wife and filling up on some eggs and carrot juice myself, it was time to start reading from where I left off the night before. Latin was much easier to translate on a full stomach and clear mind. I marked a few lines where the translation didn't seem right to me for Kalani to review later.

Towards the end of more than two hundred pages of writings was an entire section that seemed to be discussing blood. Not that I was an expert in blood work, but the book seemed to be discussing DNA in a primitive but accurate way. As I flipped to the subsequent page, Kalani strolled into the room, still wearing her revealing white silk negligee. Admiring her, I almost flipped to the following page without realizing I hadn't read the current one.

After gawking at my wife using eyes now the size of a good melon, I couldn't believe what was drawn on the pages of a book more than five hundred years old. "Kalani, tell me what this drawing looks like to you please."

Kalani sauntered over, brushing her fingers inches above her breast line. I tried to ignore her not so subtle attempt to pay her more attention than the book. But my mind was now squarely focused back on the crudely drawn image staring back at me.

"Come on, baby, can't this wait for a little longer?" Kalani fluttered her eye lashes at me. "You can read that ancient history another time."

Her playfulness was enticing but what was on the paper was too astonishing to ignore. "Take a look at this first, what does this image look like to you?"

"You really are no fun." Kalani pouted and batted her eyes one last time before gazing at the page. "What do I know? But if I had to guess I'd say it's a drawing of a double helix. The book is talking about chromosomes, big whoop. I'm trying my best to swap some DNA with you and all you care about is this dopey drawing in a dumb book."

"Kalani, wake up girl. You're so missing it. DNA wasn't discovered until hundreds of years after this book was written. This is explaining exactly why we are immune to most earthly diseases and if you remember, Winfield told me our powers are all recorded in our DNA. I'm now fairly certain Winfield has seen this book. I know the guy is smart, but he's been so ahead of the curve on so much about our past and our chemical makeup. He had to have seen this book."

"Oh so what," Kalani said in a pissed off tone. "Who cares if that quack knows all our secrets? You can go interrogate that wind bag of a doctor later. Right now, I want some more loving."

After keeping the wife happy and being delivered lunch in bed, it was time to get back to my reading. As hard as I tried, I didn't understand the medical nuances the book was describing. I couldn't quiet grasp all the concepts. Kalani's father was a doctor, but he was so opposed to anything I stood for, I didn't think he would assist me. But if my translations and assumptions were correct, this book foreshadowed the predicament our disciples were currently facing. The pages in front of me were weaving a tale of a time when our disciples would no longer want to remove souls and our existence would be in jeopardy. Even Kalani believed the writings were telling the reader how soul stealers could remove a soul and keep all the power to themselves.

Every time a disciple removes a soul, the energy of doing so is shared amongst all who share in our DNA. That energy provides us the ability to live three times longer than your average human. Because we have so few soul stealers and many more to depend on our ability to continuing to remove souls, all our life expectancies have shrunk by decades for our recent offspring.

My goal was always not only to keep our disciples focused on our original mission but also to ensure the longevity and survival of our kind on earth. The text in this book was offering me the key to our survival. Now my issue was that I didn't understand all that was being described. But I knew someone who would.

Kalani was right about one thing. I would be adding to my frequent flyer miles.

One of the few joys of visiting with Doctor Winfield was seeing the perky Nurse Simon every time I walked through the office doors. That day would be no different than all the others.

"Well howdy, Mr. Novo. It's always a special treat when you come a visiting. I was fixin to pick up some lunch for the doctor and me. Could I git you something too?"

"That is kind of you, Nurse Simon, but I grabbed something to eat on my way here. Thanks for asking though."

Nurse Simon smiled and buzzed Winfield. "You be nice to the Doctor, he's been extra grumpy since our Cowboys didn't make the playoffs again."

"I know how he feels, the Dolphins didn't do so well either." We gave each other one last smile as she made her way past me to the front door and I took the fifteen long steps down the hallway.

When I walked into his office, Winfield was sitting back in his chair using nail clippers to trim his fingernails. "Cowboy, what part of I don't ever wanna see you again do ya keep missing?"

I sat in the chair on the opposite side of his desk. "Aw Doc, you don't mean that. Besides, I recently sent you millions of dollars. Doesn't that at least get me one pleasant hello?"

Winfield shook his head with disgust. "Hallo. Now git outta ma office."

"Where's the book, Doc?"

Winfield glared at me. "I suggest ya visit our fine library not too far from here if you're looking fer books. This here's a medical office. Now granted, I gotta few medical journals here and there, but let's be honest, those books wouldn't interest a simple mind such as yours."

I wasn't going to allow this guy to get under my skin. I shot him a glare. "I'm in possession of one of at least two books that tells everything about our past and possibly our future. Now, I realize you have a mad genius mind. And I would never question your proven medical abilities. But as I was reading that book, I was struck by the idea that maybe, just maybe, you knew our powers were stored in our DNA by reading from the missing book. Quite possibly one that was owned by your father?"

Winfield put his nail clippers down and leaned back in his chair with his hands clasped behind his head. "Tell me sumtin, El-Dar Novo. Why does everyone believe in this mythical book that no one has ever seen? If you're talkin bout the same one that ole Bastian Duvaliar claimed to be hiding, well now, it's never been seen."

"You tell me sumtin, Doc-tour Winfield. Why is it that a computer whiz, now in my employ, found an online video of you giving a speech at a medical seminar about two years ago and in it you didn't have an accent? Even stranger, you were almost quoting directly from a book you claim doesn't exist? Besides, I told you it exists and I've read it from cover to cover."

"Well, if you're in possession of it, why the hell are you even in my office?" Winfield said with angst in his voice. "As far as the way I speak. Well, them Ivy League boys in da northeast, they think all us down here in Texas don't know how ta identify da back end of a Texas Longhorn from da front. So I tone down ma accent when I give speeches up yonder."

"Doctor, I won't go as far as calling you a fraud. I have no doubt that you attended medical school and do have eradicating cancer from humans as your stated goal. It's an admirable cause. And I do think you are a brilliant physician. But I also think you are in possession of a copy of a book that doesn't belong to you. I also have come to realize that sometimes when you're ticked off, your accent gets even thicker. This entire Texas twang is growing old."

"Perty strong words coming from a halfwit."

I could feel the blood percolating inside me like the pot of coffee in his front office. I knew he wanted to throw me off my game, but I had to fight the urge to blow up.

"Call me all the names you like, Doc. I know Tasha Timmons was here looking for the same book. I'm almost certain she's the abandoned girl I asked if your father raised, and you denied it. She's one of the select few who could have seen that book in your father's possession."

"Why do ya insist ma dear ole daddy ever laid eyes on your mysterious book, Novo? Let alone this Timmons woman tripped over it too?"

I offered Winfield a quick smile. "Because in the book, which was authored by someone with the surname Orcus, it clearly states that only the leader of the Council should be in possession of our written history. And last I checked, your family has ruled the Council for many generations until I removed your father's soul. It also stands to reason that since at one time your father was grooming you to take over the Council, he may have shown you the book."

Winfield snickered. "Ya do have a wild imagination dere,

cowboy. But even if all dat's true, you ain't the leader of jack shit. So from ma point a view, you don't have any more rights ta laying eyes on dat book den I do. Ain't that right, El-Dar Novo?"

I could feel my blood pressure rising even higher. I moved forward and pounded my fist on his desk. "I was the leader and I'm destined to be again! Where's the damn book?"

As I sat back in my chair, I heard the front door open. Nurse Simon made her way to the back office delivering Winfield his lunch. "I'm so sorry, Doctor. The store was outta those fancy tator chips ya like, so I gotcha some plain ones. I'll pick up some on ma way home tonight and bring em in tomorrow. I hope you're not too upset?" Nurse Simon shrugged and licked her index finger.

Winfield winked at Nurse Simon and calmly stated, "It's fine honey, you go on back ta your desk and enjoy ya lunch. Novo and I have more business ta discuss."

It suddenly hit me like a lighting strike on the vast Texas plains. "It was Timmons, wasn't it Doc?"

"Why do ya keep bringing up da Timmons woman?"

"She's the one! Timmons is the one who took Nurse Simon's soul after we met. You would never hurt your nurse. Of course, how stupid am I?"

"Perty stupid, if ya ask me, cowboy," Winfield muttered.

"No, it was right in front of me all this time. Tasha Timmons came looking for the book you claim you don't have and when you didn't turn it over to her, she removed your nurse's soul. Timmons could see you had a thing for her and she thought it would be a way to get you to give up the book. That book must be something special to you for you to have allowed Timmons to hurt your lover. But then again, you are a selfish prick."

Winfield picked up his nail clippers and started fiddling on his fingers. He refused to look at me which told me I was on the right path.

"Wow, you did, you allowed her to be harmed, didn't you? Shall I tell her you chose a book over her? Then, when that didn't work, Timmons sent the same goons after you that tried to kill me. That's how you ended up in that hotel where I had to save your ass."

Winfield growled. He pointed his little nail clippers at me. "That's a nice story, Novo, but ya can't prove it."

"Oh, but I can. It all worked out for you in the end, didn't it, Doc? Because I came wandering in here one day needing your help and you knew I could get her soul back. You were too scared to try it, even though you knew how to do it. You made me risk my life for your nurse. Wow, I can't wait to tell her."

Winfield sat straight up in his chair. "You don't wanna hurt that perty filly any more than I do, cowboy. And I suspect ya didn't come here looking for no book." Winfield frowned. "Why did ya come back here?"

"Shouldn't it be obvious, Doc? I know you read that book cover to cover. Only you did it years ago. I want you to create the sedative that allows me to keep all the strength I get when removing a soul. I no longer want to share with others. Once I know it works, I'll pass it along to the other thirty or so remaining soul stealers and we're going to cut off all who won't participate in removing souls. The system is about to change."

"And what if I choose not to make your potion, cowboy?"

"Here's the thing, Doc. You think I'm relentless? Timmons will never give up until she has that book. She already thinks she's in charge of the Council. Wait until she has all our secrets. But I'm preaching to the choir because you know all this. So if you want her off your back, help me. I'll make sure she never attacks you again."

"I can take care of myself, Novo. Besides, makes no difference ta me who runs your blasted Council. Besides, you informed me, you plan on starving me out, fool."

Nurse Simon wandered back into the office. "Doctor, I wanted to remind ya about the appointment ya have over at the hospital this afternoon." She giggled. "Well that and I heard some hollering back here and I wanted ta make sure all was ok."

Winfield gave her a reassuring smile. "Everything's great in here, honey. You call the hospital and tell em, I'll be there as scheduled." Nurse Simon smiled at me and made her way back down the hallway.

"Have I ever lied to you even once, Doc?"

"Hard to say, cowboy, now ain't it?"

"Not for you. I'm guessing you can read my soul. And if you can, you know I've never lied to you. I've done everything I said I would for you, including embezzling millions of dollars on your behalf. If I give you my word on something, you know I follow through."

"That's great, Novo, hell, then pick up your gold star on your way outta my office. There's people waiting on me."

"Doc, let's assume for a moment you have read the book. Then you must realize, if I take the soul of Nurse Simon, only I can return it. If you ever wanted your perty filly to be normal again, you would be dependent on me to make her whole. Good luck to that ever happening unless you do as I ask."

"Stop your lame threats, Novo. Ya ain't got the cojones ta hurt that woman and we both know it."

"You did, Doc. You allowed her to be hurt and you're much closer to her than I am. Right now, I have one goal in mind and I don't care who I hurt. Look deep into my soul, Winfield. Do it! Do I look like a man who lied to you?"

Nurse Simon hustled down the hallway. "What are you two boys shoutin about? Doctor, you're gonna be late fer the hospital if you don't get moving. Now scoot."

Winfield and I stared at each other. Neither would look at her or anyplace else in the room.

"Go ahead, El-Dar Novo. Take it, see if I care. I dun let it happen once, twice won't be no different."

I stood up from my chair and moved close to Nurse Simon. I gave her a soft kiss on her cheek and had decided to leave the room when Winfield shouted. "One week, come back in one week and you'll git your damn elixir. Now stay away from ma girl."

As I turned to thank Winfield, something unexpected happened. Rose reappeared. "Rose is no one's girl. And Rose does not appreciate the way you are speaking to Elder Novo. If Elder Novo wants something, Doctor, Rose strongly suggests you get it for him. Is that understood?"

Winfield's mouth was wide open. For once the man had nothing to say. I gave Rose a kiss on her other cheek and thanked her.

"No problem, sugar. Rose told you she will take care of everything and she will."

I looked at Winfield. His jaw was still on the floor. I smiled his way before offering a parting shot. "I'll be back in a week for my drug. Since you have the other book, you can look up in there how to mix it. If you don't, Rose will take care of everything." Rose pinched my backside as I left.

15

*T*rue to his word, a week later I found myself back in Doc Winfield's office collecting my elixir. The elixir's purpose was to slow down my metabolism after removing a soul to allow all the power from taking the soul to remain with me, and not be shared with the other disciples.

"I'm still madder than a hornet at you and ma perty nurse for that parlor trick ya both pulled last time you wassa here. I scolded her after ya left and she acted like she had no idea what I wassa talking about.

"You can believe what you want, Doc. It was not a trick. I admit to being fond of your nurse, but she is a disturbed creature who needs help. For a brilliant guy, sometimes you are perty dumb, Doc."

"Yes, it's that fondness that don't sit right with me, Novo." Winfield growled in a muted tone. "Here's a vile of what I made fer ya. Drink it in good health, cowboy. If this one works, I'll make ya more, but let's see how this one does first." Winfield flashed a big smile.

"Thanks, Doc. I am sure you realize I do not want just any ole chemist making this for me. I cannot risk someone asking too many questions."

Winfield smirked. "Yeeeaahhhh, I knew there had ta be a reason why you had ta come to my office. Ya don't trust other chemists, even delivery companies. We both know ya only wanna see my nurse. Now git on outta here. Ya got what ya came for."

"Thanks again, Doc. I do appreciate all you do for me and our growing respect for each other. I trust we can work together long into the future. By the way, where is Nurse Simon today?"

"Yeah, long inta da future, cowboy. Don't ya mind bout my nurse, I gave her things ta do today, far away from here."

I scooped up the small vile and headed out the door. I realized long ago not to trust Winfield, even if he hadn't double crossed me yet. My next stop was to verify what was given to me was legitimate.

Dr. Pickering wasn't exactly thrilled to see me back in England. I waited for him to leave for work. "Bloody hell, it's you again. I gave you want you wanted the last time, now bugger off for good."

"Hold on, Doctor Pickering. Hear me out for two minutes and I will guarantee you, all this will be worth your time."

Pickering stopped in his tracks and put his briefcase to the ground. He crossed his arms and stared at me. "You have two minutes and not a second more."

I reached inside my jacket pocket and removed the vile of potion that Winfield had given me along with a copy of the page from my book that described what the chemical breakdown should have been in the vile.

"I would like for you to analyze another vile for me, Doc. See if this matches what should be on this paper. If it does not match, I would like you to make a solution that does match. You can't allow anyone else access to the vile or paper and please don't ask any questions. Just do as I ask."

Pickering tilted his head and asked, "Why would I do anything for you?"

"See, Doc, now that's a question. But I will answer that one. I have been told that you are one fine tennis player."

Pickering lifted his chin and stated with a proud voice, "Club champion two years running in doubles and silver medal in singles. I would say, not too bad, if I say so myself, mate."

"Yes, quite good, Doc. Me. I'm not much of an athlete, but I love watching sports when I can. I have even seen some of the best at Wimbledon. I am guessing that if you had an opportunity to play in the championships later this year that would be a dream come true for you. Am I correct?"

"Hells bells, of course. But I'm not a ranked professional. They would never allow me to play. Besides, I've had a bit of a wounded knee over the years. I'm afraid I would be hard pressed to win a point, let alone a game against any pro."

I allowed a few seconds for the air to clear and let him think he couldn't do it. "Maybe so, Doc. But what if I had a top female pro join you in mixed doubles? Would you be interested then? You just told me you are a top doubles player."

I don't know what Pickering was actually doing for a brief moment but it was a weird combination of the snoopy dance and him playing air tennis. "I would go bonkers if I could do that, but I'm telling you, no one would play with me or allow me within ten miles of center court without a ticket."

"You start working on what I asked and let me handle your entry. As far as a doubles partner, Kristen Sammers retired from singles last year but is looking to hook up with someone to play doubles this year. She is a personal friend of mine and will no doubt play with you at Wimbledon if I asked her."

Pickering started in with that dance again. I never did completely understand the British. It didn't take Pickering long to snatch the vile and paper from my grips and drive off to work. Since I had a day or more to spend in London, I ventured over to see my old classmate Matthew Paul. He and I spent many hours together as youngsters in the compound learning our skills.

Matthew like others in our group, found he couldn't remove souls. He spent many years saving them as a preacher, but later became a businessman, and found his way to be President of Wimbledon. He knew about many of my struggles with the Council because he was one of the few I had stayed in touch with over the years. I could trust him. I called in a big favor and had the team of Pickering and Sammers be a wildcard entry in mixed doubles. In return, he asked me to remove the soul of one prima donna tennis star who always complained during the tournament. I had hoped Matthew was only joking.

Two days later, I met Pickering back in front of his home as he was leaving for work.

"I have no idea who you had to kill to get me in the

tournament, but I recieved a call from Miss Sammers as well as Mr. Paul and it appears I am going to play this year. I can't thank you enough. I only pray this isn't some sort of wicked game you're playing on me, Mr. Novo.

"Nope. It's all real. I suggest you get yourself in top form to play. Kristen hates to lose. Now, what did you find out?"

"Well, you don't have many friends do you, mate? Inside that vile was enough poison to kill a charging elephant. It's a deadly toxin from a dart frog. Whoever gave that to you wanted you dead."

I couldn't say I was too surprised. But I still felt some remorse as Pickering was going on and on about how the amount of poison could have killed me. Being immune to most poisons it's hard to say if it would have killed me or not, however Winfield was likely to know which toxins are deadly to our disciples.

"I appreciate all your assistance, Doctor Pickering. The new batch, are you sure it is exactly as described in the notes I gave you?"

"Am I really playing in Wimbledon this year?"

"Touche', Doc, but yes, you are invited to play and those people who contacted you are who they say they are."

"Well then, what I gave you won't harm you long term, but if my calculation are correct, it should slow down your heartbeat considerably for a short time. Why would you want to do that to yourself?"

"That's a question, Doc. I warned you no questions. But I do thank you for all your help. If this works, I am going to need much more of it."

"If you want more help, then I suggest you fix the seeding so that I don't have to play the top seed in the first round."

I accepted the new vile along with my notes and chuckled with the good doctor. "I won't ask Matthew to mess with the integrity of the seeding, but there is always the US Open. I have connections in many places."

With my new mixture, it was time to test the theory in the book that I could retain all the power from removing a soul. But first, I had to remove one. I logged into Bink's computer and database and found a name lower on the list. This way I knew my target wouldn't be schedule for removal for months. I downloaded a report and read it.

16

*H*er name was Treva Alexandria. She was a top runway model whose cover girl looks were also seen in many top fashion magazines. While prancing down a runway in Paris, showing off the latest in fashions, one of our spies noticed her dark soul that matched her dark complexion and darker hair. Her radiant green eyes splashed with blue were the window to her dark, broken soul. No one had investigated why Treva owned a dark soul, but she was added to Bink's database. A report on her background was completed. Since I had found some in the past on the list not worthy of losing a soul, I wanted to investigate before removing her precious gift.

The report listed Treva's father, Robert Alexandria, as a software engineer turned consultant, who was hired by a United States software company to travel to India in search of future computer programmers. He was one of the first to explore this ancient land for potential talent in programming and computer skills.

Treva's mother was one of Robert's recruits. Maya Patel was taller than your average woman in India. Her brilliant green eyes and beautiful face attracted Robert at first glance. Though never married to Robert, after Maya became the mother of Robert's child, and Robert's assignment came to a close, he moved mother and child to the States.

Maya went on to become a software programmer and moved to Washington State with her daughter. Robert remained a consultant for several companies and traveled extensively. He spent as much time with Treva as possible. Robert traveled with Maya and their daughter to India more than once. When Treva hit her teens, Robert took her with him on occasional business trips throughout Europe as well as New York City. It was in Rome where Treva was discovered.

Robert and daughter were strolling the streets of Rome when they were approached by Vincenzo Angeline, a known and respected photographer from the region. Vincenzo freelanced for a talent agency, who hired models to show off new fashions, and appear in magazines.

Robert was reluctant to allow Treva to be photographed, but after her pleas to her father, he allowed a test shoot the following day. Treva instantly played to the camera. She acted as if she had been in front of a camera for years.

The initial shoot lasted less than thirty minutes but the photographer could be heard saying "bello, bello", over and over. Angeline couldn't help but even declare, "magnifico", at the end of the session. Within three months and some training, Treva was posing for top magazines and being hired by famous designers.

Neither Maya nor Robert were pleased with how quickly it all came to pass but their daughter didn't take on a heavy work schedule until she graduated high school. It didn't help matters when it was apparent that the teenager would be paid more for her modeling in the first year, than her mother or father would make in the same time frame. Treva became independent in a short time.

Soon after her eighteenth birthday, she moved to New York City. Traveling from the west coast of the United States to Europe became too much of a burden on the young model. Her father would visit with her whenever he was in New York. Her mother would vacation in Europe following Treva as she worked the spring fashion shows. It wasn't ideal for either parent, but Treva made it known to both parents, she was in charge of her own life decisions.

Fame came quickly for the young model. Within three years, she was an international super star. Her face adorned almost every fashion magazine in circulation. Treva went on to represent everything from eye liner and designer dresses to jewelry. Her work schedule left little time for socializing. That's why it became a shock to everyone when the super star model announced she was pregnant. It was assumed her personal photographer, Vincenzo Angeline was the father, but neither would confirm everyone's suspicions. Treva continued working as a model, representing maternity clothing and furniture until three weeks before delivering her son.

That's where my report ended. I scoured the internet for stories after Treva became a mother but for more than two years, she mostly dropped out of the public eye. She reemerged for occasional work around New York City, but her career as a runway model in Paris and Rome came to an end. Many of her contracts representing products expired. The only reports I could find on her were in the gossip pages. She was seen in night clubs with rumors of her being intoxicated or worse. Treva's press agent denied every rumor.

My mission was to approach her as a publisher of a new fashion magazine, headquartered in New York City. My name would be Shaun Warren, a wealthy businessman with a desire to make a splash in the world of publishing and high fashion. I would be willing to pay the former super star model one million dollars for an interview and five photographs. Her face would be the cover of the first edition.

My initial angle to meet Miss Alexandria would be to get information from the doorman who stood watch at Treva's swanky Manhattan apartment building one block from Central Park. He was a tall, slender man who stood like a statute guarding the building's front entrance. His brass name pin saved me the discomfort of asking. I flashed a few twenties his way to catch his attention.

"Francis, what can you tell me about the habits of Treva Alexandria? Does she have any appointments she keeps on a regular basis?"

The stoic man didn't flinch. I asked again. This time he turned with a terse stare and irritated tone.

"I heard ya the first time, pal. Miss Alexandria's business is no business of yours. If it was, you'd know how to contact her, now beat it."

I pulled back a few feet to reconsider my tactics and allowed Francis to continue his duties as an elderly lady and her dog exited the building. I wasn't about to give up so easily. I watched and listened to Francis and the elderly woman have an exchange of words. Francis kept a close eye on me as he spoke with the woman, who had a firm grip on the leash holding her small pet. The woman was inquiring about the doorman's family, and in particular his son.

Francis replied. "I don't know what do to about him, Mrs. Krall. He just won't stay away from the drugs. Me and the wife, we can't afford one of them fancy private places to get him cleaned up. We don't know what to do anymore."

The elderly lady offered condolences and well wishes to the doorman. She and her pooch wandered down the concrete walkway. That gave me an idea. I started up another chat with the doorman. "I couldn't help but overhear what you told Mrs. Krall. I think I can help you."

"Yeah, and why would you do that, mister? People who live inside this building, they all have known me for years and wont lift a finger to help me and my boy. You think I'm gonna believe some stranger, who walks up ta me on the street can make it all better. I don't think so. Now like I said, get lost."

"Lighten up, Francis. I can see why you would think the way you do. But I can help. Do you by chance know who Dylan James is?"

Francis removed his cap and wiped his forehead before offering a slight smile. "Yeah, I seen him years ago at the Garden. I think he's dead now, so what?"

I laughed to myself thinking how much Dylan wouldn't appreciate people thinking he was dead. "He is very much alive and lives in North Carolina. He and his daughter own a drug and physical therapy center not far from his home. I will ensure your son is placed in his facility and you won't have to a pay a penny over what your insurance covers."

"Sure pal, and the Easter bunny is gonna come hopping down the street any moment too."

I pulled out my cell phone and spoke with Dylan. I asked him if he wasn't too dead and all, if could get the doorman's son into the rehab facility. I would owe him a favor.

Dylan responded in a mocking voice. "Jeesh, Cale. You still haven't come through with helping McAdams like you promised. Now you want another favor?"

"Relax, Dylan. I'm close to getting George's name cleared. I spoke with Speaker Corbin about George. I also have the FBI and a reporter working on it to break the case against him wide open. One way or another I will make sure to clear George's good name. Plus, I've been kinda busy trying to keep a few bad guys from running the world. But other than that, I've been sitting on my ass. You're right."

"Ok, sorry. Send the kid our way and I'll make sure he gets the attention he needs. What's the kid's name?"

I handed the phone to Francis and he spoke directly with the music legend. When he hung up, his tone was apologetic and excited. "Holy crap, was that THE Dylan James? Please don't lie to me, mister. My boy has been so mixed up in drugs for months. The idea of him getting real help would be a miracle. Please don't tell me this is all bullshit. I'm sorry I didn't listen to ya at first."

"It's real, Francis. But I sure would appreciate it if you would tell me if Miss Alexandria leaves the building on a regular basis."

He lowered his head and shoulders. Francis scuffed his shoes on the pavement a few times. "I don't have much in my life, mister. I stand here day after day opening the door for people who pretend to care, but I know they don't. All I got is this job and my family. If someone found out I gave you information, I'd be canned. Then all I'd be left with is my family."

"You don't have to give me any personal information about Miss Alexandria or her son. Your son will be admitted into the center either way. But maybe you could tell me when it might be to my advantage to be standing outside this door?"

Francis looked surprised. "Son? She has a son? Well now, maybe you're the one who oughta be dishing out the juicy info, mister. Never once have I seen Miss Alexandria with a child in this building and I've been stationed here long before she moved in the building."

Now I was the surprised one. I assumed Treva cared for her son. Could that be a reason for her soul being dark? But then again, her soul was seen as dark before the birth of her child. I stood in front the building questioning myself when Francis started to speak.

"Not much I wouldn't do for my son. The kid was all state in basketball. He had some colleges looking to give him a free ride when he got all mixed up with some bad people. I was so proud telling all the residents about my son as I hailed them a cab in the mornings. I know they didn't care so much. Maybe one or two did, but I was so proud. When ma boy got all screwed up, I stopped talking about him. Other than Mrs. Krall, nobody asks. I still don't believe what you are telling me is real. But if I was you, I might wanna sit at the bench just inside Central Park most days about three in the afternoon. Someone I open the door for likes to jog in the park about then."

"Thanks, Francis. I assure you that my offer was real and that was Dylan James on the phone. Here's my card with my number. If anything goes wrong in getting your son to North Carolina and into rehab, you call me. I promise you, I will do all I can to see that your son gets the help he needs."

Francis accepted my card and read it. "You're lucky you didn't grow up in my neighborhood with a name like Caeles Novo."

"That's funny, I was thinking the same about the name Francis."

He laughed and extended his hand. "Well, everyone away from here calls me Frank. The manager thinks it sounds more sophisticated to call me Francis. Nice to know ya, Caeles Novo. Let me shake your hand to see if you're a man of your word. But if you're lying to me, you just might meet some of my old neighborhood pals to give you that ass kicking."

"Frank, they wouldn't stand a chance."

Frank stuffed the card in his lapel jacket pocket and continued with his duties. I found my way back into the shadows.

The morning sun gave way to a steel gray afternoon. The temperature cooled and the wind picked up. I sat patiently in the chilly weather for a chance to speak with Treva. Frank's advice was accurate. Treva jogged past me dressed in gray bottom sweats and a white top with a hood pulled over her head. Most wouldn't be able to recognize her dressed in sweats, but my skills were superior to most. I sat on the bench for close to an hour until she returned.

As she made her way back in my direction, she slowed from a jog to a walk with a purpose, stretching her arms and looking upwards. Today was my lucky day. Treva sat on the bench at the opposite end where I had been waiting. She inhaled several deep breaths with her eyes closed.

"I hear taking in too much of this dirty air isn't good for your health", I quipped.

Treva took a few more breaths, then glanced my way before replying. "Possibly you need to get new advisors. Fresh air cleanses the soul."

I smiled at Treva. "I think you are the one who could use new advisors. I can assure you that is not true."

"Why not? Are you the expert in matters of my soul?"

What a line to ask me. I had to think how to proceed. "I do not claim to be the expert in much, but I do know who you are. I have been waiting for your return so we could speak. Do you have a moment, Miss Alexandria?"

She jumped up from the bench and wagged her finger at me. "If you know who I am, then you should know that I don't talk with strange men in Central Park. If you need a moment of my time, contact my agent."

Treva walked five feet away when I let out, "I'll give you one million dollars for one hour of your time and five photographs. I want you to be the first cover of my new magazine."

She turned back to look my way with a sinister smile and a

dark soul. "Contact my agent. Her name is Sharon Abington."

I replied in a firm voice. "The offer is only good if you sit with me for five minutes right now." I didn't move a muscle.

The wind picked up and blew Treva's bangs across her face. She let out a quick sigh and returned to the bench. She sat with her arms and legs both crossed implying her mind was closed before I could make my offer. "Ordinarily I would have kept going," she said. "But all this fresh air has cleansed my soul and put me in a better mood. Now who are you and what do you want?"

I wanted so badly to tell her the truth and let her know all the fresh air in Central Park wasn't going to clean her dark soul. Instead, we sat for ten minutes and I told her the lie about me wanting to start a magazine with her on the cover. Her questions and tone of voice led me to think she didn't believe a word I was telling her. It was also obvious from our conversation, she was a highly intelligent woman. I fed her my lie and off she went. We agreed to meet on the same park bench about the same time of day, the following afternoon. She would give me her answer after she spoke with her attorney and agent.

As promised, the following afternoon, Treva met me in the park after her jog. Sweat was pouring off her cheeks as she started to stretch her legs by placing one at a time on the bench.

"I don't know who you think you're dealing with here, Mr. Novo. I'm not some cute face and no brains. I called my lawyer. He's never heard of any Shaun Warren. Your company doesn't even have a web site for goodness sake.

I tried to get a word in, but she cut me off. "Francis showed me a card from someone poking around the front door the other day. Be honest, was that you? And if it was, don't go promising Francis you can fix his kid, we both know that's a lie."

Treva wanted the truth, I was going to offer her the truth. "Yes, Miss Alexandria, I was the one asking questions about you. But Francis didn't tell me anything about you. Don't get him fired."

She jumped right in. "I'm not out to get anyone fired. Those days are over for me. I come out in the fresh air to cleanse my soul of the past."

"May I ask? Why do you think you have cleansed your soul? And what did you do that your soul needs cleansing?"

Treva smirked. "Like I'm going to bear my soul to a guy who lies about who he is, just so he can try to get a date with me, please. I've told you more than once now, I'm not an empty headed glamour girl."

I'd never considered that angle. "A date?" I laughed. "You think this was all some ploy to ask you out on a date?"

Treva seemed stunned. "It's not? I've seen it all, Mr. Novo, assuming that's your real name. Guys are too afraid to ask me out. They either think I'm some stuck up bitch, or I won't go out with them unless they're a movie star or mega rich. I have money. I don't need some man to support me or treat me like I'll break easy. Almost every night, I sit home alone watching television, praying prince charming will ask me out on a real date. Not some insecure mamma's boy only wanting to have dinner with me so he can plaster our photo all over his Facebook page and impress friends."

"Well, now I feel bad, Miss Alexandria. I'll be happy to take you across the street for a nice dinner, but it can't be an official date. I don't have a Facebook page, but I do have a wife who doesn't take kindly to me dating beautiful women."

I could feel tension lift between us. Treva's eyes marched their way from my head to my toes several times, stopping only to look closer into my eyes. She had a look of confusion as her head cocked to the left, then right while squinting all the while.

"The card you handed Francis had a title of spiritual advisor. Explain yourself. Tell me who you are and what you want. If you're not a publisher or a guy looking to add to his resume that he dated a celebrity, what's your angle?"

"I want you to take a deep breath, Miss Alexandria. Take in all the air you can, then relax."

She did. She looked intently at me.

"Do you believe deep down your soul was cleansed in that single breathe?"

"Yes, I do."

"My name is Caeles Novo. I can see into your soul and I know you don't believe what you told me. I wanted to interview you because before I take your soul, I wanted to make sure it deserved to be taken."

Treva closed her eyes and she sunk lower into the park bench. "I prayed so hard this day wouldn't come, but I knew it would. I tried so hard to cleanse myself from the past. I wanted to be a good person. But you don't know how much pressure I was under. I wanted to be the one they called for the top jobs. I wanted the best outfits in the shows. I worked hard. I did believe I deserved my fame and fortune."

As Treva opened her eyes, I could see a teardrop dribble from her right side. She wiggled her nose and wiped it with her sleeve. "My mother was raised as a spiritual woman in India. We visited there when I was a child. She introduced me to a man from her community that told me that my soul would be stolen if I didn't live a clean life. Now here you are. I changed my ways, Mr. Novo. I swear I did."

In all the years of removing souls, this was the first time someone actually believed me. I felt sorrow. But I still wanted to know more. Maybe I could spare her.

"You do have a dark soul, Miss Alexandria, but my question is why?"

She looked deep into my eyes. "I would change the clocks in my apartment, so my roommates would be late for assignments. I would put things in their drinks to make them look tired. I would do anything and everything to make me look better. I lied to girls back stage about designers or what other people were saying about them to create drama and start fights between the girls and designers."

"What about your son, where is he?"

"After I gave birth, I couldn't handle not working and being a mother. I hired a nanny and I would go out late and party. I couldn't bear the crying. I hated my son for needing me. I hated life for changing me from an international star to a mommy who needed to shed ten pounds. I picked up a cocaine problem, but my father forced me into rehab. I'm clean for one hundred and eighty seven days. I told everyone my son was living with his father, but he's not. My mother has my child. I'm pretty sure I know who the father is, but I'm not positive. I had a few days off after a shoot in the Caribbean, and I hooked up with some guy for a few days. I know it was stupid. I've only been with two men in my entire life, but both within the same week. My life has been one cheating and lying day after another. I sold my soul to be at the top of the modeling world, and now I guess you've come to collect, like the man told me you would. If I could go back and atone for my sins, I would."

I viewed her soul. There had to be a way of making this right. I gently placed her hand into mine. We both gazed off into the city skyline. "Miss Alexandria, what if you could cleanse your soul? What if there was a way. Would you do it?"

"Definitely. I would do it without thinking twice."

I explained to her all about soul stealing, who we were, what our mission was on earth. She learned about the Surrounding of Souls and how her soul could be cleansed. For the first time ever, I felt I would be doing what our original mission was on earth. I had found a true believer and one who wanted to be cleansed and start her life over. We agreed she would go home and call her family and explain she would be going through a different type of rehab, but like the other time, she would be better for it in the long run. Treva arranged for me to meet her in her apartment the following morning. Her soul would be removed long enough to be cleansed and returned.

17

*T*he clouds grumbled with anticipation. That morning was unlike any other for me. I would be removing a soul with consent. No jumping from the shadows or living a double life to get close enough to my target. There was a scheduled time to fulfil my life's work with someone who claimed to believe in me. Plus, I would be able to test my elixir, to see if I would retain all the strength from removing a soul. Kalani knew what I was about to do. I would call her as I drank the potion, so she would know to anticipate if she felt the effects or not.

Frank the doorman was standing guard at his usual post. This time I wouldn't have to play twenty questions to get past him. My name was to be left as a visitor to the building. Frank looked at me sheepishly as I approached the entrance.

"No hard feelIngs, Mr. Novo? I'm sorry, but I had to tell Miss Alexandria someone was snooping around for her. There were too many people who saw me talking with you. In this economy, I can't afford to be outta work, even one day. Please don't go back on your word to get my boy help."

I had far more on my mind than being upset with a guy for doing his job. I shook hands with Frank and let him know everything was still on track. "I have a son too, Frank. I'll do all I can to get your son the help he needs. You have my number. Now, I do believe I'm permitted to enter the building."

"Yes sir, you may. And thank you again. I'll give you a call after he goes through therapy. I'm driving him down there this weekend."

Frank pulled open the large glass door and I made my way up the elevator to the tenth floor apartment. After a double knock, Miss Alexandria allowed me into her residence. I scanned the room. One large white wall was filled with photos from her modeling career. Three other white walls all had a single painting on each, created with more splashy colors than could be found in a large box of Crayola crayons. The furniture was chrome and white leather. Across the room was a large sliding glass door that exhibited a panoramic view of Central Park. The place matched the beauty of its occupant.

Treva escorted me across the spotless wood floor to have a seat on her white leather sofa. "Make yourself comfortable," she said. "But don't get too comfy, we have lots of work to do today. And how do you like my furniture? I had it all shipped in from Italy. My photographer, Vincenzo, his brother makes custom furniture. My dad tells me every time he visits I've wasted too much money on crap that doesn't mean anything. I should be investing my money better, but he forgets, I come from the fashion world. My home is a reflection of who I am."

Before she could say any more, there was a knock on the door. Treva invited in a young looking guy with more grease in his hair than all the hands in a Nascar pit crew. The next thing I noticed was his expensive looking brief case and manicured hands. The same hands that pulled several sheets of paper from a plastic sleeve that he removed from his brief case.

"Oh, Mr. Novo, I guess I didn't tell you," Treva explained. "My attorney thinks you're a, uhm, huckster, I think he called you. I don't believe him, but he wants to hold you liable should anything happen to me."

Another first for me. I was asked to sign documents to steal a soul. I had woken up in a great mood too. Before I could object, Mr. "I look way too young to have passed the New York Bar exam," is sitting next to me with pen in hand and looking at me like I had three eyes. On top of all that, he had the audacity to speak to me like I was clueless.

"Yes, Mr. Novo. As you can plainly see, I have marked the six places where you either have to initial or sign. Once you do that, I will leave you both to your séance."

Who were these people to treat what I did as trivial or attempt to hold me liable for what the spiritual world might do with someone's soul? My mind was racing with past lessons. Never once were we taught what we should do when asked to sign legal papers to steal souls, from some kid who wasn't even born when I started doing what I did.

It is funny what your mind does in that moment when you're put in situations you don't have an answer about what to do. Mine was replaying lawyer jokes over and over. I glanced over at Miss Alexandria and asked her, "What's the difference between God and an attorney?"

She looked at the young man with a wicked smile, then turned toward me. "I have no idea, Mr. Novo, what is the difference between God and an attorney."

186

"God doesn't think he's an attorney," I answered.

The attorney offered me a blank stare. Miss Alexandria giggled before stating, "Sign the frigging paper, Mr. Novo. I'm anxious to get started."

It wasn't the signature part that was annoying me. It was that I was being asked in the first place. I had no assets in my real name. I didn't have a real social security number or even a passport that was in my birth name. Everything connected to me was always well protected. My signature on those pages were worthless. But still, I couldn't allow them to think they were getting the better of me.

I asked if I could have a drink while reading the papers. I was offered a few options. I chose lemonade. I drank a few sips, then signed the documents. Before the inexperienced attorney could remove the papers from the coffee table, I allowed my drink to spill on the edge of the papers I had signed. He rushed to wipe up my mess but the acid from the drink was embedded in the fiber of the paper. Once filed away, the paper would be destroyed from the acid while no one was watching.

I guess the young guy couldn't help himself but to leave with a parting shot as he was being led to the door by Treva. "It wouldn't be wise to attempt to try to steal any money or harm Miss Alexandria in any way, Mr. Novo. And please don't embarrass yourself by trying to seduce her. And by the way, I've heard that joke a million times and it sucks every time I hear it."

"Thanks for letting me know. I will make sure I have a better joke the next time I see you." Treva shoved the lawyer and his sassy mouth out the door and proceeded to walk back my way.

"I'm sorry about all that," Treva said. "When I called my dad yesterday to explain to him what I was planning on doing, he was dead set against it. We argued back and forth until he suggested I get something signed. I don't know what was in those papers, nor do I care. I was only doing it too keep my dad off my back."

"That's fine, Miss Alexandria. I need to call my wife to let her know we are about to begin. Since everyone is affected differently after their soul is removed, I trust you took my advice from yesterday to have someone look in on you now and again, at least until your soul is returned."

"Oh, yes, thank you. That's all been arranged. I have a housekeeper who is planning on stopping by every day. She's going to make sure I have meals and I'm ok."

I made my call to Kalani and drank the elixir Pickering had concocted for me. The wind whistled through the slightly opened sliding glass door. I requested Treva sit next to me. I softly embraced her hand with mine. The wind stirred more. Her soul passed through me and off to the Surrounding of Souls. My body surged with power as hers slumped into her custom made Italian leather sofa.

Treva exhibited an upside down smile as her hand went limp. I moved from my seat and stretched her body out, lying it comfortably across the sofa. My head pounded as if I had a headache of the worst kind. My arms were tingling, but my heart was now barely beating.

I called Kalani again and she informed me she felt nothing. All the power had been retained by me. I moved to the chair closest to the sofa and fell into it. The phone dropped from my hand. I could barely hear Kalani asking me if I was ok from the speaker in the phone now on the floor.

I awoke several hours later. I looked at the sofa with blurry eyes but no one was there. No sounds were initially heard. My heart beat felt normal. I tried to stand but my legs wouldn't cooperate. I sat there for several minutes breathing in the air rushing through the wide open sliding glass door.

The first sounds I could hear were from a tiny older woman with long black hair, dark skin and a faint Spanish accent, who I had never met, trying to hand me a glass of water. "Miss Treva asked me to watch over you. She is sleeping in her room. Drink this."

I shook the cobwebs from my brain and accepted the tall glass of water. I could see my cell phone sitting on the coffee table. I asked the woman to hand it to me. I called Kalani to let her know all was well. I informed her that I would be spending one more night in New York, then I would be off to finish up my promise to Dylan in helping George McAdams. The next morning I headed off to meet up with a few people in the Washington D.C. area.

Josh Simpson was a newspaper reporter who had been leaking secrets on behalf of the current administration to assist in the President's reelection efforts. I was assigned to remove his soul and did. Unfortunately, in order to help my old buddy Nestor, I was forced to return Simpson's soul. The oddity about Josh's soul is that I didn't return his soul.

When I visited the Surrounding of Souls, the soul of Josh Simpson was being guarded by the gatekeeper, who took on the likeness of Josh's father. The gatekeeper refused to allow me to take Josh's soul and instead offered me his twin brother's soul who was killed in a car accident. The same accident that killed his father, but spared Josh, who was in the back seat at the time of the accident. Josh now carries his brother's soul. The effects of carrying his brother's soul, who was always the more mature and wiser twin, had made Josh attempt to dig up the truth in his stories, and not rely on information being spoon fed to him by the President's staff.

I proved to Josh that I stole his soul, but returned his brother's to him by answering questions about his past that only he and his brother would know. After that, Josh had agreed to help me in proving George McAdams was innocent of murdering a history teacher named Desmond Danker.

It had been everyone's theory that McAdams and Danker both were investigating a slush fund used by politicians to keep women silent, when they had affairs, or even out of wedlock children, who were fathered by top politicians. When neither would stop investigating it, Danker was murdered and it was set up to appear as if Congressman McAdams did the crime. The only problem was there was little motive for McAdams to kill Danker. The night before the jury was to render a verdict, all charges were dropped as long as McAdams never claimed his innocence or spoke about the case in any way. Washington insiders were stunned with the outcome of the case. McAdams bright future in politics ended abruptly.

I had been asked by Dylan James, who was a friend of McAdams to clear his name publically. Dylan knew I had abilities beyond most investigators, because of my connections and powers. Plus, Dylan knew I had stolen and returned his soul long ago.

I contacted Simpson and met him at a small coffee shop near

his office. He appeared fit and happy. Carrying his brother's soul seemed to be working for him. Josh explained how busy he was and the stories he was working on over coffee, but I only cared about one story.

"My cousin worked for the secret service, Cale. Once they realized she was feeding information to Danker and McAdams, the secret service had to keep her quiet. They shipped Paula out west and set her up in a nice house and new job. But she's feeling real guilty about McAdams."

"Hold on, are you telling me you have a cousin who knows this was a setup?"

"I'm not sure what I'm telling you. I'm trying to put it all together myself. Paula won't talk freely on the phone because her phone is likely being tapped. I'm not even sure exactly where she is out west. But if I deciphered what she was trying to tell me correctly, she thinks Danker is still alive."

Now this was getting interesting. I loved mysteries, even when I didn't really have time to solve them. "Ok, Josh, if Danker is still walking upright, whose body did they find in his apartment?"

"Well, I'm not really sure. But I am following up on a hunch I had. The police blotter had a story about three bodies being pulled from the Potomac River the night Danker was supposed to have been murdered, but only two ended up in the morgue."

"Ok, so if Danker is still alive, who is hiding him? Do you have any ideas, Josh?"

"I would look hard at the secret service. They protect the President. Paula did tell me before they moved her that Danker was investigating if the President had a child out of wedlock."

I thanked Josh and we parted. We promised to keep each in touch if either of us found anything. My first action after leaving Josh was to contact Iza Tappen and see if Iza could hack into the secret service emails to investigate if Danker's name popped up. Or attempt to discover the file to show us where all the people in protective custody were being held. I was contacted back letting me know my bill increased by five hundred thousand dollars for that job because of the complexity and danger of jail time. I agreed to the fee.

The next thing I did was call Special Agent Nesstor. At first, he wasn't going to meet me. I had to convince him this had nothing to do with the hockey star. We met later that evening for dinner.

As Elliot entered the restaurant, he appeared tired to me. His hair was now completely grey, his back arched slightly. He walked with a limp I hadn't noticed the last time we met. Sometimes I would forget how much quicker humans aged compared to our kind. I had known Elliot for close to forty years. We met when he was a young officer on the Chicago police force. As he sat at the table, I remembered seeing Elliot for the first time. He was assigned to a homicide case, I presumed, committed by the man who owned the first soul I ever stole. We formally met while I was working on removing the second soul I ever stole. I was going to miss him after he retired. He sat across the table from me.

"Since I was in town, I wanted to buy you dinner, Elliot. In all the years, I don't think we have ever actually shared a meal, have we?"

"No, I don't think we have. It's the least you can do after all the headaches you've given me, Soul Man.

The waitress came over and handed us each a menu and some water. The longer I sat across from Elliot, the heavier my heart became. My dinner partner sat quietly as well until the drinks arrived.

"Do you remember when we met back in Chicago?" I asked Nesstor.

"I do you son of a bitch. Didn't you get mixed up with some lady killing off guys for money?"

"Yes. But I knew you before that lady and I never told you."

"Oh, how so?" Nesstor asked.

"You were promoted to detective and one of your first cases was the murder of an older lady. You suspected the piano player, Johnny Jackson did it. You followed him and his band to North Carolina. One of his band members who you wanted to question, drowned before you could get to him. Do you remember that?'

"Hell yes, I remember. I know that kid killed the old lady. I don't know what prompted him to kill her, nor could I ever get enough evidence to bring charges, but to this day, my gut tells me he did it."

"I suspect your suspicions are right, Elliot. I took the soul of Johnny Joe Jackson. He was the first soul I ever removed. I suspect he murdered his band mate as well. Jackson knew sooner or later you would get the truth from his band mate. Johnny wasn't asleep in his hotel at the time of the murder like he claimed."

"Well shit, Cale. Why didn't you tell me this forty years ago? That coulda really helped me prove my case."

"I don't have any proof Jackson killed anyone. I only know the guy was bad news with a black soul. If it's any consolation, his career was essentially over after I removed his soul. The only woman he ever loved refused to marry him, and he never had another hit song. He plays small venues to this day, just to pay his bills."

Nesstor leaned back in his chair and frowned at me. "Do you have any other secrets you're keeping from me?"

There was my opening. "This is not a secret, more my intuition at this point. The history teacher that McAdams was on trial for, the guy is still alive. The larger part of the story is that I believe the secret service is hiding him and the President was the one who approved it all."

Nesstor could only shake his head. In a tone of disgust, he said, "I knew we couldn't have a nice quiet dinner without some crazy ideas being thrown my way. So I guess now you want me to walk into the oval office and arrest the President of the United States for what, conspiracy? Where do you come up with these insane thoughts of yours?"

"You know what, Elliot. I'm starting to be happy you're retiring. Maybe I can work with someone who won't call me an idiot every time I give them a solid lead. I've given you and your agency some great leads, which have led to some of your biggest convictions. I don't remember you calling me a fool then!"

A regal older looking man dining at the table beside us, with a much younger woman, covered in expensive jewelry, gave me a sneer as if to ask for quiet. Nesstor gave me that same stare that Winfield and Kalani give me when they're upset with me. I had become immune to all of it. I could understand to a point why

Elliot wouldn't believe me, but over the years, a high percentage of my leads became success stories on his fat, successful resume. I was growing weary of him disrespecting me and my information.

"Cale, you need to come to grips with something. I'm too tired to come charging in on the white horse any longer. I wanna find some quiet pond in Florida and go fishing. I don't have the desire to go searching for bad guys any more. I especially don't need to accuse the President of the United States of fixing a murder that never happened because you think there was a conspiracy to bring down a two bit congressman who woulda been beaten in the next election. I'm done. It's over."

He was correct. I didn't want to hear it. Maybe he was going to retire, but I wanted him to tell me I was more to him than some low level informant. I wasn't giving him tips about a guy passing bad checks or a foreign diplomat with a bunch of parking tickets. I found him notorious bank robbers, large scale drug dealers and high finance cheaters. He owed me more than his now constant insistence that I had become a nuisance.

"What about the Clinkard woman, Elliot. I handed her to you on a silver platter. Don't I get a thank you for that one?"

"That reminds me, Soul Man. I now get a daily email from the old lady's daughter, letting me know that she has placed a curse on me. She claims the next arrest I make will end badly for me, unless I release her mother. So, now I've got that going for me. So yes, thank you, so much, for all you do for me."

This wasn't the way I anticipated the evening would end, but it finished on a sour note. It was time to take satisfaction in knowing I did help in bringing many to justice spiritually, as well as in the court system. Nesstor didn't need to tell me my own self-worth. I had contributed to making society a better place, even if he had turned into a crabby old man looking forward to cashing his pension checks and baiting a few hooks.

The following morning I was to meet with the Speaker of the House of Representatives, John Corbin, in his office at the Rayburn building. The Speaker was on a tight schedule but this was a conversation best had face to face. I would have preferred we meet away from prying ears, but Corbin insisted he needed to stay close to the Capitol building because of a busy congressional schedule.

The second I was escorted into Corbin's cramped office, it was obvious he needed a new tailor. The guy had either lost some weight or wore suits two sizes too large. This was the second time I visited with him where he looked more like a struggling insurance salesman than one of the most powerful men in the world. His office staff was dressed impeccably, he appeared as a frumpy old man. We exchanged greetings and a handshake inside his office before Corbin went and sat behind his desk, offering me a seat on the other side.

"You know, Mr. Speaker, if you ever want to become President, you are going to have to step up your game with your suit and ties."

"Eat shit, Novo. I'm busting my ass trying to get four hundred and thirty five house members to pass several appropriation bills today. I have a President who thinks budget is a dirty word, and a Senate majority leader who refuses to negotiate, claiming because Morrison was reelected, we should keep spending like drunken sailors. Do you think I have time to worry about what color my tie is? Now whaddya want?"

I could take a hint. My time would be short. "This is a private conversation, sir. I suggest you clear the room."

With a wave of his hand, his aide, who I recognized from the last time we met, and a young woman left the room and closed the door behind them. I continued. "Your sister goes by the name of Tasha Timmons. She is doing her best to take over the Council. I have had my disagreements with her, and I believe she had a hand in attempting to have me killed."

"Do you see a conspiracy everywhere you look, Novo? I mean seriously, the last time we spoke you were convinced the President was framing a congressman for murder and now you think my sister is out to kill you. Maybe you need to take a long vacation."

"I didn't come here for your insults and lectures, John. I didn't want to advertise about your sister over the phone. You never know who might be listening on the other end."

"There you go again, another conspiracy. Do you think our government would record conversations from our own citizens? You have gone bonkers, Novo."

"Keep mocking me, John. One day everyone in this town is going to wake up and realize the landscape has changed and not for the better."

Corbin looked at his watch then back at me. "Whatever. Now, how do I get in touch with my sister?"

"A powerful man like you, John, you can't find one woman? Our deal was that I would get you a name and I did. She travels the world removing souls. Occasionally, she shows up at the compound for meetings. I suggest you start with any connections you might have with people inside the compound and get her a note."

Corbin looked at his watch again. His aide knocked on his office door. "Mr. Speaker you are wanted over at the Capitol. We need to go now, sir."

Corbin grumbled at his aide and waved him back out. "As you can see, Novo, I don't have time to chase her all over the place. You bring her to me or no deal."

I scoffed sarcastically at Corbin. "Yes, it seems only people in this town are busy. I'll get your sister here, but I'm calling in my second request. I need you to tell me how I can get five minutes with the President, or better yet, can you arrange it for me?"

"Now you have lost your mind. I'm supposed to get you a sit down with Morrison? The man barely speaks with me, and I'm on his side."

"Listen carefully to me, John. You get word to President Morrison that I want to meet with him privately for five minutes, or I will showcase Desmond Danker on every cable station in the country telling his story."

Corbin shook his head and stood up. He walked over close enough that our bellies almost touched. "Danker is dead to the world, and he's going to stay that way."

I poked Corbin in the belly with my finger and moved back slightly. "Not according to my sources, John. So you can either get me my five minutes with Morrison or when I find Danker, he can tell the world it was you who set up McAdams. I'm not looking to hurt you or the President. But I will."

The door to the office flung open again. "Mr. Speaker there is less than four minutes for you to place your vote. We need to go this instant, sir."

Corbin sounded exasperated. Yeah, yeah, let's go." Corbin looked back at me one last time before clearing out of his office. "I'll be in touch."

While driving back to New York to visit with Treva Alexandria, I received a text from Iza Tappen.

Forwarding address for Danker.

I pulled over to the side of the road to write it down. I deleted the note. You never know who is reading your emails. I sent a note back asking Iza if Iza recieved the entire file with several names or only one.

Have friends in high places who needed cash, got one address for a price.

I guess it didn't matter how Iza discovered the address, as long as it was accurate. After dealing with Treva, the priority was to find Danker. Once back on the highway, I did start to reflect on what Corbin had told me. Possibly I did need a break. The image I had in my mind was being the captain of a rudderless ship. Where was this ship taking me? Every time I thought I was back on course, the winds shifted. But that's the beauty of life. If you have faith, then you realize the winds shift for a reason. And if you look closely, you can always find your destination on the horizon. As long as you keep your faith that your destination exists.

18

*T*reva Alexandria was a mess. Her housekeeper met me at the door of Treva's apartment. "Miss Treva does nothing but eat and sleep. Please help her, Mr. Cale. Something is not good with her." I followed her to the back room where I sat next to Treva, who was sitting on the sofa staring at a television screen.

"How are you feeling, Miss Alexandria?" She turned her neck slightly away from the television, her puffy red eyes now trying to focus on me, as her head swayed back and forth. I could see remnants of orange cheese puffs around her lips, her clothes wrinkled. I wanted to grab my camera and record a photo for the gossip pages, but I knew better. This person put her trust in me. I didn't want to let her down.

"I feel like a cow," Treva said in a whiny tone. "I now understand what hell must be for a super model. I feel so fat and unattractive. How long before I get my soul back?"

After removing a Twinkie from her clutches and cleaning her sticky fingers, I decided not to wait any longer. The time had arrived to restore her soul. I asked her housekeeper Gloria, to lock the front door and turn off all the phones. I had restored souls, but never one who asked to be sent for redemption. I had no idea if there was any time limit. My book with all our secrets didn't mention any time frames. I turned off the television. She would have to wait to see who was voted off the Island.

I asked Treva to close her eyes and hold my hands as we each sat sideways facing each other on the sofa. Her housekeeper was sitting in the chair a few feet behind me. I relaxed every muscle in my body. I moved my right thumb so that I could feel the pulse emanating from my subject's wrist.

The wind stirred on the balcony. A small chair was tossed against the sliding glass door. Gloria gasped for air as Treva remained motionless. With closed eyes, the spirits were summoned to lift my soul to the Surrounding of Souls. My heartbeat raced. Then a calmness hit me as my body temperature rose. My limbs became frozen.

My soul was lifted to the Surrounding of Souls by the spirits. My mind envisioned a long runway with bright white lights lining the edges along the floor. My soul continued its journey down the runway, as large theatre lights crisscrossed back and forth along the black floor. At the end of my souls journey, near the end of the runway, stood a woman with dark framed glasses dressed in a white blouse and black pants. Her hair was cut with bangs hanging straight across her forehead. From her neck hung a pearl necklace.

"Are you the gatekeeper?" I inquired.

"A gatekeeper" the woman replied. "I am Edith Head. I have never been nor will I be anyone's gatekeeper, thank you very much."

"I apologize, mam. No disrespect was meant. I seek the soul of Treva Alexandria. Her soul was sent here to be cleansed. She has asked for forgiveness and seeks redemption. Please release her soul so that she may continue her modeling career back on earth."

I never knew what form the gatekeeper would take in advance. So I had learned to never have preconceived ideas who I would be bargaining with for the release of a soul. But I did enjoy meeting some the world's great leaders.

Edith started to rant. "The world doesn't need another creature comprised of only skin and bones. I have it on good authority, the woman has no regard for my era of fashion. Sure, she had no problems wearing her little spring collections from Cardin or Lang, but try catching her in one of my creations. Only a woman like Liz Taylor or May West know how to wear my designs. Why should I unleash another malnourished model back into society?"

"Mam, the woman has been eating nothing but Ding Dongs and Tasty Cakes for days. She was never confused with Twiggy, even in her prime. Truth be told, Mrs. Head, every time I have returned a soul, I always had to bargain with someone who my souls earthly body greatly admired. I am not doubting whoever offered you advice about Miss Alexandria's taste in fashion, but I am willing to bet Miss Alexandria is an admirer of your work. I ask you again, please release her soul to me."

The lights went out on the runway. Only the lights crisscrossing remained, but they lost much of their luminosity. Time was short. If my soul remained away from my body too long, I ran the risk of it not returning and being trapped in the Surrounding of Souls. My body started to weaken.

"My name needs to live on," Edith declared. "I was commissioned to design the uniforms for females enlisting in the Coast Guard. Despite being honored for my work, few know of my design. You may return the soul of Treva Alexandria, but only if she contacts the Coast Guard and models my uniforms in recruitment ads. If you believe she can wear my designs with large appeal, prove it."

"Done, I will convince her to do it."

"If not, the next time you visit our home, you will be turned away without regard. I have spoken to some of the others you have made promises to here, like General Washington and Mr. Ansel Adams. Don't think we don't keep track of you, Caeles Novo. Now leave me. I promised Grace Kelly that I would make her an evening gown for her date with Paul Newman."

My body shook violently as the soul of Treva Alexandria linked with my soul. Both souls returned to my earthly existence. My eyes opened with Treva's green and blue eyes staring directly at me. I gave her a quick smile and with a warm embrace. My subject's soul was returned.

She let out a long sigh as Gloria jumped from her seat and raced into the kitchen getting an ice pack that she placed across Treva's forehead. I sat feeling relieved and stronger for the experience. But one obligation had to be fulfilled.

"Miss Alexandria, do you know who Edith Head is per chance?"

"Oh my goodness, yes. My mother and I would sit and watch old movies just for the costumes. In my younger days, I would complain to mom about having to watch those old black and white movies but as I grew older, I have come to appreciate the work Edith did. Why would you ask?"

"The gatekeeper who returned your soul took on the appearance of Edith. I gave her my word that you would model the uniforms she designed for the Coast Guard. If you are serious about starting over, I need you to do that for me. I gave Mrs. Head my word."

Treva removed the ice pack from her head and placed it on the end table. "I'll call my agent to see if she thinks that's a good place to kick start my career. However, before anything happens, I want to visit my mother and son."

I didn't like her response. "Hey, I risked my life for you lady! The last thing you want to do is upset me or the spirit world right after your soul was returned. I really don't care what your agent says, someone will contact the Coast Guard the moment you return from seeing your mother and son. You will honor her request."

"Mr. Novo, as much as your assistance was greatly appreciated, attempting to bully me isn't your best strategy. I do things on my time schedule and only if they benefit me."

This woman was stepping into dangerous territory. She needed to be reminded of my abilities. "Miss Alexandria, one of my father's favorite quotes goes like this. I brought you into this world and I can take you out of it. You will make every effort to model those uniforms, or trust me, we will meet again."

"I'm really not a fan of your tone, I think you should leave now."

"That's fine, Miss Alexandria. However, keep one thing in mind, there is a small army of soul stealers looking to feed on dark souls. Some still employ cameras as a weapon of choice. For someone who makes a living in the public eye, you might think twice before disappointing me. You sought redemption from being a selfish, self-centered brat. The spirits granted your wish. You can now either pay back the spirit world, or every time you look into a camera lens or brush against any stranger, you can wonder if this is the day you lose your soul again. I won't be around to save you a second time. You think about what I said. Take care now."

Gloria the housekeeper ushered me to the door. I glared at Treva one last before exiting. My body still felt as if I had downed several gallons of energy drinks. I needed a place to chill. I headed over to the hotel and started to research Desmond Danker.

Danker was a history professor from American University who was born and raised in the District of Columbia. His wife died from breast cancer several years ago. They had one son. I couldn't find any information about the son online. I did find a few photos using social media of Desmond. I also found his biography on the university web site.

It seemed Desmond Danker was well respected within the world of academia. He had won several awards for his writings. Danker published two books about President Washington and the revolutionary war and one about the civil war. From his personal web site, he wrote about how he was working on a new book concerning President Lincoln.

The next day, I boarded a plane for Las Vegas, Nevada. If Iza Tappen was correct, Danker was not only still alive, but hiding in plain sight. The Vegas airport was bustling with fortune seeking dreamers arriving in town and exhausted faces heading through security returning home. Kalani and I made an occasional trip to Sin City, mostly for entertainment reasons in the past, but it had been a few years since our last visit.

The address given to me, took me to a side street not far from the famous strip. The street was a concrete jungle, lined with similar three story apartment buildings, all painted with earth tone colors of browns and greens. They blended into each other without the glitz and glamour only a few blocks away. I found the closest parking spot and walked the street until I found the exact building and apartment number where Danker was supposed to be living.

The name on the outside door of the address I was searching for read, Thomas Edwards. I knocked but no one answered. I questioned a few neighbors who were coming and going from the building. No one would tell me anything about the person living in apartment 2F. I waited a few hours but to no avail. I left and checked myself into the Bellagio for a good night's sleep.

One of the joys of visiting Las Vegas was the food. You could always find me in the buffet line, first thing in the morning. It was also a wonderful place to people watch. I could sit for hours attempting to figure out where people had come from by their accents or mannerisms. I could also remain busy removing souls right from the breakfast table, if I was so inclined. But I had other plans for the day.

After a few hours of sitting outside the same apartment building, I was at the day before, a man who looked similar to Danker came walking out of the building. His hair was darker and the man was thinner by twenty pounds than in the photos I had seen online, but I was confident the man who strolled toward the street was Desmond Danker. I was about to get out of my car to speak with him when a cab pulled to the curb. Danker jumped in. I followed them to The Sahara Casino, near the end of the strip. The cab pulled around to the back of the casino, where Danker got out and entered the building. I found a place to park and went inside.

Inside the Sahara, it was difficult to find anyone. People were lined up checking in, others were either playing games of chance, or going on the Nascar ride at the back of the casino. I strolled back and forth several times looking for any sign of Danker. I was tempted to purchase a ticket to see "The Amazing Jonathon" who Kalani and I had seen the last time we were in town, but I ended up perched in the keno area for an hour. My patience was rewarded. Not only by winning two hundred dollars playing keno, but getting a glimpse of Danker. I followed him to a black jack table where he was taking over as the dealer.

Being an observant person, as well as having above average math skills, blackjack was my game of choice. It is also a game that if you play every hand perfectly, it slightly favors the player, not the house.

During my training as a soul stealer, one way we were taught to focus, was learning how to count cards, using eight decks of cards, similar to many casinos. The purpose of the training was to hone our ability to focus for several hours at a time.

Card counting is a simple, yet proven theory where you assign different cards in the deck to have different values. Depending if the sum of the cards played are high or low, will determine if the odds are more or less in your favor, each time a hand is played.

It's the reason why many casinos use multiple decks now instead of a single deck. More decks water down the value of card counting. Though counting is not illegal, casinos have methods of evaluating if people are counting cards. One being if your bets vary as opposed to playing the same amount each hand.

One time after stealing the dark soul of a casino employee, I stayed an extra day to play black jack. I wanted to test my card counting skills. I knew playing at a five dollar minimum table, early in the morning with few players put the odds more in my favor. At night there were too many players to screw up my odds by taking hits when they shouldn't or vice versa.

After two hours, I had taken my initial fifty dollar buy in to over five hundred dollars. Many would think this wouldn't alarm any casino boss, but casinos don't get built so lavishly by allowing players to increase their funds tenfold. No matter the denomination.

My winnings continued to increase throughout the morning. The dealers were about to change shifts. I was the lone gambler at the table. The silver haired, sixty something year old dealer, who didn't utter a sound, was replaced with a red headed beauty who could have been mistaken for the latest centerfold. I did everything I could to keep my focus, but she kept asking me questions like my name, where I was from, what I was doing later in the day, and so on. Within fifteen minutes, I had given back more than half of my winnings. I knew then what the casino had done. I looked at the eye in the sky and smiled, letting them know their plan to disrupt my winning streak had succeeded. As I stood up to leave, the pit boss looked at me and said, "Kinda hard to concentrate with Kelli dealing, now isn't it? You have a nice day."

Since that day, I hadn't played blackjack. Being someone with a large ego and a competitive nature, the thought of losing money, only to get close to Danker irked me. But I had little choice. My assignment of the day was to ensure the man I suspected was Desmond Danker, truly was him. I sat at a twenty dollar a hand table, where he was dealing and bought two hundred dollars in chips. I noticed the eye in the sky and gave it a wink.

It was late afternoon. The sounds of a busy casino were everywhere. The clanging of coins hitting the bottom of slot machines. The loud yells from nearby tables when the dealer dealt themselves black jack. The scantily clad waitresses taking drink orders. Even down to the dealer taking my wad of twenties and calling out to the pit boss, "cashing two hundred." But the smells were worse. I was never a smoker, so the smell from people smoking cigarettes at my table was giving me a headache.

I pushed out two ten dollar chips to the betting circle in front of me. Then came one of the other sounds, the whishing the cards make while flying out of the shoe at the corner of the table and striking it. The dealer placed the cards in front of me and the other four people playing the hand. My cards were a six and a five. Two players before me took cards and busted, but several of the cards were lower numbers. My odds improved. The dealer's long index finger was now pointing right in front of my cards. Most dealers in search of tips won't move that finger until they think the odds are no longer with you to take another card. The dealer's finger didn't budge.

"You would like a card, sir?" He inquired.

I looked up at the dealer, who I suspected was Danker, then

flipped out another twenty dollars in chips in order to double down. The next card was a nine. I stayed with twenty. The player behind me stayed with his two face cards. The dealer was showing a face card. He flipped over a six. The rules state the dealer must take cards until they reach seventeen. He took another card and busted with twenty three. I was off to a good start. My competitive nature was now fighting my mind to stay focused on my mission and not on my cards.

The dealers name tag read "Thomas" with the word "California" underneath. Some casinos put the name of the state from where the employee is from under their first name. After winning the second hand, I looked at the dealer as his finger was again pointing at my cards for the third time. "So, Thomas, how long have you been working here in town?"

"A few months." He kept pointing at my cards. I took a card and busted out.

"Are you originally from California, Tom?" I was trying to get him into a conversation. The next hand, I was dealt black jack. I tossed the dealer a ten dollar chip as a token of my appreciation.

"Thank you, sir." The dealer said offering a quick smile. "I've moved around the country, but I plan on staying here for a while." He tucked my chip off to the side after banging it on the edge of the table and peeking at the pit boss.

"You have any kids, Tom. Me. I have a boy, good kid. I wish I could see him more often, but I travel a lot."

The dealer offered an inquisitive look. I started to think maybe my questions were getting too personal. Though he did answer me. "Yep. I've got a son, I get to see him every few days."

I smiled at him before busting out again. I played for another fifteen minutes, listening for clues, as the dealer chatted with the other players. When the dealer was moved from my table, I took my winnings and went back to the keno area. I watched him from a short distance, until he headed away from the tables. I moved a few feet behind the man known as Thomas, as he walked toward the back of the casino. I don't think he noticed me following him. He was about to exit behind a door when I called out. "Mr. Danker, may I have a moment of your time, please?"

The man stopped in his tracks, paused briefly, before turning around. I knew the instant he turned by the look on his face, he was Desmond Danker. "You have the wrong guy, pal. My name is Thomas Edwards. Sorry."

Before he could open the door, I called to him again. "Did you know two of Abe Lincoln's boys where named Thomas and Edward? And did you know that the man I'm looking for was writing a book about Lincoln when he was presumed murdered?"

The man who I was now confident was Danker moved a step towards me. "I don't care about any names of any dead Presidents or dead authors. I'm not the guy you're looking for, so stop following me."

"My friend George McAdams trusted you, Desmond. I don't know why you ran. But his life has been destroyed by I suspect, the same people, who have banished you to dealing black jack. Please help me."

Danker vanished behind the door. I started to walk away to figure out Plan B. Normally I would have pressed harder, but the guy had a clean soul and didn't need my harassment. There was always another way. Before I could exit back into the shadows, the door opened.

"Yo pal, come over here, hurry up. I only have a thirty minute break." Danker had reappeared.

I walked briskly back toward his direction.

"I don't like what happened to George," Danker said. "I followed his trial as much as I could. If they had convicted him, I woulda come forward. What they did to that poor guy was disgusting and I do feel a twinge of guilt. But I'm curious, why the hell did they stop the trial?"

"Not sure," I told him. "But his reputation has been ruined. Most still think he killed you and his political cronies cut some back room deal. He is having a hard time finding a job despite being innocent, besides being an honest guy. I am trying to help him out. What really happened from your perspective?"

Danker pulled me away from the door and toward the back exit of the casino. "I shouldn't be telling you any of this," he said. "But I'm afraid you're going to go tell someone I'm here. I can't leave this town, not right now. My son is in a nearby prison. Please, whatever you do, don't tell anyone you found me. I beg you."

"Ok, Desmond, I promise. But you have to give me something that can help out George."

A few patrons walked in and out of the casino. Danker gave each a long stare before continuing. "I didn't have any idea they were going to fake my murder and pin it on McAdams. You gotta believe me. The secret service moved me out here overnight. George and I discovered a line item in the federal budget that's been associated with the secret service since President Lincoln's last days. I ran across it while I was researching my book. I suspect it's now being used as a slush fund to keep politician's mistresses quiet. I was planning on exposing the fund in a new book. McAdams was asking too many questions in open hearings. Next thing I know, the secret service was telling me, that if I stay quiet, and stop writing my book, the President will pardon my son his last day in office. But I had to get out of Washington that night. They made it sound like bad shit was going to come down all over me if I didn't take the deal. They gave me my place rent free for six months, and paid for me to go to dealer school. That's all I really know. I swear it."

I became giddy inside. I had all the information I needed to get what I wanted from the President. Plus, I knew he was telling me the truth by reading his soul. My curiosity got the better of me. "What about your son, Desmond? Why does he need a pardon? Why not serve out his time?"

"Frankie always had a wild side. But I never suspected he would go off the rails the way he did. He moved out here with some college buddies saying they were going to make money in real estate. He was doing pretty good too, but try telling a young kid to save his money. Nah, he splashed it all around the night clubs and one night ran into the wrong woman. He was convicted of drugging and raping her. I refuse to think of my boy in those terms. My boy would never rape or drug anyone."

"That's rough, Desmond."

"Shhh, don't call me Desmond. My name is Thomas, and besides, what's your name?"

"Me? My name is Caeles Novo. I can tell if your son is innocent or not. If he is, we can try to get him a new trial. If not, you had better hope the President does what he promised."

Danker looked at more patrons walking in and out. "I never know who might be watching me now. It's a shitty feeling, always thinking big brother is watching you.

He looked around again. "Whaddya mean, you can tell if my boy is innocent or not? He told he is innocent and I believe him."

"I am really not here to judge him, Des.. err, Thomas. I am only letting you know that I have some special abilities that might allow you to have some piece of mind, that's all. I can look into his soul, like I have yours and know if he's telling the truth or not."

"You're joking, right? Who sent you? Look, pal, I don't know how you found me or who you really are, but I beg you, leave me and my boy alone."

I laughed at Danker. "It seems so few ever believe me. I am really not looking to hurt you or your son. I am only letting you know that I have connections more powerful than the President. I will be at the Bellagio for one more day if you are interested in knowing the truth."

19

$\mathcal{K}$alani called me as I was preparing to check out of the Bellagio. "Did you contact a real estate agent about land in Nevada?" She didn't sound happy.

"I was looking at some web sites and inquired about a property the other day, yes. Why do you ask?"

"Bill Goldstein called me last night. He sounded like the two of you have been friends for years. Bill claims that he has the perfect site for sale to fit your needs. The location isn't far from downtown Vegas. He wants to set up a time to show you the property. I'm not moving to the frigging desert, Cale. That's not happening."

"Will you chill out and give me Bill's number please. This has nothing to do with moving our home."

"Then what's going on? You've been keeping far too many secrets from me lately. It's starting to concern me."

"Baby, please relax. Once I get everything set, I will fill you in on what I've been doing. But for now, you're going to have to trust me. You do trust me don't you?"

There was far too much time before she replied for my liking. She rattled off Bill Goldstein's number. Then with a soft voice said, "I want so much to still trust you, but you've changed." She promptly hung up.

I couldn't blame Kalani for being upset, but after all the years we had been married and all we had gone through, she should have known she could trust me. My master plan was coming into view. Meeting with Goldstein would be the next step in destroying the people who tossed me from power and attempted to permanently remove my ability to steal souls. I thought I was protecting Kalani from the Council by not offering her too much information.

The phone in my room rang again. I picked it up hoping it was Kalani. Sadly, it was Danker. He sounded perplexed. "Tell me straight, Novo. Do you plan on shooting my son with drugs so that he will tell you the truth?"

"Mr. Danker, I realize it's not easy to believe me. I can assure you, I am not a spy. I do not work for any government. My methods are spiritual."

"I'm not looking to get my son hooked up with some cult behind prison walls." Danker stated with a twinge of anger in his voice. "I shoulda know better than to make this call."

"Slow down, Mr. Danker. I'm not the leader of any cult. Quite frankly, you have already given me all the information I need to help McAdams. I no longer need you, so if you don't want my help, so be it. But, let me ask you something. Do you believe in God?"

"I do. What does that have to do with anything?"

"How do you know that God exists, Mr. Danker?"

"I dunno, faith maybe?"

"I would never suggest to you that I am a God, Mr. Danker. By I am suggesting however, that you allow me to help you with the same faith that you have in believing that your God exists. After I do what I do, you will either become a believer or you won't."

"Mr. Novo, President Lincoln was quoted as saying, 'I do not think much of a man who is not wiser today than he was yesterday.' I'll be visiting with my son Frankie at the High Desert State Prison from noon till one this afternoon. You're invited to join me."

Prisons have always freaked me out. Being surrounded by so much darkness was never my idea of a good time. I would rather stand in line for an hour at Disney World and be inundated with, "It's a small world", than feel trapped inside prison walls. But I had made the offer. We all do things in our lives that we don't want to do.

I met Desmond Danker outside the prison area. We were led through an outside gate. When it locked behind us, I cringed. The feeling of no longer being in control of my circumstances made my heart race. My palms started to sweat. Breathing became more of a chore.

I did my best to not look at the prisoners playing basketball and standing in groups behind the high fences. But it was like slowing down to view a car wreck on the highway. You are driven to witness other's misery. Only the misery was my own. Surrounded by a sea of dark souls was my worst nightmare. This time the nightmare was very real.

Once inside the facility, we were taken to a small room with three chairs and a table. Danker and I each sat on one side of the table. A few minutes later, a tall, slender good looking man in his mid-twenties was led in by a prison guard. Danker's son sat on the other side of the table in his orange jumper with the number

NVP937845, printed in black, on a white rectangular patch sewn on his prison attire above his heart.

"How you holding up, Frankie?" The elder Danker asked.

Frankie rubbed his red puffy eyes as if he had woken up from a nap. "It sucks as much today as it did the last time you were here, Pops. I'm doing all I can ta keep my bones from getting broken in the yard. If I stay outta trouble a few more weeks, I'm hoping they'll let me work in the library. That's about all I know."

"I'm sorry you have to go through all this, son." The father paused. "I want to introduce you to my friend, Cale. He might be able to help you get outta this place. Please answer all his questions as best you can."

Frankie leaned back in his chair and rubbed his eyes again. He looked at me as I looked deep into his soul. I was looking at a man that even if he was innocent of his convicted crime, wasn't a good guy. Darkness filled his soul. It was getting harder by the minute for me to be in a place surrounded with so much evil. I wiped away beads of sweat from my upper lip, despite the room being quite cold.

"Who is this guy, Pops? He some kind of detective or fancy lawyer?"

Danker responded to his son, "Please, answer his questions."

"Frank, like your father said, my name is Cale Novo. Consider me a lie detector machine without being hooked up to any wires. I am not here to hurt you. Your father believes in you and loves you very much. He's looking for some piece of mind and the truth. If what you have told him and others is accurate, I have friends that might be able to obtain your release. But first, you have to prove to me you're innocent."

Frankie smirked at his father. "I'm not talking with this whackadoodle, Pops. If you don't believe me, then you can both leave."

Desmond raised his chin and with an irritated tone declared, "You will speak with this man or I will leave. But if I leave without answers, you can rot in here for all I care. Now talk with Mr. Novo."

Frankie crossed his arms and let out a deep sigh. "Whaddya wanna know, dude?"

I needed to leave as quickly as possible. I couldn't feel like a sardine sealed in a can made of sin much longer. There was no time to attempt to outsmart the creep. "I only have one question, Frank. How many women have you sexually assaulted in your life?"

Both Frank and his father sat up straight in their chairs. Each yelped out simultaneously, "What kind of question is that?"

"It's a very simple one, gentleman. I asked Frank how many women he has sexually assaulted in his life time."

Desmond looked at Frank. "Don't answer him, Frankie. Now I'm sorry I brought him here to see you."

I let his words clear the stale air. My stomach churned inside. My head pounded. But I did all I could to remain calm. I looked at the father. "Maybe you're not ready to want to know the truth, Mr. Desmond. I guess coming today was a mistake."

Desmond closed his eyes. He lowered his head to his chest. It was barely audible but he did say, "Answer the man, Frankie, for me."

Frankie cried out in a strained voice, "Pop's look at me. You know I didn't hurt anyone. Yes. We had sex. I admitted that long ago. But she wanted it, Pops. She couldn't wait to get to my apartment. That woman wanted me."

He was lying. My head pounded even more. My patience had run out. I yelled at Frank. "How many, Frank? How many women have you abused?"

Frankie cried out again, "Pops, look at me. Look at me."

Desmond couldn't. A tear fell from his eye. "Please, Frankie. Answer the man's question.

"I'm not answering shit to either of you. I can't believe you, Pops. You bring this guy in here telling me he wants to help and he's got the balls to ask me how many women I've assaulted. That's plain bullshit."

The father lifted his head. He examined Frankie's welled up eyes. "Fine, Frankie. You don't have to answer Mr. Novo. But answer me. How many, Frankie?"

Frankie waved to the guard standing at the door. As the guard walked in I couldn't take the pressure any longer. I reached out and grabbed Frankie by the arm. One more black soul was on its way to the Surrounding of Souls.

Frank Danker was led out of the room by the guard. His father was left sobbing next to me at the table. Frank left too quickly for me to gauge if he understood the magnitude of him losing his most prized possession. However, that was the least of my concerns. I did have empathy for the elder Danker, but I also needed to get out from behind the prison walls and fast. The moment another guard appeared to lead us out, I jumped from my seat imploring Desmond to quickly follow.

Power was surging throughout my body from removing Frank's soul. The guard escorted us back past the outside recreational area for the detainees. I wanted nothing more than to be a greyhound sprinting to the outside walls. Desmond was scuffing his feet with every stride. Sadness was etched across his face. None of that mattered to me. Between the energy of removing a soul and the heaviness of the surrounding evil, I was going to explode.

"You ok? You don't look so good." The prison guard asked as we inched closer to the final exit.

"Must be the dry heat." I responded. "I'll be fine once I'm outside these walls."

"We get that a lot around here," the guard answered back. "Most people do feel better once outside. Usually the ones with something to hide though. You have something to hide?"

Fantastic I thought. After spending my life trying to eliminate evil from society, I had a correctional officer playing Dr. Phil assuming I was the one with a guilty conscience. He needed to stick with herding bad souls back and forth from their cells. Desmond Danker was five feet behind me, apparently not sharing my same sense of urgency to depart.

Once outside with the prison door closed behind us, I filled my lungs with fresh air. Despite being energized from stealing a soul, my heartbeat slowed. I had been inside prisons before, but this time, was especially unnerving. I didn't know why, but it was.

Desmond's shoulders were slumped, his eyes filled with tears. He leaned with his back against his car, staring at the hard gravel beneath his feet. He remained motionless for several minutes before he began to speak.

"You don't need to tell me, Cale. I could see it for myself. Maybe you were right. I didn't want to know. But for the first time, when I looked into my son's eyes, I saw the pain he inflicted on others. I'll never forget those eyes. They'll haunt me forever."

"Some say the eyes are the window to the soul. I'm sorry, but you did get your answer. "

Consoling people was not my forte. I could listen, but words never came quickly in disheartening situations. Standing next to Danker, knowing it was impossible to fully understand what must have been going through his mind, all I could do was put my arm on his shoulder and wait.

"I'll never understand it," the grieving father said. "His mother and I gave that kid everything. He was raised in a loving home. He graduated with honors from every school he attended. Frankie could have done anything he wanted. But not this, not this."

Danker looked up into the blue sky and blazing early afternoon sun. I removed my arm and stood next to him. A coyote was chasing a rodent in the nearby desert as a bird screeched. Danker began to sob. The coyote won the race. I was again reminded how everything and everyone in nature has a purpose. Without evil, goodness doesn't exist. Without sadness, you can't comprehend happiness. Without the weak, there is no strong.

"I'm not sure what I can offer to make you feel better right now. But I do know one thing. If Frank ever does decide to repent, and can come to grips with what he has done, he will be forgiven. His soul will be cleansed."

"I wish I could believe you, Cale. But right now, I need to go home and figure out where I went wrong with my son."

"Your son chose his own destiny. This isn't on you. Granted he's going to have to pay for his sins behind those walls. But he's still a young man. He has time. You're going to have to have faith that he can turn his life around. But that will be on him to do so."

"There you go again, you're talking all spiritual on me. Who are you? No one goes around confirming lies by peeking into souls."

"Go home, Desmond. Take solace in knowing you're one of the good guys. Even if you and Frank are connected by blood, he is still his own man. Realize that and I'll return to tell you my story. But today isn't the day. Go be the person I know you are."

Danker looked at me as if he were still a non-believer. We walked around to the other side of his car. He got in and rolled down his window. "I guess I should be thanking you, but it's still too painful."

I tapped him on the shoulder. "You and I are like so many here on earth. We're only trying to make sense of it all. Good luck, my friend. You are free to be Desmond Danker again."

He drove into the horizon. As I turned and walked back to my car, I watched the coyote munch on his prize. I hoped Desmond realized he was still one of the strong and that nature always has a plan.

Glancing at my watch, I realized I was running late to meet Bill Goldstein. I drove toward Boulder Highway to the site where approximately twenty five acres were being offered for sale. When I arrived, I could see a car parked off the side of the road. I pulled behind it. Bill was pacing in the sand and rocks. He was wearing a blue blazer, white shirt and tie pulled up so tight, I thought he might choke.

"You're lucky, Mr. Novo. I was going to give you two more minutes and I was outta here. I git tired of people dragging me out here and then not showing up. I've ruined too many dress shirts in this heat."

"I guess it is not my place, but why not sit in the car with the air conditioner running?"

Bill Goldstein, was larger than the average man in height. He walked towards me. "Maybe you haven't noticed the price of gas these days, sir."

We weren't off to the best of starts. I introduced myself and we shook hands. Bill opened his trunk and took out an aerial map of the site. He closed the trunk and placed the map across top of it. He pointed out all the setbacks as to where building would be permitted on the dusty land. After his initial disappointment with my tardiness, he converted into full on professional sales mode. A few times I thought he would unbutton that top button and loosen his tie, but he never did.

"What can you tell me specifically about the zoning, Bill? I know on your website you had it listed as residential, but how dense can we build? What about utilities and water? Also, can we construct one building that is similar to a golf clubhouse?"

"No, no, no. We already have enough water issues around here. They would never allow you to build a golf course out here."

"Bill, I don't want to build a golf course. It will be a training center, where between fifteen and twenty people live and we have one building with classrooms and a large conference room. Can we do it?"

Goldstein looked out across the expanse of dirt and sand. He then folded up his map and dug back into the trunk of his car. He took out the zoning code for the property. I already knew the answer but I wanted him to earn his commission.

"I hope you guys aren't some kind of cult group. Who builds a training center in the desert?"

"They said the same thing about casinos, didn't they, Bill? How did that work out? And no, I don't consider us a cult. We are a small group of people who like our privacy, that's all. Now what about the zoning?"

Goldstein looked at me, then the paper. "Well, I can't guarantee anything, but I think you can do what you are talking about here. I would suggest you make an offer and put down a deposit."

I instructed Bill to write up an offer for five million dollars. He balked since that was close to seven hundred and fifty thousand less than the asking price. I previously had Iza do some homework. I knew the owner was cash poor. The land was his only asset of real value. His home was about to go into foreclosure and his business needed an infusion of cash.

The land had been on the market for over a year. I presumed the owner might accept even less, but I was anxious to strike a deal. I knew from the few land sales there had been in the past year, my offer was fair. We had an agreement with a letter of intent before dinner. After haggling with the agreement and the discussion on zoning, Bill asked me how I knew so much about putting the deal together. I told him, "In a past life, I was a commercial real estate agent." He nodded.

The next task was to call Dylan James. After spending ten minutes apologizing to Lorenza, his wife, for not calling more often, she put Dylan on the phone. He was excited to tell me that he was working on secret recordings with his daughter. It was his first time in the recording studio using the same Martin D-45 that hung in Gordy's Guitars store front when he was a kid. The original owner sold it back to Gordy and Dylan immediately scooped it up. After all, it was Dylan's Holy Grail while growing up.

"Yeah, that's great, Dylan. But enough music talk. I need an attorney to set up a corporation for me and review a sales contract on some land I plan on buying in Nevada. Can you call your law firm and grease the skids for me please?"

"Yet another favor? Did you take care of clearing George's name yet? What's the use of having super powers if you can't fix one little problem for me, huh?"

I knew Dylan was partially teasing, but after the day I had, it didn't need to end with more grief. "I'm in Vegas right now handling George's problem. I suspect in a week or so, things will be cleared up. Now can you please give me your attorney's number and let him know that I plan on calling him? Please,

Dylan?"

"Who peed in your corn flakes today? I'll call Carl in the morning and have him call you. But whatever you do, be nice."

True to his word, Carl Peterson, Dylan's agent and attorney, called me the next day. Carl was also partners with Dylan in several real estate holdings. Along with a group of investors, they owned several shopping centers, mostly in the northeast section of the United States. We scheduled a face to face meeting in his New York office for two days later.

Carl was in law school when he met Dylan, who at the time was singing in local New York bars. Dylan was Carl's first client. Carl's father, a record executive, suggested Stu Edrich change his name to Dylan James. The idea was that Stu would have the "Words of Bob Dylan and the soul of James Brown."

Dylan had explained his relationship with Carl to me several times about how they had become great friends and business partners. Before I ever walked into Carl's swanky office, I recognized this was more than your average agent and artist relationship. Carl welcomed me inside his office with a friendly handshake.

"Please have a seat, Caeles. May I call you Caeles?" Carl Peterson inquired.

"I've been called worse." I said before smiling at Carl.

The first thing that caught my eye were all the photos of Carl Peterson yucking it up with famous athletes and recording artists lining one wall. Carl's law firm offered many services. His main function in the firm was to recruit clients so the firm could act as their agent. The next thing I realized was that Carl spared no expense on his large cherry desk and more than suitable black leather chairs. His office also had the smell of jasmine, rare for an attorney's office.

He smiled and sat behind his desk that had nothing more on it than a phone, a computer monitor, one red legal size folder and a Mont Blanc pen. His hair was outlined with grey around his temples, but Carl appeared fit for a man thirty five years removed from law school.

"So I understand you're looking for some help with a land contract in Nevada? Why not use an attorney out there?"

"Privacy is important to me, Carl. For this contract, using my usual attorney would not be prudent. When speaking with Dylan he has always said nothing but glowing things about you and your firm. I also know that George McAdams used one of your defense attorney's in his criminal case. You all come highly recommended. Besides," I said after smirking, "if I only wanted a simple contract, you are correct, I would have used a real estate attorney in Nevada."

Carl looked at the clock on the side wall. "I'm a very busy man, as I'm sure you are as well. My time is valuable and your clock is running. So let me be very clear with you. I have no intention of representing you until you tell me how you managed to get Dylan on that jet from England all those years ago. How did you convince him to enter rehab? And don't you dare lie to me."

"What did he tell you?"

"He's stuck with the same story for close to twenty years now, that you returned his soul and made him feel whole. That you made him see the beauty in his life again."

"Why not believe him?"

Carl squirmed in his seat and rubbed his face. "I'm paid to be skeptical and find the truth. I'm also paid handsomely to protect my clients from con artists looking to separate them from their assets."

I moved forward and folded my arms across the edge of Carl's desk. "So tell me Carl, how much money have I ever extracted from your precious client, Dylan James? Better yet, how much have I ever asked him for, ever?"

"My records show not a dime."

"Exactly, not a damn dime. Now you can either take me at face value that I'm looking for assistance from your group in putting together a substantial real estate deal, more than some two bit contract that could have been handled in Nevada, or ask me to leave. Because, you're right about one thing. I'm a busy man. But more than anything else, I especially don't like to be called a con artist."

Carl never apologized. He sat in his chair eyeballing me long enough to make me feel uncomfortable. Good vibes were not filling the room. As I placed my hands on the edges of my seat to get up, he barked at me.

"Sit down, Novo. What do you want from me?"

Leaning back in my chair, I served up the pitch. "You are to set up two corporations. One will go by the name of Fortunate Souls, which will be a minority shareholder in the second one. The investment group can name the other company. The initial investment from me on behalf of Fortunate Souls will be five million dollars plus your fees. That should be sufficient to cover the land acquisition costs.

"Why the second corporation?"

"The parent corporation will be responsible to build a development to my specifications on the land Fortunate Souls will purchase. Once built, the parent company, comprised of your investors, will rent the development to Fortunate Souls at rates that would allow the investment group to make twenty percent on their investment."

"Come on, Novo. No one is going to pay a twenty percent return with times being as tough as they are right now."

"Pay attention! I am a man of special needs, so right now I'm willing to over pay to have my demands met. Now, shall I continue or not?"

"Go ahead," Carl said with an exasperated tone.

"The lease will be for twenty years, but Fortunate Souls would be permitted to buy out the parent company any time after five years for all the costs to build, plus a twenty five percent return on the investment, not counting any collected rents."

Carl was skeptical. "Why not build it yourself? This deal seems too good to be true."

"Again, I don't want to draw attention to who owns the property. Are you in or out?"

We went back and forth for another few minutes until he agreed to speak with his group of investors to see who might be interested. I was pleased and started to stand when he spoke again.

"Tell the truth. How did you get Dylan to clean up his act? Anyone who cared about him talked to him till we were blue in the face. Hell. I even cut off his money supply. Then he comes up with some bullshit story about some guy sitting next to him on the steps of The Royal Albert Hall and whallla, he's on the next flight back to the States. He immediately enters rehab without even one grumble. What really happened?"

"I take it you're a non-believer, Carl?"

"You might be able to bullshit Dylan, but you can't me. I only took this meeting because he asked me to hear you out. I don't think you have the resources to come up with five million dollars. And I especially don't buy his story that you returned his soul."

"Tsk, tsk, Carl." I looked into his soul. "I've seen worse, so your soul shouldn't be taken but if you stick your arm out, I'll be more than happy to prove to you that I'm for real. Come on, test me. Let's see how much you don't believe in me."

He frowned and scooted his chair further away.

"Yeah, I didn't think so, Carl. You'll have your money before the end of business tomorrow, including your fee. I suggest you start believing our mutual friend, Dylan, and write up my contract. I would hate to offer total strangers a sweetheart deal like this."

I was escorted out of the office by Carl's buxom secretary and back into the shadows.

20

*E*ach year, when the school year has ended, Washington D.C. becomes saturated with families on vacation. That time of year was my preference to visit, since my presence in town was less conspicuous. Meeting Agent Nesstor near the steps of the Lincoln Memorial allowed us to blend in with the crowds. I requested to meet with Nesstor after meeting with Carl Peterson in New York. Elliot needed to be updated on the entire Danker saga.

"Here is your opportunity to retire breaking open a high profile case. I found Danker. Remember, he's the guy I told you about the last time we met? He's the guy who Congressman McAdams was supposed to have murdered. Do you remember me telling you about him?"

"How many times do I have to tell you, Cale? It's over for me. I'm going to retire to Florida and find a quiet fishing pond. I wouldn't care if even Jimmy Hoffa himself was found working the hot dog stand outside of Yankees Stadium."

"Ok, I get it. I will tip off Groden that Danker is going to come forward and tell the world that he was never murdered while you get in line for the early bird special with the blue hairs in Boca. I suspect Danker is going to say that President Morrison not only knew about the fake murder, but ordered it. But you enjoy your fish sandwich at the Grumpy Grouper."

Elliot yawned. He did appear as a man ready to retire. I was handing him a case potentially larger than the Watergate scandal, but my old friend was uninspired and worn out. While we sat on the steps overlooking the bustling crowds, remorse was the only emotion remaining for my friend.

As Nesstor stood to leave, I could hear his knees crackle and see him wince. "Do yourself a favor and don't make a fool of yourself in front of the President of the United States," he said. "I know you've tracked bad guys all over the world. But if there is one thing I've learned about this town, our bad guys aren't always who you think they are."

Nesstor smiled. He carefully walked two steps toward the main walkway before turning back around at me. "Jim Groden has been working with the information you gave us about that hockey player. You might be right about him." He didn't have to say another word. I knew that was his way of saying he was sorry for ridiculing me the last time we met.

The main reason I went to Washington was because Speaker Corbin arranged for me to meet with President Morrison. We were scheduled to meet on the terrace roof of the Kennedy Center on the President's wedding anniversary. He was treating his wife to a performance of "Cats", but scheduled fifteen minutes to meet with three large donors before the show began. Corbin informed me that he had sold the President on the idea that I was a large donor. I would be allotted five minutes of private time with the President.

I was the last of the three scheduled to meet with Morrison. I had been waiting on the other side of the building with a secret service agent until it was my turn. A secret service agent was assigned to lead me around the terrace where the President and two others were waiting.

The sky grew darker as evening was turning to night. The moon was beginning to leave a shine on the Potomac River which was in perfect view from the Presidents vantage point on the terrace. I had dealt with many world leaders in the past, but this was the first time I was meeting face to face with a sitting President of the United States. The agent who escorted me was much taller and by my estimation more than thirty pounds heavier than me. The men surrounding the President were also taller than me, and the President. I started to question my motives. Sure I wanted my friend George to be cleared, but the actions of accusing the sitting President of a crime was at that moment very real. But it was too late for second guessing. I was standing so close to the President, I could gather a whiff of his Canoe aftershave.

"Thank you for meeting with me, Mr. President and happy anniversary. I know my time is short, so I will get right to my reason for being here. I know Desmond Danker is alive."

President Morrison looked at the agent to his right then looked at me. "Who the hell is Desmond Danker and why should I care if he's alive?"

The agent assigned to escort me moved into my private space. The two other agents who were standing on each side of the President each gave me a wicked stare. For one of the few times in my life, I was scared.

"Let's be clear about something, Novo. Yes. I know who you

are." The President stated. "I assumed you were showing up to apologize to me for getting in that young reporters head with your whacky tale about removing his soul. My chief of staff told me that we had a good thing going with that kid, till you screwed it all up. So unless you're going to apologize for all the harm you did to my reelection bid, this meeting is over."

Hearing his condescending tone strengthened my resolve. I had lost all worries about who he was and only cared about getting my point across. No man was going to bully me. Not even the President of the United States.

"Pretend all you like, Mr. President." Then I decided to take it one step further and lie. My hands were trembling. "The FBI will soon have Danker in custody and you will be exposed for ruining Congressman McAdams career. Plus, everyone will know you are the father of that youngster in Florida."

"What the hell are you talking about? Child? Danker? If you think I had anything to do with McAdams, you're crazier than what's listed in our reports about you. My children are all accounted for and belong to my wife and me. Never once in all my years of marriage have I ever stepped out on her. How dare you accuse me on my wedding anniversary!"

"I apologize, Mr. President. But George McAdams is a close friend of mine and someone ruined the man. I have it on good authority that the secret service has money set aside to buy off women who had affairs with top politicians. McAdams and Danker were both going to expose that fund. When they were about to expose your love child, Danker was presumed murdered by McAdams. Now you tell me who has the muscle to pull off something like that in this town using the secret service? Danker also told me that you were going to pardon his son on your last day in office."

Morrison shook his head and let out a scary laugh. "I only met you because I had heard what a strange little man you were from Corbin. I had to meet you for myself. But not only are you a sad excuse for a human being, you're delusional with your accusations. Let this Danker guy say anything he wants. As far as McAdams, I've never even met the guy. I had jack shit to do with the charges brought against him. And a child I don't know about, that's hilarious. Like I said, I've never once cheated on my wife. And not that it's any of you frigging business, but after our last son was born seventeen years ago, I had a vasectomy. So let me warn you one time. If you ever utter those accusations against me again, they will be your last. Now excuse me, but my wife has been more than patient waiting for me."

A secret service agent bumped me as he passed. The President was led indoors as I was led back around the other side of the building and out a back exit. My head was swimming with thoughts of what had happened. The agent who escorted me downstairs told me, "If you are smart, you'll never show your face around here again. That took balls, but it was so stupid." He laughed at me, before shoving me out the door.

Maybe I should have listened to Nesstor. I was always accusing him of not trusting me, yet I never listened to him. A break from all the scheming was in order. I caught the first flight in the morning down to my parent's house in Florida. Mom's home cooking was what I needed to recharge my batteries.

My mom and dad put up with me hanging around their house for a few days, until my dad talked me into heading to Miami with him for a baseball game. The Marlins were playing the New York Mets. By the fifth inning the Marlins were already trailing by seven runs. The team had once again been decimated with trades and allowing veteran players to leave when their contracts expired. The team was comprised of players with little major league experience.

After watching another young player strike out, my dad turned to me and said, "If I ever do take another soul, the owner of this team will be at the top of my list." I agreed. I was introduced to baseball several decades before while taking a soul in Chicago. However, I rooted for the Marlins since it was my dad's favorite team.

Carl Peterson called me the morning after the ballgame. "Much to my surprise, your cash arrived yesterday. My investors still want more proof you'll be able to pay the rents if we build your project. Any suggestions on how to appease their concerns?"

Carl irritated me because he couldn't close the deal. "Carl, you have to do a better job of selling these folks. Now, if you want more collateral, then fine. But your return on investment goes down with every extra dollar I have to come up with. If I'm taking all the risk, why on earth should your group make the over the top profits I suggested earlier?"

"Don't tell me how to do my job." Carl screamed in my ear. "I've been putting together deals before you were born. But yes, since you don't have any credit to speak of, come up with another ten million and we will build the project."

"I'll get you the damn money. But the terms are now more in my favor. Do your job and close the deal."

Carl and I debated back and forth over the new terms until everything was settled. My only issue was coming up with another ten million dollars and not drawing attention to what was taking place right under the Council's nose.

It didn't take long before Dylan James dialed me. "What did you say to Carl? He yelled in my ear this morning about what a pain in the ass you are."

"Can I help it if your hot shot attorney can't convince people of a good deal when they see it? I sweetened the pot this morning by putting up almost half the money. If he can't sell this project now, I'm moving on. I have a real estate agent asking for the deposit and an executed contract for the land sale every day. I need this done, Dylan."

"Ok, ok. You won't lose the land contract. And I'll call whatever investor is holding up the deal and assure it gets done. But that's not why I was calling you. One was to thank you for fixing the issue with George and the other was to invite you and Kalani on a cruise."

Now I was confused. I hadn't told him anything about Danker or George McAdams. "Don't thank me yet. I made a total fool of myself in front of President Morrison. Danker is alive, but the President looked me straight in the eye and told me he had nothing to do with harming George or a fake death. He also convinced me he has never once cheated on his wife. So. I am afraid so far I have failed George other than proving the trial was a farce."

The other end was silent until Dylan chucked. "Whatever, dude. All I know is all day on the cable station, NUTS, Carlin Masterson has been promoting tonight's show 'Talking Crazy' and

Danker is his guest. So obviously once it airs, everyone will know the trial was a set up. Are you telling me you had nothing to do with this?"

"I did speak with Danker. I suggested he look into his soul and make things right with his conscience. But I don't know anything about Masterson having a live chat with him. A few months back I robbed Masterson of his soul and he belched in my ear. We are hardly on good speaking terms."

"Well, whatever you said to Danker musta worked. Now my big news. I'm putting the band back together and next spring we're performing on a cruise ship. We're jamming out a few sets between while floating around in the Caribbean. The Dan Lampman band is joining us along with an Eagles tribute band. You wanna join us? Bring the wife along."

"I don't know, Dylan. I'm busy reclaiming leadership of our disciples and saving the world right now. Besides, I thought you were sick? Didn't you tell me you had the onset of Alzheimer's and the doctors advised you not to stress yourself out?"

Dylan laughed. "Dude, get this. Some hot shot kid doctor my daughter hired over at the rehab center; ran a ton of tests on my brain. Turns out I have some brain damage from all the pain killers and other drugs I took after my surgeries. Well, plus my crazy times."

"I guess that's a good thing," I replied.

"Yeah, so now they're giving me drugs cause I took too many drugs." Dylan laughed. "Is that wild or what? So I decided to put the band back together. The cruise was Carl's idea, this way no long bus trips. The best part is when I screw up, I can blame it all on the drugs again. My buddy Keith might be a surprise guest joining us on a few songs. I called him to ask how he can still be performing after all the crap he put in his body. Come on, man, it's gonna be a blast."

I remembered thinking that Dylan usually didn't sound so rushed and scattered in his thoughts. Was it the medication the doctors had him on or the brain damage? But heading off on a cruise did sound like a good respite. It would depend on the timing. "What about Linda? I thought she had Parkinson's?"

Dylan's voice changed instantly to a low murmur. "I've known about her condition for a while. Lorenza and I go out to California every year to visit with her. When bad shit happens to good people, it shakes my faith. But don't worry, I refuse to fall again. No more losing my soul. Please come, it's gonna be a blast. Oh crap, I gotta run. My daughter has me doing a public service announcement for her friend Kristen Perry for some group called NOPE. You know, to warn people about mixing drugs and alcohol."

"Ok, I'll let you go. Get me the exact dates. I will do my best to make it. What better way than to sail off into the sunset watching you do what you enjoy best, playing your music with a live audience. Good bye, Dylan. I wish you all the best."

After getting off the phone, my mom flipped on the news. Dylan was correct. It was being reported that Desmond Danker was in the custody of the FBI. The talking heads on the television were all questioning where Danker had been and why the set up in the first place. Since I knew much of the backstory, I could only snicker at how off base many were in their conjectures being reported as facts.

The White House spokesman was fending off reports the

President had a child out of wedlock. Reporters were stationed outside the homes of George McAdams and Nicole Hunter. Hunter was the mother of the child now being speculated about on national television. The media was now latched onto the latest "Story of the Century."

A text arrived from Nesstor. "You had to stir this all up, didn't you? Danker's not credible. He only knows the information fed to him from the secret service."

Doing the right thing was not always popular or easy. But assisting in clearing George's good name was a promise I had made to Dylan. He had helped me several times, including admitting the doorman's son into his daughter's rehab center at a reduced fee. My debts were paid.

While enjoying a tuna sandwich carefully prepared by my mother, my phone buzzed again. This time it was George. "Dylan called me to say that you found Danker out in Vegas. Is that true? Josh Simpson woke me up last night claiming that Danker had turned himself in to the FBI. Simpson sounded like he knew the entire story and now some staffer from Masterson's show is calling me every five minutes trying to get me on camera tonight. What's going on, Cale?"

"Yes, it is true I found Danker. But I didn't coerce him into anything. Whatever he is doing, it is all on his own. But I will tell you this, George. President Morrison is not the father of Nicole's child. I spoke to the President in person. He is not the father."

"I'll call you back," George replied. The phone clicked. I finished my sandwich.

All afternoon the news channels had little on but speculation surrounding Desmond Danker and possible connections with McAdams and how the President fit into the equation. Politicians were lining up to get themselves in front of a camera. Some were calling for the President to resign with little to no facts. One report even had speculated that Morrison would be resigning in the morning. I wanted to call the media and set the record straight about the President. But I realized no one would believe me, so why draw that much attention to myself for nothing?

Masterson's show started at 7pm. He immediately started into a dialogue with, "What did the President know and when did he know it?" He continued with, "I never voted for the man nor do I support his grand party, but he will get a fair reporting on my show. I don't think he's evil like his associates, merely misguided by the whackos in his party."

Masterson's words dripped with insincerity to me. But I had to admit, I didn't have much time for television except for Miami Dolphin football games. Was it possible the media had lost any desire to be objective and I missed it? After more of his ranting, the show went to a commercial break.

As the show returned, Danker's face was front and center. He was not in studio but on video. Masterson introduced Danker and allowed him to tell his story of being whisked away in the middle of the night with the promise that the President would pardon his son. He claimed he knew nothing about his death being faked until days later.

Masterson interrupted. "Did you speak directly with the President about your son receiving a pardon before starting a new life?"

"No, Carlin. There was little ....."

Masterson cut in again. "Despite not speaking with the President directly, how guilty is the man and are you in favor of him resigning?"

Before Danker could speak, Masterson turned his attention away from the video screen and to his left. "Let me introduce a contributor to NUTS, Devin Melvin from Mamma Smith's Tribune. Tell me, Devin, after hearing what Mr. Danker had to say, can the President survive?"

"Carlin, it's obvious the President is a racist homophobe who likely drinks tea before he goes to bed. He needs to go and go now."

Masterson turned back to the video screen. "Have you seen the President drink tea, Mr. Danker?"

Danker stared back. He didn't say a word. Masterson again turned to his in-studio guest. "Talk with me, Devin. Is it possible the American public reelected a man who drinks tea?"

Devin Melvin answered. "As distasteful as that sounds, Carlin, I suggest the man was born in Canada. What has our country come to that we elected a tea drinker who was born in Canada? That alone proves he's guilty of something. I say, if he doesn't resign, we petition our politicians to have him impeached."

The camera panned in for a close up of Masterson's face. He frowned. "Hmmm, you make some good points, Devin. That's why we always love having you on Talking Crazy. You're objectivity astounds me.

I could hear Danker's voice in the background. "Carlin, may I say something, please? I've not accused the President of any crime. I was asked to come and tell my story. I feel like you're putting words in my mouth."

"No, no," Masterson replied. "We heard you loud and clear. The President is a tea drinking racist homophobic criminal, who ripped you from your home and fell short on his promise to pardon your son. Thank you for joining us. Next up on Talking Crazy; how trillion dollar deficits are good for the economy."

My dad grabbed the tv remote. "I love that Carlin Masterson. He has such a way of getting to the heart of a story. But it's time for the Marlins game." I looked at my mother. She was rocking in her chair, doing her needle point work. I looked back at my dad. It was time to go home before my head exploded.

21

*H*igh humidity across the land had given way to sweater weather in Northern California. Sundays were spent watching football, while the remainder of the week was used doing chores around the house. Kalani came and went on assignments. Nic was in school.

Josh Simpson was making a name with his reporting surrounding the quick reappearance and disappearance of Desmond Danker. Danker had not been seen in public since the Masterson show. Simpson was one of the few reporters who didn't write stories condemning the President. His stories were investigations as to why Danker had to go into hiding not once but twice, and a small town congressman was charged with murder that ruined his career.

Pressure mounted for President Morrison to resign. The President was steadfast in his assurances he was not an adulterer, nor knew anything about Danker or McAdams. The media combed the guest list at the White House speculating about each female visitor.

After several months, George McAdams contacted me. "Nicole fessed up. She was ticked off at me for not paying her more attention after I started my new job. She made up the whole story about sleeping with Morrison when he was running for President to make me jealous. Once her lie was told in public and she turned up pregnant, money started rolling her way. She didn't know what to do. Lentz advised her that if she didn't tell anyone about her tryst with Morrison, the money would keep coming."

"Holy crap, George. What are you going to do now?"

"What am I supposed to do? How can I trust her? I couldn't take her word that I was the only person she was with after her divorce. So I took a blood test. It's a match. I'm Michael's father."

"Does anyone else know?"

"Are you nuts, Cale? How's it all gonna look? People are gonna think I was blackmailing the President for any number of reasons, including helping me get reelected to congress. I can't come forward and tell everyone I'm the father. Simpson is calling me every day trying to sniff out a story. I'd like to clear the President's name, but the media would crucify me. I don't want to get back into politics, but this would seal my fate forever."

"I don't know. You didn't do anything wrong. Nicole knows you had nothing to do with her getting payments from the slush fund you were investigating. Let me make some calls and see what I can find out for you."

I called Nesstor for advice. He didn't answer. I sent a text, but received no response. Even when he was upset with me, Nesstor would respond. I then called John Corbin. It took three calls and two days, but eventually I reached him.

"Mr. Speaker, what's the inside story surrounding the President? And thanks for selling me out to him by the way."

"Get over yourself, Novo. Do you honestly think the US Government doesn't have a record of your existence? You've been giving tips to the FBI for years. Of course they have a record of you. As far as the President, I'm staying far away from that one."

"It's not the President's child, John. I knew it the moment I looked into the President's soul."

Corbin laughed. "Please, everyone inside the beltway has always known the guy's squeaky clean. I would be shocked if the President was involved with any of this mess. My guess is that someone has an axe to grind and is trying to make political hay over this story. There's not a politician in Washington that wants the press to know we have a slush fund to keep affairs quiet. The President's taking one for the team until the FBI can figure out how things got so out of hand with Danker and McAdams."

"But who else has the political muscle to get the secret service to have done all they did in hiding Danker and incriminating McAdams? Is there anything I can do to help find out?"

"There's not many who coulda pulled this off. And if you really want ta help, stay outta town, Novo."

Sitting around the house doing nothing but handyman work was not a pleasant experience. Especially since I was a horrible handyman. The only thing keeping my mind busy was overseeing the project in the desert. The land deal had closed and a site plan was approved. A construction company had been hired and groundbreaking was weeks away. If the next step in my master plan didn't work, everything I had been working for would end in the barren land a few short miles from downtown Las Vegas.

Several messages were left on Nesstor's phone until his partner Jim Groden reached out.

"Sorry I couldn't get to ya sooner. Elliot's been shot. It's not looking good."

"What the hell are you talking about, Jim. I've not seen anything on the news about any FBI agents getting shot."

Jim spoke in a soft tone. "The brass is keeping this hush hush. It's all my fault. Elliot and I were up in Boston investigating a gambling syndicate with ties to the DC area. Before heading back, I talked Elliot inta heading over and speaking with that hockey player, Larsson. We didn't follow protocol. Damn, it's all my fault."

The phone went silent. I was waiting for him to continue but I could hear him sobbing. "What happened when you found Larsson," I asked.

"I only wanted to ask the guy a few questions. You know, see the expression on his face. We were invited in and the three of us were sitting in the living room. Then all hell broke loose outta nowhere. Someone came in from a backroom and started blasting away. We was ambushed big time. Elliot took two in the gut and one in the shoulder. I took one in the leg before I could react. I think I hit the guy who fired at us, but I never did get a good look. I was more concerned about protecting Elliot. The two of em got away."

"When did all this happen?"

"Awe, man, three days ago, I guess. After the hospital released me, since then, I ain't left Elliot's side. His wife's here now. He lost a lot of blood before they could get to him, Cale. He's been in intensive care since they rushed him here. Anyway, I noticed you've been sending him messages, so I thought you would wanna know what happened."

"Give me the name of the hospital. I'll be there as quickly as possible."

"There's nothing you can do, man. The doctors are doing all they can."

"What about Larsson? Where is he?"

"Who knows. Every cop in the land's looking for em. We're hoping he didn't get across the Canadian border before we could get the notices out."

I took the red eye across the country and landed at Logan Airport in Boston the next morning. The entire flight I was beating myself up for giving them information about Larsson. Elliot told me over and over he wanted to close out a few more cases on his desk and retire in one piece. I should have handled Larsson in my own way.

When I arrived at Massachusetts General Hospital, Nesstor remained in intensive care. His wife approved of me seeing Elliot for a few moments. "If you have and other magic tricks," she said, "Do what you can for Elliot."

Guilt overwhelmed me. The noises from all the machines Elliot was attached to, pounded my senses. He laid under the sheets, eyes closed, motionless. Tears rolled down my cheeks. His hand was limp as I held it. His wife entered the room and sat next to me. We sat for an hour without a word between us. Only the sounds of the machines beeping over and over could be heard.

Groden darted into the room and hovered at the foot of Elliot's bed. "They picked up Larsson and his accomplice in Maine. The Marshalls will be delivering them both back to Boston day after tomorrow." He was beaming from ear to ear. As I felt the coldness in Elliot's fingers, I realized Groden's idea of justice couldn't match mine. The government would fight to incarcerate the two of them for life on earth. My form of justice would be to send their souls into oblivion for all of eternity.

Special permission was given for me to sleep in Elliot's room. Groden and Elliot's wife went to the hotel for a few hours rest. I assured them if anything changed, I would call immediately. Neither had slept in a bed for three nights.

Most of the night, I held my old friend's hand and prayed for his wellbeing. Kalani called to check on me a few times during the early morning hours. None of my training or abilities were any use to Elliot. It was a long night and an even longer following day.

Doctors and nurses would wander in and out of the room with little to say. The best one could offer was, "He's stable, for now. That's a good thing. He's been through two long surgeries and needs to heal." His wife, Groden and myself took turns holding his hand waiting for the occasional moments Elliot would open his eyes.

As darkness set in, Groden pulled me outside of Elliot's room. "Caeles Novo, I would like to introduce you to our regional director, Anthony Moore. He asked to meet with you."

Moore looked to the floor before offering a weak, clammy handshake. He was shorter than me, with pale skin and rail thin. Not what I would have expected for a man in his leadership position. I sensed a nervousness in his initial words. "I've heard much about you, Mr. Novo. I understand your work is of a spiritual nature. Am I correct?"

I peeked at Groden. He looked away. My thoughts were filled with suspicions. I looked back at Moore. "Why do you ask, sir?"

"The Bureau has a special request. We appreciate all you have done for us over the years and recognize your special relationship with Agent Nesstor."

Moore finally looked me in the eye. With a nervous tone stated, "We'd like to guarantee that Mr. Larsson and Mr. Seger never testify in court. I have been told that you can help us. No doubt it would mean a lot to Agent Nesstor for his attackers to be served justice."

Groden jumped in. "Please Cale, help us out. You're the one who tipped us off that Larsson was a murderer. We can't take any chances he's allowed to walk free."

I wasn't sure what the problem was, so I grilled Moore. "Shouldn't this be an easy case to prosecute? Why do you need me to ensure justice?"

Moore again looked down. "I know what you're capable of, Mr. Novo. We'll make arrangements for you to meet with Larsson and Seger tomorrow. It's imperative they never leave our custody. Please, will you help us? For Agent Nesstor?"

The thought of Larsson and his buddy being delivered to me would make the task of removing their souls simple. Despite not understanding why the FBI seemed overly concerned about justice being served, a meeting was arranged for me to meet face to face with Larsson and Seger.

Jim Groden picked me up and drove to the Suffolk County Jail in Boston. Anthony Moore didn't join us. My head was pounding from being surrounded with darkness as we were led into the main building. We were escorted into a large room filled with a few small chairs surrounding several tables. One prison guard stood watch in the opposite corner from the door. A few other prisoners were meeting with guests at other tables as Larsson was led in and seated at the opposite side of our table. Groden and I sat down after Larsson.

"You tink you're going to get something from me now?" Larsson declared with a defiant voice. "Rot een hell, asshole."

At first I wasn't sure who Larsson was talking to. He was staring at Groden but I assumed Larsson was talking about his soul. The two of them stared at each other until I began to speak. "Why should you be allowed to keep it? I took it once, if I steal it again, your soul will never be at peace."

Larsson turned his attention my way. He studied my face. "I remember you. I'm not the evil one at this table, he's on your team."

"Hurry, Cale. I wanna get back to the hospital," Groden said.

Larsson sneered at Groden. "Why ees your partner still alive? Should have been you, asshole. You the dirty cop."

"Do it, Cale," Groden said with a forceful tone. "We only have five minutes."

"Do what?" Larsson questioned. "My lawyer will have me out of here before my dinner gets cold. You come to my home, my home, and try to rob me. Den you shoot at my roommate in my home and I am the one sitting in jail? No, no, you cannot do to me anymore then you did. Go, dirty man."

My head was pounding from sitting inside another jail. Larsson waved to the guard to be escorted away. Groden repeated several times with an anxious voice, "It's now or never, it's now or never."

Larsson made a fatal error. As he was standing to leave the room he looked at Groden and stated, "I hope you die in hell along with your thieving scumbag partner."

That was the line Larsson shouldn't have crossed. Nesstor was a good man. No murdering thug was going to tell the world otherwise. I grabbed his arm. The guard escorting Larsson noticed and latched onto my arm. He attempted to remove my arm from Larsson. He did it as Larsson's soul was being forever lost into oblivion. The guard let loose as if he stuck a wet finger into a power socket. He stumbled two steps backwards before regaining steady footing.

I fell back into my chair as did Larsson. He then vomited on the table. The guard who had been standing in the corner called someone on his radio as the other guard leaned with both hands on the table, now covered with Larsson's spillage. Larsson started to speak, but it was in broken words, half in Swedish and half in English. His eyes rolled into the back of his head.

Two custodians entered the room with cleaning supplies. Three guards came in behind the cleaning people, clearing the room of the other prisoners and guests. Groden pulled me out of the chair and pushed me towards the door. "We need to git and right now," he said. I became disoriented. It wasn't until I was staring at the Charles River from the passenger side of the car that Groden was driving along Storrow Drive, before I began to feel in control again.

"I was starting to think I was gonna have to check you into a bed next to Nesstor if you didn't snap out of it soon," Groden said. "I don't know exactly what happened back at the jail, but it was obvious we needed to check outta that place. What the hell did you do to that poor guard?"

There were still a few cobwebs in my brain but I could speak. "The guy grabbed me at the wrong time. Did he say anything to you?"

Groden replied, "It wasn't in our best interest to hang around and find out. I could tell the guards were starting to figure out something wasn't right, they didn't know what. I wasn't gonna still be there with you when they did."

"We didn't finish the job. Seger was the guy who shot Nesstor. That is if you're telling me the truth."

Groden turned his attention from the highway long enough to smile at me before stating, "I guess I'll have to figure another way to handle him. It won't be easy getting you back inside that building after today's circus."

I asked to be dropped back at the hotel for some rest. Lucky for me, daylight savings time came to an end for another year. The extra hour of sleep before heading back to the hospital was a welcome event. When I arrived at Nesstor's room, a nurse was cleaning his wounds. She offered some encouraging words. "Your friend is healing well. The doctor will be in to check on him soon."

I perched myself in my usual position in the corner of the room. That way I could view anyone walking the hallways while keeping a line of sight on Elliot and a side view of the window. The clock hadn't been turned back yet in Elliot's room. It still read five thirty a.m. Once the nurse finished her duties, I was alone in the room with Elliot. My eyes were still heavy. Despite a good night's rest, they began to close. I noticed Elliot wiggle a few fingers on his left hand. He was motioning me to come closer. I did.

Elliot kept motioning me closer until my ear was almost to his mouth. The only sound was the occasional beep from one of the machines still hooked to his body. Elliot struggled to offer even a few words. "Don't...let...him...near...me."

I pulled back to get a better view of Elliot's face. "Who? Don't let the doctor touch you?"

Elliot waggled his head to say no.

"Is there a male nurse who is upsetting you?"

He offered another no. I scratched my head and scanned my memory for any male who might have been in the room the past few days. The only other was a technician checking on a machine and the employees dropping off food that Elliot never touched. Plus Jim Groden.

"Groden?"

Elliot's eyes grew wide as he barely moved his head up and down one time. I told Elliot I would sit watch until he could speak with authority. I sat back in my chair wondering what all this meant. Elliot closed his eyes and fell back asleep.

An hour later, Mrs. Nesstor returned. Dark circles had formed under her eyes. I knew she hadn't eaten much for days. I handed her the fruit cup from her husband's breakfast tray and encouraged her to finish every last piece.

"Has Elliot spoken with you yet, Mrs. Nesstor?"

"No. He opened his eyes a few times last night. I think he's alert enough to watch the news. And he did smile when I told him I was leaving to get some rest. But he hasn't tried to speak that I know of yet. Why do you ask?"

"Has he acted annoyed at the doctors or nurses in any way?"

She gazed at Elliot for a few moments, then looked back at me. "Not that I can think of, Mr. Novo. I have noticed once or twice him act like he's having nightmares. I spoke to the doctor about it, but he wasn't alarmed. It's the only thing I can think of. My husband has gotten very good care here. Though I will admit, I'll be much happier when he can come home." She smiled.

"That must have been it," I said to Mrs. Nesstor. "Elliot must have been having a nightmare while I was napping. Maybe that's what woke me."

"You and I have known each other a long time, Mr. Novo. The odd expression you had tells me that maybe I shouldn't be so quick to believe you."

As she finished speaking, Groden entered from the hallway and greeted us. I noticed Elliot open his eyes and look at me. He shook his head no. I looked at Elliot and mouthed, "Ok" without the others in the room noticing. Elliot's wife turned on the news as Groden sat in the chair near Elliot.

Midday was upon us and Jim Groden insisted I take Elliot's wife out for fresh air and a hot lunch. "I'll sit with Elliot for a while. Go. If he talks, I'll come and find the two of you." Elliot opened his eyes wide and glared at me.

After much back and forth, no one left the room. Groden paced the floor for hours. I sat quietly listening to the news from the television with one eye on Elliot, the other on Jim Groden. Mrs. Nesstor would move from peering out the window to sitting in a small chair next to her husband. She would hold his hand and smile at him from time to time.

We were playing a live chess game with each side waiting for the opponent to make one bad move so the other could capitalize. Being a former chess champion, I would not be the first to make a faulty move.

"Hey, Jim," I said to Groden. "Why don't you go down to the cafeteria and grab us each a sandwich. If you fly, I'll buy."

Jim Groden licked his lips. "Sounds like a plan. I have to make a few calls anyway." I handed him a twenty, and off he went. The time would give me a few minutes to rest my mind and catch a quick nap.

I was in that state where you are close to being completely asleep, yet not. In my groggy condition, I heard a news commentator talking about how an inmate had been found dead in a local prison. I opened my eyes in time to see the name, "Steven Seger" flash across the screen.

The commentator continued. "Seger was killed this morning in Suffolk County Jail after an apparent fight with other inmates in the prison yard. Our on the scene reporter, Jim Crockett has informed WBZT-12 news that a small riot broke out during a morning basketball game. By the time the authorities could regain control of the yard, Seger was found dead. Stay tuned for more information on this and other breaking stories during the seven o'clock evening news."

I sat up in my chair and observed Elliot. His eyes were staring at the television screen. Beads of sweat had formed on his forehead. He motioned to have me come back towards him. I leaned in. He whispered, "Grrooden."

His wife enthusiastically jumped from her chair and shoved me aside. "Elliot, you can talk, you can talk." Elliot glared at me.

I immediately attempted to correct her. "No, no, Mrs. Nesstor, you were mistaken. I was the one speaking. Elliot still can't speak. He's far too weak."

"That's enough, Mr. Novo. I know my husband's voice, even in a whisper. What's going on here? I deserve to know why you two are keeping secrets."

Elliot curled his index finger to motion his wife to move closer. I moved closer too. "Truuuusssstttt, Novo," he said before closing his eyes.

I looked at Mrs. Nesstor. "No one can know your husband is well enough to speak. No one. Not even his doctor. Do you understand?"

She stood straight up from leaning over the bed and crossed her arms. Her voice was one of disgust. "No. I don't understand. Why on earth must I keep it a secret that my husband's health is improving enough to speak? Explain it to me, sir."

Elliot moved his finger across his lips. "Ssssssshhhhhh," he said. His wife took notice and went back to her chair after delivering a frown my way. The three of us remained in the room with only the sound from the television and one of the machines monitoring Elliot until Jim Groden returned with the sandwiches, chips and drinks.

The three of us were eating when the evening news began. The lead report was concerning the death at the prison. I turned to Groden. "That's pretty convenient for you, don't you think, Jim?"

Groden snickered then said, "Yeah, saves me a ton of paperwork, so what. The poor bastard. I guess he messed with the wrong guys."

"Who might those guys be, Jim?"

Groden snapped. "You don't wanna go there, Novo."

Mrs. Nesstor glanced at me with a raised eyebrow. Her mouth opened ready to speak when I shook my head no, asking her to remain quiet. Her eyes darted between me and Jim several times before she stared at her husband.

We each finished our meals without another word. Elliot's doctor arrived. He picked and prodded Elliot for a few moments before saying, "We're going to change one of your medications, Elliot." He then turned to Elliot's wife. "Don't be alarmed when the nurse comes in to change his IV, Mrs. Nesstor. I ordered it."

Groden followed the doctor into the hallway. I watched from my viewing position as the two of them exchanged words. Drawing suspicion, both disappeared from sight. Elliot's wife placed her hand on my wrist. She had a tear in her eye.

"Caeles, if there is something I need to know about my husband's safety, please, let me know what it is. I know I don't understand all you do and what your relationship is with Elliot to the fullest extent, but don't take me for a fool."

I put my hand on hers to offer comfort. "Elliot asked me to keep Jim away from him. I suspect something happened the day they were shot that Jim wants to keep quiet. I have my suspicions but that is all they are. Until then, I'll keep a close on Jim when he is in the room. Once Elliot can speak with more authority, I'll know what to do. But for now, stay quiet about Elliot speaking with me, until I know who to trust."

22

*A*nother sleepless night was spent in the hospital room. Elliot's wife and Jim Groden each refused to leave the hospital all evening. The nurse came to change Elliot's IV medication. I watched intently as she scanned and changed the bag. Groden spied the nurse as well.

My senses had become dull from lack of rest. The mental chess game had gone on too long. Groden was weary as well. I watched as he dozed off several times during the early morning hours. Mrs. Nesstor remained awake all night, refusing to leave her husband's bedside. As daylight hit, Groden tried to coax her away.

"Maria, please let me take you back to the hotel for some rest. If you don't start taking better care of yourself, you'll be admitted here too."

"I'm perfectly capable of caring for my husband, Agent Groden. Don't you have some bad guys to catch? You're the one who refuses to leave Elliot's side. Why is that, sir?"

Groden looked at me as if he was asking for help. I shrugged. I was too tired to argue with either of them. My grumpy side appeared. "Why don't both of you get the heck out of here and let me relax for a few hours. Nothing is going to happen to Elliot."

Mrs. Nesstor fired back. "No one is asking you to stand guard here, Mr. Novo. Maybe you should be the one to leave."

"That sounds like a great idea," Groden said. "Nothing personal, Novo, but you look like shit. I think Maria is right, a few winks at the hotel will do you some good."

"I'm not going anywhere either," I declared. The three of us began a staring contest switching from face to face. As exhausted as I was, I had made a commitment to Elliot and wouldn't leave his side. It had been several days since the shooting. I assumed Elliot would be capable of putting together cohesive thoughts in short order. I was trusting Elliot would come around soon since I had personal business to attend to back in Nevada.

A voice called from the hallway. "Agent Groden, may I speak with you?" Agent Moore was standing outside the room. Groden left the room with Moore. I couldn't see them. I went to the hallway to see them talking a few doors away. The meeting lasted less than a minute. Groden headed back as I could see Moore hit the elevator button across the hallway.

"I gotta go check on something, Novo. I'm uncomfortable leaving Elliot alone right now. If anyone Maria doesn't know comes to the room, watch them carefully. I'll be back as soon as I can."

"What? Why?" I asked. "Who would be coming to see Elliot?"

"Trust me, Novo. The less you know the better. I'll be back in a few hours to relieve you and take care of Elliot."

I went inside Elliot's room to find his wife sitting in the chair next to her husband's bed, sobbing. She took her lovers hand then looked up at me. "I apologize for raising my voice with you," she said. "I've been married to a cop for forty-two years. I always knew the risks. When Elliot told me he would be retiring, I started to think this day wouldn't come. I allowed myself to believe no harm could come to my husband." Tears streamed down her cheeks.

She leaned down and placed her head across her husband's chest. Elliot lifted his arm and began to stroke the back of her head. He opened his eyes and started to speak with a low tone. "It's all going to be fine, my love."

She picked up her head. "Elliot! I've missed you so much." She kissed his cheek before lowering her head back down to his chest crying tears of joy. He wrapped both arms around his wife. I stood several feet away allowing them a semi-private moment.

Later, Elliot focused on the television off and on for hours but never uttered a word. His wife ate his dinner. I left the room long enough to grab a meal from the cafeteria. I later slept for more than four hours in the corner chair before the sun cracked open a new day.

I awoke to the sound of Maria insisting to her husband, "After you get outta here, no more field work. You find a way to park yourself behind a desk and don't move." Elliot smiled.

"When did Cale arrive?" Elliot asked his wife as I rubbed the sleep from my eyes.

"He's been here for days, honey. You don't remember talking with him?"

Elliot hit the button to slightly raise the back of his bed while examining the room. It was the first time I had seen him in anything but a horizontal position since I had arrived. He glanced at me, then back at his wife. "Huh, I spoke with Cale? When?"

"A couple of days ago, sweetie, you don't remember?"

I stood up and moved to the foot of his bed. "Yeah, you whispered to me that you were concerned about Jim Groden, you know, your partner. You led me to believe he wanted to kill you!"

Elliot rubbed his cheek and said, "My wife informs me that I was shot multiple times, endured two surgeries and have been hooked up to a morphine bag ever since. I hardly think anything I said while tripping on pain meds can be held against me. I was stoned out of my mind."

I was flabbergasted. I spent several sleepless nights worrying about a guy who was on a private magical mystery tour? "You don't remember telling me to keep Groden away from you and telling your wife to trust me?"

"Have my wife trust you?" Nesstor asked. "Hell, Soul Man, I've never been convinced I should trust you." He ended his words with a big smile.

The nurse entered the room before I could strangle the guy. She fluffed his pillows. I had visions of smothering his face with them. I sat in my corner perch and watched the nurse continue her duties. "The doctor will be in later this afternoon, Mr. Nesstor. Are you having any pain?" The nurse asked.

"Only from the stares I'm getting from the guy in the corner," Nesstor replied.

Elliot slept off and on during the day and didn't want to talk about the day he was shot. I convinced Elliot's wife to get a good night's rest in the hotel. I went too. I slept until the following morning. When I arrived back to Elliot's room, his wife was trying to get a few sips of juice down his throat.

I made plans to fly to Las Vegas at day's end. But I still wanted Elliot's version of what happened the day he was shot. Plus I wanted to say my goodbyes to his wife and Jim Groden, who I hadn't seen in over a day.

Elliot was complaining to his wife about the juice being too cold and not a kind he would normally drink. His foul mood wasn't going to deter me. He owed me his story before I left. I left a text message for Groden to see if he was going to return by midafternoon with no response. My time was running short.

"Talk to me, Elliot. What's the truth about what happened at Larsson's house?"

"What did Jim tell you?"

"It doesn't matter what he told me. I want your version of it."

"You know, Soul Man, sometimes things are none of your business. But I will tell you this. Jim and I are investigating a gambling ring with connections from Boston to Miami. We have evidence that your buddy Larsson along with athletes in other sports are throwing games for profit. It's an ongoing investigation and that's all I'm gonna tell you."

"Wait, you weren't there because of the information I gave you about Larsson murdering drug dealers?

"No! How many times do I have to tell you, I don't want any part of that case? This gambling case was the last one I wanted to clear off my desk before retiring." Nesstor began coughing. And one more thing, this is all your fault."

"My fault?"

"Yes, you had me arrest that Clinkard woman and her daughter put a curse on me. Remember? She told me that a bad thing would happen the next time I made an arrest."

"First of all, Elliot. You didn't make an arrest. You were shot before you could do anything. Second, you asked for my help to get the Clinkard's on American soil and I did."

"That's enough, from the two of you," Maria said. "Mr. Novo, I refuse to have you upset my husband. Can't you see he's still struggling to speak? Now if you won't stop talking about police work, I'm going to ask you to leave."

"I'm fine, Maria," Elliot said, still coughing up a fur ball.

I let the air clear and allowed Elliot time to stop coughing before continuing. "Are you aware some FBI big shot had me take the soul of Larsson and that Seger was killed in prison?"

Nesstor looked surprised. "Who the hell is Seger?"

"Hello, he's the guy who filled your belly with lead."

"Strange," Nesstor said. "Who spoke with you from the FBI?"

"A little smarmy looking guy by the name of Moore. Do you know him?"

"Never heard of him. But then again, there's plenty of people with the agency I've never met."

"Stop it," Maria Nesstor said. "Elliot you need your rest and Mr. Novo, I do appreciate you being with us the last few days, but you are doing more harm than good now. Please, let my husband rest."

After looking at my watch, it was time to leave. I had a meeting to attend in Las Vegas. I asked the Nesstors to give my regards to Jim Groden. I said my goodbyes and headed for Logan Airport. I called Kalani and had her stop at home to pick up my best suit and tie. I realized all was on the line in a sand pit in the desert. Kalani pressed me for details but I didn't budge. I wanted her reaction at the same time I would see the reaction from the others who were willing to show up when I proposed my plan.

Kalani met me at Mclaren Airport in Vegas. We checked into The Mirage, where I slept for several hours.

Late afternoon struck and Kalani and I drove to the land I had purchased months earlier. When we arrived, a few construction workers were moving dirt with heavy machinery. I could see posts, marking areas where I knew buildings would be rising in the near future. Kalani kept pressing me. "I assume this is why that real estate guy was calling the house? I'm telling you again, I'm not living out here."

"Don't worry, you won't be here anymore than you are at the compound now, and if I get my way even less." Before I could say more, the bus I was waiting on arrived. Twenty-four men and women unloaded. Most were strangers to each other. They ranged in ages from late sixties to over two hundred, yet no pure human would ever guess. Some had dark skin and hair, others, fair skinned with freckles.

I asked them all off the side of the road overlooking a large open area with a few construction workers and equipment. "Thank you all for joining me," I said. "I would imagine some of you spoke with each other on the bus ride out here and figured out who you all are. If not, let me explain. My name is Caeles Novo. For a short time, I was the leader of the High Council. By counting the number of you who got off the bus, with a few exceptions, we are the remaining soul stealers on earth. I was the one who sent you the request to join me. I have met some of you, but not all."

Each sized up the other. Most had never met each other before getting on the bus. Unless we took training classes at a young age together or in rare cases, married one another, we were rarely seen together. We were a solitary group.

When the invitations were sent out, each was offered a free stay in Las Vegas as a thank you for hard work. Since it was fairly common for the Council to give free holidays after doing a good job, I assumed not many would think twice about taking advantage of the free time off and some gambling chips. But I also realized few if any would get on the bus before knowing where the bus was heading and why. A text message was sent to each of them an hour before the bus was leaving asking them to join me. The text informed them that it was me who offered the paid vacations, not the Council as stated in their initial notes. I was requesting an hour of their time.

I allowed them to walk around the mounds of dirt and markings in the ground before asking them to join me under the temporary patio built for workers to get away from the sun while on breaks. They sat on the benches provided. My nerves flared. I loosened my silk tie and began my plea.

"My fellow disciples, how many of you think you know our true mission as soul stealers?"

All raised their hands. "I am here to tell you, none of you do." I removed copied pages I had stashed in my brief case. "These pages are from a book documenting our true mission on earth. I searched until it was recovered. Every step of our past and our future resides in the pages of that book."

I went on to tell the lessons I learned during my time of being the leader of the Council. I spoke about why few soul stealers remained. I told them about all the businesses we owned as disciples, yet few knew the real truth. I continued with how we would be all gone from earth if we didn't change our ways. I implored them to realize they were all working longer hours than necessary, while others who could steal souls refused. I told them about Dr. Winfield and his discovery about the unique gene in our blood lines. I told them I wanted to return us to our original mission and lessen their work load. Some in the group applauded while others never twitched a muscle.

"How many of you have families and would like to spend more time at home?" Most raised their hands. "Put your hand up, Kalani," I said as I continued. "Look around you. This is our new training facility and compound. We will not forget our past but learn from our mistakes. We will begin anew and rise again!"

A splattering of applause but not the rousing cheers I had imagined. An older man began to ask questions. "Does the Council know about this site and approve of your plan?"

"What good is a Council if there are no followers? I have taken steps to remove the power from the Council. But I need all of you." I then continued by telling my audience that I had someone develop a drug where we could retain all our power when removing a soul. We no longer needed to share. In doing so, it would force others to take souls if they too wanted to continue to live three hundred years.

Another member from the group shouted at me. "My father worked for hundreds of years as a soul stealer and is now retired. I refuse to abandon him and others like him."

"I agree," I said. "The same doctor who developed the drug to keep the power when removing a soul has developed a drug that will allow us to share, if we decide to administer it. We can control who shares in our power and who doesn't."

Some in the group started to squirm. "All of this was not only predicted in our history book, but the methods to share and not share powers are documented as well. I have personally tested the drug to keep the power to myself while taking a soul. The other will be tested soon."

Then the real news was delivered to the group. "We were never taught by our leaders that redemption was always our original mission. I have restored souls."

"Liar," was shouted from the group. Before I could refute his words, Kalani came to defense.

"Caeles has restored many souls and I have witnessed it. He has also shown me the book that tells of our past and our future."

More disapproval from the group ensued with calls of liar and fake. I had played out many scenarios in my mind before this day, being called a liar was not one of them. "Am I to believe that some in this group can't tell if I am lying or not? That claim might work in other surroundings, but not among us." Soft laughter could be heard in the group.

Some of the curious started to ask questions about the book

and returning souls, while others listened without a word. A few
fiddled with their electronic devices while three walked off
whispering among themselves. After a brief discussion, all were
invited back to the casino for a catered dinner.

Before I could stand for an opening toast at dinner, Kalani
stood and began to speak. "I realize many of you have never met
my husband or even know of his struggles with our leaders. I'll bet
many of you don't know the Council attempted to kill him. They
also removed his ability to remove souls for a period of time. It's a
big reason why he stumbled into ways to keep our power to
ourselves when stealing a soul. He can be a giant pain in the ass. I
live with him, I know. Despite his flaws, I would love to see him
more often, so would our son. I'm willing to bet your family
members would love to see more of you as well. Please listen to
what he has to offer and keep an open mind tonight. Thank you."

She sat back down, her hand shaking as she took a sip from
her water glass. Knowing public speaking was not one of her
strengths, it meant even more to me. But it was now my turn. I
played this speech over and over in my head for weeks. Show time
had arrived.

"Our destiny as true disciples has been taken us off course by
leaders I once trusted. My journey has been a long bumpy road,
but one with purpose. However, over the past several decades,
our leaders have taken us down a different road. One filled with
greed and opulence. Your only decision now is if you want to
remain a true disciple or chose to be led down a dead end. My
choice is clear. I ask you to join me back on the road where all
disciples work for the common good and no one takes the fruit of
our labor who has not earned it. Living off the toil of others may
look to be an easier road, but that is a road with no end. You will

walk it, until one day you wither away. We are soul stealers. We do not apologize for this because it was a power granted to us from the Lord of Life centuries ago. But in order to survive, we must force all with the power to take souls to choose our road. If they continue to follow a different road for the sole purpose of selfish deeds of greed and opulence, we will no longer work to maintain that road. Those who have traveled our road but are now too tired to continue, will be given support and a free toll. But those looking to travel their own path for selfish means can no longer be part of who we are as soul stealers. I have made my choice, now you must make yours."

Conversations with many continued over dinner about how this was not a power grab on my part. Every soul stealer would have a vote on who would comprise the new council. People in our bloodlines who never could, or lost the ability to steal souls, would continue to support those who could steal souls in the form of a tax. The elderly would be exempt from taxes as long as they were soul stealers at one time. We would encourage others to still be leaders around the world and in local communities, but our mission as soul stealers would again take priority.

Most at the table were in favor of my proposals and were eager to get started. Some of the older members feared repercussions from the current Council and wanted assurances our move to Las Vegas wouldn't jeopardize them or their families in the future. I didn't want to give away any more details, since I didn't know who could be trusted in the group. I kept chipping away at the core problem that so few of us were working to support so many others. We were losing incentive to want to steal souls. I had to convince them that it was not only our duty, but the duty of everyone. The burden shouldn't only be on the few of us who were active soul stealers.

Some questioned the time line for the move to Las Vegas as well as why we should leave our old compound. Why not overthrow the old regime and start fresh where we had resided for generations? I knew those answers but had to side step offering the truth until I could meet with my former leaders.

By dinner's end, I felt confident many in the group would join me in restoring our numbers as well as forming a new coalition. Feeling confident that enough our mission would get back on track to its original intent, it was time to get our new facility completed and finish destroying the existing Council.

23

A text came from Nesstor via Iza Tappen requesting I return to Boston. It took me a moment to remember that Nesstor had put me in touch with Iza in the first place. I was curious why Nesstor didn't call me. I considered the idea he was day tripping on morphine again, but maybe there was more to it. I sent a note back to Iza that I would return to Boston in a few days. Another text arrived soon after, asking me to return immediately.

A few of my fellow disciples still had questions about how to convince others to participate in soul stealing among other things. The timing of Nesstor's request wasn't ideal. The disciples and I decided to set up another time where we could all sit and work out more details in the future. I explained to the remaining disciples still in town that this initial meeting was more to introduce my ideas and gauge interest. Most had assignments and had to leave town. After making a promise to Kalani we would spend a few days in Vegas, she wasn't thrilled I was off to Boston again. Assurances were made that I would make it up to her by taking her on a cruise in the spring.

Boston was cold and miserable when I returned. An early

winter storm had blanketed the area with snow. Before heading to the hospital from the airport, a trip to Filene's was in order to pick up a winter coat and gloves. Rumors were swirling that the store was heading into bankruptcy.

Seeing Filenes fall on hard times made me realize that one of my goals, once we convened our new administration, should be to institute an economic development committee. Since we owned so much stock and other holdings in companies around the world, I felt it necessary we have our disciples with business experience have some oversight. I was bitten once by not paying attention to our financial situation. That wasn't going to happen twice.

When I arrived at the hospital, Elliot had been moved. He was no longer in the intensive care area and was in a standard room. It was early evening and his wife had left to grab dinner. Elliot wasn't sure if she would be returning later that night or not. He had insisted she get some rest at the hotel. There was talk of him being moved to a rehab center closer to their home in Virginia in the coming days. That was why Elliot requested to see me sooner rather than later.

The color had returned to his face. His voice was strong. It had been three weeks since the shooting and Elliot was healing faster than his doctor's anticipated. "I'm a tough old goat," he quipped. "There's a few reasons why I asked you to come back. For one, I wanted to thank you for looking out for me and Maria. I also wanted to apologize for lying. I knew you here all along. I knew what I was saying when I whispered I was concerned about my partner. But I didn't expect Maria to hear. I knew I couldn't protect myself lying here close to death, but I knew I could count on you."

My emotions were split in that moment. Elliot and I coexisted for many years. Every time I allowed myself to consider him a true friend, something would happen to question my trust in him. Because of my lifestyle, there were few people in the world I considered a true friend. I wondered if I would even recognize friendship when I saw it. Was this Elliot's way of extending the hand of friendship? Or was there a buzzer in his palm ready to zap me and be humiliated? He seemed sincere. I had been trained in many things, being a social creature who understood emotions was never one of our lessons.

Elliot continued. "I'm concerned, Soul Man. Jimmy hasn't been back to see me since you said Moore sent him on an assignment. Plus, odd, but no one from the Bureau has come to see me. I received a few cards and some flowers, but other than Jimmy Groden, no one has stopped by."

"I don't know, Elliot. Your office is located hours from here and I'm sure they are all busy. You know how people are. I would not be too concerned about it, unless there is something you are not telling me. And since you felt you needed protection, I assume there is."

"That gambling ring I was telling you about, well it goes much deeper. Jimmy was working the angle trying to find the athletes who were throwing games for profit. My angle was to see who was in charge of the operation. I was coming across some disturbing information that has led me to believe organized crime has their hooks into some at the highest levels of our government."

I had to laugh. "I think you call them lobbyists. All you have to do is watch how politicians vote sometimes and you can figure that out, big guy."

"I'm serious. I'm starting to think President Morrison has ties with organized crime. If I pursue that angle, Maria could be a widow much sooner than I had planned."

"I don't think it is Morrison you need to investigate."

Elliot gave me a strange look. "Why do you say that?"

"Because. I met with the man, not that long ago. For a politician, he had a relatively clean soul. I don't think he's your guy."

"When did you meet the President," Special Agent Nesstor asked before offering a twisted smile. "Hey, wait a minute, that's right, you can tell if someone's a criminal by looking at em. Hell, I was gonna call in a favor and ask you to look up any politician who might be on the soul stealers naughty list, but you have the magic eyes. I forgot about that."

"No you didn't, Elliot. Don't play me. You didn't forget I have skills that you don't possess. And I met the President for five minutes a few months back. He didn't like me too much." My emotions were again mixed, questioning if this was a friend of mine or he was only wanting me to assist him in his latest case?

Elliot reacted with a rushed tone. "Maybe you missed all the gadgets I'm still hooked up to, including the morphine drip. How bout cutting me some slack and realize I'm still not a hundert' percent. Yes, I did forget you could look into people's souls, not just take em."

"Ok, maybe you're right. I'm overreacting. I have my own issues I'm dealing with right now. So, what's the real reason you had me fly across the country again? You could have told me all this over the phone."

Elliot gazed out the window. He looked back at me. "Go close the door." I closed the door to his hospital room. I went back to my corner chair and sat looking at Elliot.

"Jimmy Groden is dead. I can't prove it yet, but I feel it in my bones. I know he's dead. When we went to Larsson's place, Seger answered the door. We knew Seger was there. He was sitting on the sofa right next to Larsson the entire time. Jimmy was pressing Larsson to come clean about throwing games and Larsson admitted to missing shots on purpose and not playing up to his abilities all the time. In exchange for not scoring in big games, the street corners around schools in Boston would be free of drug dealers. You were right, Larsson admitted to killing some low level hoppers. Once he started popping drug dealers off corners, the mob figured out who was doing it and assigned Seger to kill Larsson. But Larsson lucked out because the head of the family in the area is a huge Bruins fan and season ticket holder. Rather than kill Larsson they had him throw games. Seger was then assigned to make sure Larsson showed up for games and stop killing hoppers.

"So why the gunfight?"

"Seger admitted we were chasing some people we didn't want to be chasing. He knew far more than Larsson did. We did all we could to get them both to admit everything on paper and they refused. My guess is that Larsson wanted out of the entire mess, it's why he was confessing. When we went to cuff them, it all went bad. Seger hit me three times before I could draw. I might be tough, but I've gotten slower in my old age. I don't know much about what happened after I was hit, but I have no doubt the mob killed Seger to keep him quiet. I suspect whoever this Moore fellow is, wanted to get you to keep Larsson quiet, but not kill him. He didn't know much. Seger was the real target."

The room went silent. The information was a lot to take in. I still wasn't sure where I fit into this mess. This was a problem for the FBI and others to resolve, not me. I had a wife madder than a hornet for leaving her in Vegas, a group of soul stealers conflicted on where they fit into the world and no doubt by now, former leaders of mine who were aware of my plans to ruin them.

"Cale, I don't know who I can trust inside my office. If I retire to Florida knowing what I know already, I'll blow my brains out one day. I'm not wired to walk away with this hanging over me. Will you help me?"

"I'd like to but there's not much I can do. Your government leadership is in turmoil but so is mine. I wasn't put on this earth to settle the world's problems. I take the souls from people who no longer deserve to keep them. It's what I do. It's your job to solve crimes. It's mine to make sure criminals and others acknowledge what they have done wrong, and if they repent, offer redemption. Maybe we should both retire and let the others fix the corruption that's surrounding us."

Elliot gave me a blank stare for several seconds before clapping his hands. "Bravo, Novo. You're a lotta things, but I neva took you for a quitter. So stop feeling sorry for yourself and help me. Look at you. I've known you for what, going on thirty-five, forty years and you look almost the same as the day we met. Though I will admit you have some pudge around the middle now. You have a beautiful wife and you get to see things in this world so few will ever witness, including me. Me, I have grey hair, slow reflexes, a lousy pension, and a wife up my ass begging me to quit every day. I have a boss I don't trust, a missing partner who I assume is dead, and I'm tied to frigging machines I have no damn clue what they do. Yet, I'm the one who wants to keep going? Maybe you need to look inside your own soul before you end up on someone's list, ass-hole."

"Are we friends, Elliot?"

"What kinda question is that?"

"An important one. Do you consider me your friend, a real friend?"

Elliot scowled. He dug all the earwax from his left ear and looked out the window. "I neva had times for friends. I was born to get bad guys off the streets. I love my wife. I love my daughter. Besides those two people, you might be the only other person who has neva let me down. I always knew I could trust you. That's the only answer I have for ya."

In all the years I had known Elliot Nesstor, it never occurred to me how similar we were.

"How can I help you get one last bad guy off the street, Special Agent Nesstor?"

Elliot smirked. "I know you're buddies with Danker, McAdams and that kid reporter. Remember that time we had dinner and you told me I needed to investigate if McAdams was set up? Well, I did some digging right before I came up here to Boston and I suspect that case is tied to mine. I need you to call those three and see if they have any more information regarding that secret fund, other than what Simpson has already reported in the papers."

"If Simpson starts snooping into top level people, he's likely to suffer the same fate as you fear happened to Groden. I'm not so sure I want to put him or the other two in the crosshairs, Elliot. Besides, Danker went missing right after he did that spot on the Masterson show. I went looking for him, to thank him, when I was in Vegas the other day, and he has vanished again."

"I'm not asking you to get any of them to investigate. I'm only asking you to call them and see what you can find out for me. I have no idea who's watching or listening to me from this room. I can't ask anyone from my office since I don't know who to trust right now. Will ya do it?"

"When this is all over, Nesstor, dinner is on you. I don't care how small you think your pension is."

I stepped outside the hospital and made calls to Josh Simpson and George McAdams. Simpson asked me more questions than I asked him. He desperately wanted to make a name for himself as an investigative journalist. Simpson's first inclination was to suspect President Morrison, but I attempted to sway him elsewhere in his thinking. "I don't know much else, Mr. Novo. But I'll try to contact my cousin Paula. Remember, she's the one I told you about who worked at the Secret Service. Maybe she has seen something that might help us. And I'll check the public records for the White House, the Capitol and the Vice President's residence. Maybe something will turn up there."

When I called McAdams, he was no help. "Leave me out of it. I don't want any part of politics any more. It's one large cesspool. Since the truth about Danker being alive is out there, I've gotten so many calls to run for office again, even for the Senate seat in a few years. But I have new responsibilities knowing I'm a dad.

Nicole and I are going to try and piece together a relationship for our son."

"George, maybe you didn't hear me. I am not asking you to get back into politics. I am only asking you to think about what you can remember about that slush fund and maybe who had access to it. You did ask questions about it in a congressional hearing. Maybe you can remember something for me by looking over your old notes."

"No, I heard ya. What you don't understand is that I want nothing to do with that part of my life any longer. I don't even wanna think about it. I'm sorry, Cale. I realize I owe you a debt for finding Danker, but I was put through hell in trying to do the right thing. I hope whoever set me up rots in hell, but I can't be part of the investigation.

"I guess I understand. From what I have seen, I would not want any part of Washington either. It is a shame though, that town could use a few honest politicians. Too many go there and lie only to advance an agenda."

"I agree, Cale, I've seen it firsthand, especially with that health insurance bill. Hey did I tell you? Tomorrow morning, I'm driving up to North Carolina to spend a few days with Dylan. I think I'm going to work with him in running his record label. Again, I'm sorry but now that I'm away from Washington and had time to think about it, that town is not who I am as a person."

"Good luck, George. Maybe we can catch up in the spring on Dylan's cruise. I'm going to try and make it. Anyway, if you do think of something, let me know, otherwise, take care."

This wasn't going to be much help to Elliot, but I went back inside to give him the news. "Not much to go on I'm afraid. The only thing that might be of any help was that Simpson has a cousin who worked with the Secret Service. As you know, if you read the file on McAdams and Danker, the slush fund was on the books with that agency."

"What's the cousin's name?"

"Paula somebody."

Elliot's ears perked. "Paula, Paula Green?"

"I think that's her, you know her?"

"Hell yes, I know her." Elliot said. "Her mother reported her as a missing person and her name showed up in the McAdams file as someone he and Danker had contact with at the Secret Service."

"Well before you go all crazy with your mob hit theories, from what Simpson tells me, she's very much alive. She was paid to move out west somewhere."

"Yeah, yeah. I know it might not seem like it, but you were a big help getting Paula's name for me. It confirmed what I suspected in who is behind all this. Now, I know you have better things to do than to watch an old man heal in a hospital room. I've kept you long enough. So before I send you packing, one last thing I need to tell you. I do consider you a good friend, Soul Man, thanks."

24

$\mathcal{T}$he journey would continue. A meeting had been arranged for
me to meet with my former Council members. But before my
flight across the Atlantic Ocean, I made a stop to visit with Skip
Stanton, who was the owner of the water company now supplying
water to the compound. Stanton assured me he did as asked,
after I secured his company a large government contract. He
claimed he mixed in what Pickering had sent him into the water
being shipped to the compound in Italy. It was all I needed to
know. But I wanted to see his soul when I asked the question. He
knew he couldn't get away without being truthful.

After leaving Stanton's office, I drove to the airport and
boarded a flight to Italy. Travels to the compound were an anxious
time for me. When visiting, I knew I would either be struggling,
working hard learning my craft or being admonished by the
Council for something they never approved. Even as leader, it was
an uneasy time visiting the soul stealers training center and home
to the High Council. But this time, I slept the entire flight. I
checked into a hotel near the compound only long enough to
make a few calls, grab a hot shower and put on a fresh suit. My
trip wouldn't be a lengthy one. The cab ride was a peaceful ten

minute journey.

After being frisked at the gate, which was a first for me, I was taken to the same conference room I had been in many times. Two windows allowed in what little light could find its way through the steel grey sky. The heat blasted through the tired ventilation system. The white walls with only a few paintings added little sense of color to the room. I was asked to be seated at the oak conference table with the crimson leather seats. I should have been nervous, but I wasn't. These men and women I was about the sit across, attempted to kill me at least once that I knew of, and had removed my ability as a soul stealer. I was unsure of what might be in store for me. But I was calm.

After a few minutes, a handful of men and one woman entered the room. Included were my former fellow Council members, Elder Baruch Robus and Reuel Polus, as well as a member elected after I was deposed, Tasha Timmons. There were two other men I didn't recognize who were introduced as new Council members, Norman Brown and Curtis Urlacher. I stood and shook everyone's hands before we were all seated.

The five of them were seated on one side of the table, opposite of me. It was done to intimidate me. It didn't work. I sat and waited for someone to speak. Before anyone did, the door opened and the man who I battled on many occasions, entered along with Brandon Bink. I had once stolen and returned the soul of Charon Orcus, one of the two men who were now also sitting across from me. I remained quiet.

The first to speak was Elder Robus. We had little regard for one another, especially once I was appointed leader of our High Council. "Caeles, why won't you do everyone a favor and leave us alone. I thought we had come to an agreement that we would leave you to live your life without any more harm coming to you, and allow your wife to still be a member of our family, but only if you would stop insisting on being a thorn in our side."

My first inclination was to jump across the table and strangle the guy, but that emotion soon faded. "I was unaware of any agreement. The last time we spoke in this same room, the High Council removed me as its leader because I was eradicated of my ability to confiscate souls. I don't recall executing any agreement. But, I do remember me threatening several of you seated across from me."

Seven sets of eyes were staring at me. Tasha Timmons jumped up from her seat and placed a bottle of water in front of me, before returning to her seat. "Drink up," Orcus insisted. "It's fine water from North Carolina. We have pallets of it sitting in one of our warehouses."

"No thanks, I'm not thirsty," I said.

"No Caeles, you will drink the entire bottle before you leave," Tasha stated.

I shoved the water off to the side. "I am not thirsty, but thank you, Miss Timmons."

Orcus spoke. "Caeles, we have heard some nasty rumors that you have purchased land in the United States and have told members of our soul stealing community they are welcome to join with you. Is this true?"

"Yes, it is. I fully intend to restore our mission of offering redemption to those souls who seek it and lessen the work load on our current group of soul stealers."

I sat casually in my seat as the seven across from me talked among themselves. I could overhear them discussing what penalties they would impose on me. I leaned back in my chair and stretched my arms. My stretching irritated them, so I did it again. I loosened my Jerry Garcia tie designed for the Christmas holidays with the reindeer on it and yawned loud enough to annoy them even more.

Robus asked with a defiant tone, "Why would any of our disciples follow you? You have no financial backing to support flying them around the world. You have continued to rant on about us leaving our original mission and that you somehow are the savior of us all. Why are you so delusional?"

Keeping my tone in check was harder the second time, but I managed.

"Elder Robus, first of all, I only intend to be the savior of some, no one in this room is included. Secondly, last time I was here, Elder Orcus told me about how for decades, the older members have decided that running large corporations and being leaders in our local communities has overshadowed the goal of removing dark souls. Your inept management has left but a mere thirty soul stealers. This is not some baseless claim on my part. Every one of you have abandoned our true calling here on earth. Now, I am not here to sway you into believing being in control or having power is a bad thing. But to what end? We can have both without running the remaining soul stealers into the ground. Once they realize they can have both, some will soon join with me. The ones who don't initially, will show up at my doorstep once they realize my place in the desert is their only salvation."

Tasha Timmons spoke up again. "You really are a cocky little prick, aren't you, Novo?"

"Tasha, for the first time in my life, I am a man at peace with who I am. I have struggled internally with my destiny for decades. No more. I am a soul stealer, a husband, a father, a leader of disciples and a man who believes in his cause. Maybe not in that order, but it's who I am. My grandfather has told me that I was put on earth for a reason. That reason was to rebuild my fellow soul stealers and restore our numbers. My destiny is within reach and there is nothing any of you can do about it now."

Robus yelled. "YOU HAVE NOTHING, NOVO, NOTHING."

Lowering my voice to a near whisper, I told them all, "I have peace of mind and I have the truth on my side. What is it that you think any of you have?"

Charon Orcus moved forward in his chair and stared at me. "Why do you keep insisting you are sitting on the side that is somehow morally correct and we are so wrong?"

"Because, I have read the truth. I read the book documenting our history. The same book a former Council voted to have banished so no one knew our job was to offer redemption. I searched for that book, read it, and now I have acted upon it. The book predicted all of this. All that you have done was in plain view on the pages for me to read. The book foretells of your destruction and now our resurrection. That is why I know I am right, Elder Orcus."

Robus spoke in a loud voice again. "What makes you think you will ever leave this compound alive, Novo?"

"Section two, article one of the bylaws reads that no weapon of any kind shall be permitted inside the compound walls. If any such weapon is found it calls for the immediate removal of the leader of the High Council. So stop embarrassing yourselves with hollow threats. There are no weapons on the grounds. Plus if you kill me, the antidote for what is ailing all of you right now dies with me. When we are done with this conversation, I will walk out the gates and never return. You can all live here for the remainder of your fading days. That will be my gift to you."

"And what exactly ails us?" Orcus inquired.

"Well Elder Orcus, you would be the only one present who wouldn't know since you lost your ability to see into and take souls long ago. But the other six are all hiding the fact that somewhere over the past few months, they have all lost that ability. And as Elder Polus so eloquently told me the last time I was here that section one, article six in the bylaws clearly states that only those with the ability to see into another's soul and remove it when ordered, may be a member of the High Council. Once the remaining soul stealers are informed of your short comings as they were of mine, a vote will be taken to install a new High Council."

"You're a crazy ignorant bastard," Timmons declared.

Orcus jumped in, "We know about the water, Caeles. Did you honestly believe that Stanton wouldn't call me the moment you struck the original deal and left his office? My only question is, what is in those bottles? Our chemist had several bottles analyzed and all they could find was pure water. How did you mask the poison?"

I opened the bottle next to me and drank a large portion.

"This water? Why I had Stanton put in a dash of refreshing water from Scotland. Every bottle is one hundred percent pure water."

The seven all talked amongst themselves again. I fiddled with my tie and finished the bottle of water. But I couldn't resist treating them as poorly as they did me.

"I told all of you the last time I was here, I would ruin you and now I have. It's over. I checked on your last two victims, Tasha. They both still have a soul. You know it, and so do I."

"Liar!" Timmons exclaimed.

"It's documented in Bink's database who your assignments were, Tasha. For the past three months, I have monitored every one of the souls scheduled to be taken. I know none of you sitting across from me still has the ability given from the heavens. None of you wanted to admit it to one another because you had hopes your abilities would return. They may, in roughly ten years. By then, Elder's Orcus, Polus and Robus will have returned to dust. You others can come and work for us when your ability is restored. Or you can plead your case to the new Council and ask for redemption. If the Council allows, an antidote will be provided."

Orcus laughed. "How, Caeles? How did you do it?"

"Your creaky old ventilation system was under constant repair. I bought the repair company and paid someone to insert a tasteless, odorless gas in your heating and air conditioning system. You have been breathing it in for months. It's everywhere now. Once the remaining soul stealers find out this place is contaminated, they won't return. The poison is in your lungs, your clothes, your food, it's everywhere.

"You're lying!" Timmons said.

"No, Tasha, it's all true, and by the way, it also stops you from sharing the strength gained when we do remove souls. And the best news of all is, that all of you will die three times faster than expected. Yes, Tasha, your exterior beauty will age the same as ordinary humans now."

The look on Timmons' face was priceless, though Elder Polus tried to act calm. "Caeles, my time on earth is waning. By the time you can prove your accusations that our abilities are faded and a new Council is elected, I won't care. But since I doubt the younger members in the room will feel the same as me, we will crush your plans. We have far more financial resources along with political and business connections than you could ever dream to have. We will hunt you down and kill you like I insisted last year."

Timmons rose from her chair and pointed her manicured finger at me. "I'm going to rip out your soul then club you like a baby seal."

"Sit down, Tasha," I said. "You always were a bit of a drama queen. If you could carry out your threat you would have already done so. All of you would. Proving my point that you are all impotent soul stealers and not fit to sit on the High Council."

One of the newly elected members, Curt Urlacher spoke up. "Mr. Novo, your past with us and what has gone on around here has never been explained. I have only served for three months on the Council. I want no part of this war and will offer my allegiance to you if you restore my abilities."

"See how polite this man is, Tasha? You might want to take some charm lessons from Elder Urlacher here." I then looked at

Urlacher. "You will be given a chance at redemption."

I focused my attention back at Elder Polus. "Funny thing about computers and finances these days. You can transfer billions of dollars in mere seconds."

Polus shouted at Mr. Bink. "Shut down all our systems. Hurry!"

I continued. "Sit down, Bink. Let the truth come out. I asked for Mr. Bink's trust a few months ago. Bink asked your former chief financial officer for a couple of transfers of a few million dollars in exchange for a favor from me. For his loyalty to me, Bink was promised a seat on the new Council."

Bink stood up and walked to my side of the table. I continued. "It is a shame however that Mr. Bink could not remain loyal to me. I know he remained loyal to all of you. I can't say that I am surprised since he has been a faithful servant. But since we hacked into Mr. Bink's computer, I read every correspondence between everyone in this room and Mr. Bink.

Bink fell into a chair on my side of the table and cupped his face.

"I know the Council had been made aware that I removed millions of dollars from your account with Mr. Bink's assistance. I have no doubt you thought you were setting me up somehow. Early this morning, I returned the initial amount of money taken from the account. I suggest you use that money to maintain this compound and pay for your living expenses in your last days."

I stood up and proceeded towards the exit. I turned and offered one last fatal strike. "But I did embezzle all the other money and assets. Your former CFO, who is safely on a private jet with his family, was my roommate during my training here. He is one of the few in my life who I never lost contact with, and believes in restoring us to prominence as much as I do. Between what he could do on his own and what my computer hacker did, this morning, we cleaned you out of your cash holdings. We even moved the precious metal you own to another site. And Mr. Brown, hitting on the CFO's wife, nasty business that stuff. Once George's wife told him, he couldn't wait to clean you boys out. Like I stated earlier, live the remainder of your lives in peace."

Timmons and Norman Brown charged at me as I moved closer to the now open exit door. Four armed men charged through and wrestled Timmons and Brown to the ground as they were both screaming vulgarities their mothers wouldn't appreciate.

"Just because you guys didn't arm yourselves, what made you think I would abide by your laws any longer?" I made a mental image of all their faces as I returned to the shadows.

25

*N*ews spread quickly among the disciples. The few soul

stealers, who were ready to join my crusade when we met in the desert, were now calling reaffirming their decision. Some who were in a wait and see mode, waited long enough and were flocking to our side. Panic extended into our small but expansive community. Rumors among our bloodlines, who weren't soul stealers, were racing through the ranks that I had marked them to be shut off from their money and our extended life cycle.

Stock markets plummeted around the globe. Analysts attempted to explain it as a result of this indicator or that indicator, but they didn't know it was caused by what was happening within our private world. Our disciples were leaders in major companies around the world. They had become jittery. Insider information was creating a massive sell off of stocks within companies led by members of our bloodlines. Once the downfall started, I directed our CFO to purchase stocks that were trading below where they were at the beginning of the day. We added a small fortune within a few days in undervalued stocks. I tipped off Iza Tappen, who was happy to pad their wealth by buying stocks at a reduced value, then selling once the stock stabilized a few days later.

An emergency meeting was set for a week later in Geneva among our remaining soul stealers and business leaders. I wanted to assure everyone personally they would be in no danger from me, or anyone else. I directed Iza Tappen to send an email to the entire list of disciples in our bloodlines that we took from Bink's computer. All were invited to attend.

The message outlined that the current Council had been removed and a new one would be elected. Our headquarters would be moving for the first time in over one hundred years due to maintenance issues. The goal of the email was to calm frayed nerves. All other news would be delivered when we met.

Iza Tappen had remotely wiped clean the entire computer system within the compound from wherever it is that Iza resided. Another fee would be added to my bill. I hired a detective agency to watch the compound and report to me who came and went. Many inside never left once. I knew that would be likely, since the older members hadn't left in decades. They had no place else to go. Some of the younger disciples like Timmons were coming and going from the site. I could only imagine the shock and turmoil within the ranks of the former leadership team.

The meeting in Geneva involved close to one hundred of our finest, including all remaining soul stealers. I attempted to squelch thoughts that my takeover was purely for revenge or a power grab. I assured everyone in the audience it was done on the grounds that we must return to our original mission and produce more soul stealers, or our entire race would be extinct within one or two generations. I had statistics to back up my words.

Another announcement was made that a committee would

be assigned to select the new Council members. I would not serve on the committee nor would Kalani. The committee would be free to choose any six members from our ranks who fit the criteria set out in our by-laws. If any in the audience could demonstrate they too had the ability to see into and steal a soul, they would be eligible.

Tasha Timmons attended the meeting. Towards the end of my discourse she expressed, "That man poisoned the Council. He should be tried for treason. Chop off the head of the serpent before he bites again."

"Yes, thank you, Miss Timmons. I see the charm and acting classes are working nicely for you." My few words had the place chuckling but I knew it struck a chord with some. I continued.

"She speaks the truth about being poisoned. I will not deny what I have done. But when I tried to reason with the Council while I was still the leader, attempts were made on my life, and I too was poisoned. Your leaders were dying men when I was elected. Every time I discussed making life easier for our soul stealers by insisting we increase our ranks, I was shut down. We can no longer continue to steal enough souls to keep us all alive for three hundred years. It's mathematically impossible. It's why we are dying a slow but inevitable death."

Timmons rose from her seat again. "And under your leadership before what was done to improve our numbers?"

It was imperative I contained my composure. "Maybe your memory has disappeared with your skills, Miss Timmons. My time as leader was cut short because you and a few others attempted to kill me. However before that, many things were suggested on my part but were voted down every time. Orcus admitted the main goal had become to acquire wealth, not souls."

Tasha lashed out again. She was asked to remain seated or be escorted away by our Sargent in Arms. The meeting concluded with a question and answer session. The group appeared satisfied that I had no intention of hurting anyone more than the former Council members, but there would be major changes. The necessary changes would be discussed in open forums like this one in the future.

After the meeting I searched out Tasha. "Tasha, I made a promise to your brother that I would do all I could to have you meet with him. In case you are not aware, his name is John Corbin and he is a very powerful man. If you meet with him, I will make sure the new Council shows mercy on your soul."

"I don't need your mercy, your pity or your good intentions. You might believe the heavens look upon you as a savior, but you would be mistaken. As far as my brother goes, ask him why he didn't search for me long ago, when I needed him."

"How do you he didn't? I'll let John know you will think about. Take care, Tasha, always my pleasure to see you."

After my love fest with Tasha, I left Geneva with one last score to settle.

When I entered Doc Winfield's building I was in for a big surprise. I didn't know who it was behind the front desk, but it wasn't Nurse Simon. "Hello, my name is Cale Novo, is Nurse Simon around?"

The young lady who couldn't have been out of nursing school for more than a year, looked perplexed. "Nurse Simon? There is no one who works here with that name. My name is Florence Morningale, may I help you?"

Before I could say anything, Winfield spoke from down the hallway. "Florence honey, escort our guest to my office. But don't talk to him."

By the time I walked into his office, Winfield was sitting behind his desk. He looked down his nose at me as I ambled further in to his office. "I gotta admit, cowboy, ya were the last person I was ever expecting ta see round these parts. And don't go talking all sweet with my new assistant. Ya already dun ruined the last one."

"I didn't ruin anyone, Winfield. Where is she anyway? Believe it or not, I didn't come here to see you, I came to see her."

"Yeah, I'm sure ya did, cowboy. Truth be told, that perty filly walked outta here weeks ago and she ain't been back."

I became concerned for her safety. "What happened?"

Winfield slurped from the cup on his desk. I think he did it intentionally. "Maybe ya didn't hear me the first time, El-Dar Novo. I dun told ya, she walked outta here. Broke my heart, thanks ta you. Her and I got inta a few shouting matches cause she took a likin ta ya. Then just when I thought the girl wassa simmering down, my health insurance was cancelled. I sent her off ta that dang government website and she dun threw up her arms and quit. Now, how hard could it be ta sign up fer insurance on a website I ask ya?"

I couldn't believe anyone would have a hard time getting insurance over the internet with all the modern techniques available, but what did I know. "Since I am here, Doc, I will tell you that there will be no repercussions for you trying to poison me. I have used you over the years and I have helped you. Let's leave it at that and know that I won't be back."

"Hell, Novo. I gotta admit I wanted ta poison ya for taking my girl ta that football game and bringing her gifts. But that's not why I changed that formula. I mixed up what ya asked but that Timmons woman can be persuasive. She offered me twice da cash you did. I figured, why not? I git ya outta my life and I git me enough cash ta set up me and my girl forever."

"Timmons? She was here paying you to poison me?"

"Cowboy, git the cow dung from yer ears. I said Timmons, yes. Now why don't ya make good on your promise and not return. If ya do find that old nurse of mine, you tell her from me, she was easily replaced."

"I don't think so, Doc-tour Winfield. You dun traded three fer one. It's been nice knowing ya." I left his office for the last time. I drove straight to Nurse Simon's apartment but no one answered. I called her phone several times with no response. Later that evening, I ventured to the bar I knew Rose frequented, but no luck.

The next morning I went to the library where I had met Isabella. Of the three personalities that lived in this woman's head, Isabella was her true persona. From the documents Nesstor had acquired for me in the past, the woman who I had come to know was Isabella Bernard, who was raised in Maryland, became a school teacher, and her mother and father died from a gas leak in their home right before Isabella found her way to Texas. Her high school photo matched closely to this Isabella.

I eyed her sitting in the children's section, straightening up some books on a lower shelf. I couldn't help but notice how peaceful she looked sitting on a small round seat with wheels and her smile as wide as the Rio Grande. I stood there for several minutes before she noticed me.

"Oh, hello. I'm so sorry, I didn't see you. May I help you select a book? Are you looking for something? For your child possibly?"

"No. I came to see you. We met several months ago and I told you that I would occasionally stop in and say hello. Do you remember me? My name is Cale."

She stood up from her seat and inched closer. She studied my face. She frowned. Then a small smile creased her lips. "I do know you from somewhere, yes. Let me think. Your face seems familiar."

Isabella continued to stare at me. She tilted her head a few times. With a saccharin voice she said, "Now I remember you. You were new to the area and wanted to learn about the classics. That was a long time ago, Cale. But I never forget a thing. I am excellent at putting names and faces together."

"That's right. I did inquire about the classics. How have you been? Are you doing well here?"

"Oh yes, in fact, I must have finally impressed my boss, because he hired me full time. I started two weeks ago. Don't tell anyone, but I volunteered last weekend too. I love it here so much." She giggled. "My boss said it was ok, but not to make it a habit. Do I need to have my head examined or what?"

I could only think of how profound her statement was, but I

let the comment stand. She told me she was about to go on lunch break and we could speak more on the bench outside. Once outside, she continued. "Speaking of classics, it's the strangest thing. One morning a couple of weeks ago, when I woke up, there was this tired looking book on my night stand. I had no idea where it came from. I checked to make sure I hadn't removed it from the library and forgot, but nope."

"What did it look like? Did you read any of it?"

She offered me half her sandwich but I graciously declined. She took a bite and kept talking. "Oh, I was cautious with it. The book musta been printed hundreds of years ago. It had a leather cover outside and all the pages were yellow and crinkly. The strangest part was it said it was printed on the Gutenberg Press. Now that would be remarkable if true, don't you think, Cale?

"Did you read any of the book, Isabella?"

"How could I resist? It took me three longs days, but I did finish it. Someone read it before me too. It had little sticky notes on certain pages. The story was about these one hundred people who take souls from others who don't appreciate their lives. Can you imagine such a thing?"

"That is something, isn't it?" I said.

"I don't think it was meant as fiction. I do believe it was written as some sort of history book."

"I sure would love to see that book. I would bet it's a real classic read." I said.

Isabella looked concerned. "I can't do that. But I did take good notes if you want to read those. I'm kicking around the idea of writing a novel. I'm gonna write about the soul people. They look like you and me but they remove souls from bad people. It's gonna be set in modern day. I'm gonna have this guy who is always fighting with his board of directors. He's gonna think he has to save his people from extinction or something. There will be some crazy doctor and there has to be heroine, don't you think? I'm still outlining it. I'm going to call the first one Soul Intentions. If I try hard enough, I might get three books from it."

The veins in my neck popped. Wait, wait. The book, where is it now?"

"Oh, Cale, I have no right to own such a tome. It belongs in a museum. That's why I sent it off to the Smithsonian. But don't worry, I'll make sure you get a signed copy when I finish my story."

I didn't know what to do. Maybe she was right. Maybe the safest place for it was buried in the archives of a museum. I had to remind myself that I was the new and improved Caeles Novo. The one who was at peace with himself.

"I have to be on my way, Isabella. But before I go, I was looking for an old friend of mine, Taylor Simon. I had promised her that if Dylan James and the Overture ever performed again, I would get her a ticket and introduce her to Dylan. Since I can't find Taylor, I would like to know if you want the ticket. It's for a cruise, not a typical concert. It's all expenses paid, if you would like to go."

She put her sandwich down and placed both of her hands over mine in my lap. "Oh, that's so sweet of you. But won't Taylor be upset?"

"Something tells me she would be happier if you took the ticket."

"I would love to go. I haven't been on a vacation in years. Are you going too? I think I remember Dylan James from when I was a little girl. He wrote a beautiful song that my mom loved to sing. My mom said he wrote it about his daughter and that's why she would sing it to me."

"Yes, I'm planning on going as well, so I do hope you can make it. I might visit with you again before the cruise to see how your writing is going. But I have to go now. You take good care of yourself."

"I know it's all in my head, Cale, but for some reason I feel like I have a guardian angel who lives with me. So between you and my angel, I have two who watch over me."

I stood up and took three paces when from behind me I could hear, "Thanks again for the ticket, sugar. I didn't need to turn back to know who was speaking. I smiled wide and returned to the shadows.

26

*C*onstruction in the desert was in full throttle. The budget was increased to step up the completion date. Government officials were paid off to ensure the project didn't suffer any setbacks. The new administration building was first to be completed. A row of four townhomes were next. My grandfather, James Spia and Kalani's grandfather, Jair Rex relocated from the old compound to the desert area.

I selected those two men to oversee the selection process of a new High Council as well as the committee to review our by-laws. Since both men were former Council members, many welcomed the idea for continuity purposes. Some disciples grumbled that the two were chosen to rubber stamp my decisions. The ones who did complain weren't aware of all the times I had been lied to by both men, and all the times both had fought my suggestions when I too was on the Council. In my opinion, it was a fair trade off for both sides to have these men oversee the process.

I visited the construction site a few times a month. I didn't want to give the impression I was being heavy handed in hanging around too often. Much of my time was spent at home with Kalani and Nic. Since the computer system had been erased at the old compound, for over a month, no assignments were being handed out. All soul stealers were given some time away.

The logistics of setting up the new network and restoring the data was done by three disciples trained in computer science from top universities. A deal was struck with them, that if they did a good job, they wouldn't have to steal souls. Their jobs would be to take over for Mr. Bink and run our Information and Technology Department. Iza Tappen hacked into their network soon after it was running. Trust yet verify. I had heard that somewhere and thought it was good advice.

Several meetings were held with many of our disciples who chose to attend. Incentives were being put in place to encourage others with ability to remove souls, to become a trained soul stealer. New tax structures were being put in place for those who still refused, yet wanted to share in our strength from removing souls. I sat in on many of the meetings but allowed others to lead the groups. Former Council member Curt Urlacher attended the meetings. His abilities had not been restored, but it was under consideration. No one else from the former leadership group attended. With my vision in place of returning soul stealing as our priority, as well as considerations being given for souls seeking redemption, being cited throughout the new committees, I returned home.

Kalani had been shopping for our upcoming cruise. I wasn't sure how manufacturers could charge so much for clothing that used so little fabric. But it made her happy and she still looked beautiful. She also reminded me while prancing around in her new outfits that her biological clock was ticking. Time was running short on having another child, something we both wanted. Her attention grabbing parade of outfits didn't go to waste.

The following day after doing some long overdue yard work, I sat down to watch television. Before I could flip the channel I heard, "Good evening from Washington, I am Carlin Masterson and we are going to talk crazy. Let me begin our program this evening with the scandal that is rocking our nation. It has come to our attention here at NUTS that a senator from North Carolina did not properly footnote a speech he gave to a local chamber of commerce. Can you imagine our horror when this was discovered?"

Carlin turned to another camera angle and continued. "Let me bring in a regular member of NUTS, Devin Melvin from Mamma Smith's Tribune. Devin, can you think of a bigger scandal than a politician not properly footnoting their speech?"

The camera flipped to Mr. Melvin. His mouth was agape. His eyes were the size of overstuffed meatballs. There was silence from Mr. Melvin. Masterson eventually filled in the dead space. "Talk crazy with me, Devin. Is there a bigger story than a tea drinking, plagiarizing senator?"

Melvin's mouth began to move. "That is no doubt crazy, Carlin. But I was informed we were to talk about the Vice President of the United States resigning today over allegations of ties with organized crime."

Masterson frowned right into the camera. "Now you are talking crazy, Devin. The Vice President has never been suspected of being a tea drinker. I am sure he had good reasons for associating with people who are only suspected of being involved with organized crime. The man is brilliant. He's a true believer in the cause. Let's roll the tape in slow motion of Senator Paulsen allowing what we suspect are words not written by him to roll off his tongue. Shall we? This is scandalous!"

All I could wonder about was if news organizations could correlate their credibility with their sagging ratings. I dialed up Nesstor to get the real story about the Vice President.

"Elliot, sorry I have not been around to see you lately, but I have been busy setting up shop. How is the rehab going?"

"Hey, Soul Man, it is going fine. But I know you didn't call for that. Yes, it is true about what is being reported about Vice President Giocare. I received a tip from an old buddy of mine back from my Chicago detective days that the Vice President has been collecting bribes and delivering on payoffs since he was in city government in Chicago. The mob has been in his back pocket for a long time. I've told people for years now never to allow a politician to rise from the communities of Chicago and make it to the national stage."

"So the guy gets to resign, that's it?"

I had the feeling Nesstor wanted to say more. He remained silent for several seconds before responding. "The Vice President's dealings were all connected with the case I was working on before I was shot. I was even close to making the connection to your McAdams case. I now suspect it was supposed to look like the President was setting up McAdams and the Vice President was behind it all. Plus several women were being paid off to pretend the President had kids all over the country. All this was an effort to disgrace Morrison and stick Giocare in the White House."

"Again, if this is all true, the guy can walk away, Elliot? I don't get it."

"I didn't know who I could trust with such a wild accusation. I took it directly to the Attorney General's office. The next day, a guy shows up telling me he speaks for the President. He asked me to stop investigating the case. He told me that our nation shouldn't wave our dirty laundry in the wind. Hours later my retirement papers show up for me to sign."

"So no one is ever going to know the truth?"

I could hear Nesstor laughing. "Well, a few of my notes found their way to that reporter Simpson's hands. The Vice President has resigned and I suspect more heads will roll soon. I have one more week before I'm officially signed off by my doctor. Me and the Mrs. are heading to Florida. I can sleep comfortably, Soul Man. Let this one go."

This time I was the one laughing. "You know me far better than to think I can let all this go, Special Agent Nesstor. You did your thing, one day I'll do mine. Oh, one more thing my dear friend. For a man who spent his entire career dealing with criminals, you would think you would be smarter about hiding your money."

"What are you talking about?"

"Over the last few months, I have been meeting with our top disciples from around the world. As you know, I have connections everywhere. There is a bank account in Switzerland that has deposits made to it exactly on the same days I make payments to Iza Tappen, and for the same amounts. Care to explain?"

The other end of the phone remained silent, so I continued.

"There are two signers on the account, one is you and the other is your daughter. The same daughter that has a Master's degree in computer science. Your secret and hers is safe with me, Elliot. I am the only one who knows the connection. But I started to suspect something after you were shot and Iza took extra special interest in your condition."

"Can you tell if I'm lying over the telephone? If so, I deny everything." I could hear the smile in his voice.

"I paid for services rendered and have no desire to stop paying or employing Iza. She does a great job. However, next time I see you, dinner is on you. I don't want to hear another word about how hard it is to live on a government pension, ever again. And whatever you do, Elliot, don't pay cash for your new home in Florida."

"Every last dime of that money is hers. My name is only there for emergency purposes."

"Dinner is still on you. And I don't want some early bird special either. I want the real deal." We joked back and forth for a while longer before I said my good byes to Elliot.

Kalani and I left later that day for a brief stop in Las Vegas. I wanted to make sure the elections for the new Council were still on schedule for the following week as well as receive a firsthand view of the construction. The committee had restored returning souls worthy of redemption to our by-laws. Major changes were in place to ensure others strong enough, and with the ability to remove souls, would do so, or be subject to a harsh tax. If they chose neither, they would no longer share in our strength from removing and returning souls.

Dr. Pickering, whose identity would remain with me until the new Council was in place, had converted the chemical compound that controlled who we shared our strength with, into pill form. We would distribute the pills to our disciples who remained loyal to our cause. It was seen as punishment from some, but to us who worked tirelessly to keep our disciples from becoming extinct, we knew it was a necessary evil.

With assignments to remove souls again being handed out, and our new computer systems running smoothly, I felt confident to leave for two weeks for a side trip to Jamaica. I looked forward to setting sail on the cruise I had promised my wife.

There were two books that told our history. One was in my possession. Assuming Isabella was telling me the truth, the other was stashed away in the bowels of the Smithsonian Institute. My copy had for several generations been guarded by my old friend Doc Duvaliar's family in Jamaica. That is how I came across it. A message was sent to my home telling me where the book was hidden. To this day, I have no idea who sent the message. Some mysteries are never known.

After two days in Vegas, Kalani and I flew off to Jamaica. She was on assignment to remove the soul from a world leader who insisted the world needed to destroy the cow population because they were emitting too much methane gas after eating grass. Even if true, he made our list because sometimes you can't fix stupid.

After landing, I headed over to the office of the Custos Rotulorum, or keeper of the roles. I returned our history book from where it sat for decades for safekeeping. The man in the tiny building told me that he knew one day it would return. This time however, it had several pages of notes added to it. My story.

After dropping off the book and feeling relieved for doing so, I had one last person to see before boarding the cruise ship now in harbor. The cruise had started in Miami but Kalani and I wanted to finish our business before enjoying the remainder of the cruise.

I wanted to visit with Otis Buffet and see if he spent the money I'd given him as promised. I drove along the coast, to the last place I dropped off Otis. I entered the small town. With still with little more than a dozen wood framed buildings hugging the dirt road, I noticed a new building. There stood my old friend.

"Otis, my man. So good to see you again."

"Mista Cale, I'ze been expecting ya. How do ya like my new preaching place?"

"I am proud of you. You used the money for what it was intended."

Otis kicked pebbles in the road. "I did git me a new color screen and hooked it up to da satellite television company. Even a preacher man like myself needs ta stay in touch with da world, ya know."

I couldn't help but share a laugh with him. He showed me around the A-framed church that would seat fifty in the congregation. He invited me to stay overnight and hear his sermon the next day, but as the ship would be leaving port early the next morning, I couldn't.

"Mista Cale, thank you fer believings I was a spiritual man. And the people round here thanks you too."

"You forget. Your soul told me that you were a good man. I'll return one day to hear you preach. I promise."

Kalani contacted me to let me know she was safely on board the cruise liner after taking the soul of the cow hater. I said my goodbyes to Otis and a few of the locals who wandered by during my visit. I had to get back to Kingston and return my rental car before the ship set sail. As I drove along the back country of the island nation, I again reflected upon all that I had accomplished over the past year. But now it was time to get on the ship and enjoy some time with family and friends.

Seconds after arriving to my room, I thought maybe I should have taken a longer route to get to the ship. Kalani was in my ear. "Can you please explain why some beautiful woman wearing next to nothing knocked on our cabin door looking for some sugar?"

My dilemma didn't improve with my response. "Dylan's not the only one with groupies onboard, you know."

"That's all you have to tell me?" She asked.

"What is it you want me to say? Oh yes, I invited my mistress on board knowing my wife was only a few feet away? In all the years we've been married, never once have I broken our vows. Go ahead, look into my soul. Do it. You can see whether I'm telling you the truth."

"I don't like secrets, Cale. Who the hell is that woman?"

"I'm not real fond of secrets either. Let's not forget I've never pressed on you how your old drug dealing neighbor back in Hawaii had his soul returned after I took it. It had to be you. You admitted to working for the guy, and he claims you were his lover. So if you want to talk about secrets, let's come clean. Since I don't know, I'll guess that was Winfield's old nurse, Taylor Simon. I have told you all about her, so your guess is as good as mine what persona she was when she came to the door."

Kalani's stare was menacing. Her tone filled with anger. "You wanna know the truth, fine. I worked for Kopono so that he would stay away from my cousin Aleka. When she was young and stupid, she hooked up with the wrong crowd. I asked Kopono to leave her alone and keep her away from dealing drugs. My payback was taking a few souls from his competitors. Aleka was so upset when you stole Kopono's soul. She returned his soul because she never stopped loving him. We kept the secret from you that she could return souls, so that you didn't make her do it all the time. She wanted to retire from working for the Council."

Kalani was telling the truth. I felt bad, but then again she attacked me the moment I walked through the door. So much for a romantic evening with my wife. But she wasn't done with her explanation.

"And as far as that scumbag being my lover, stop being a jealous idiot. He knew your soft spot was me. Kopono was a trained cop and a low life drug dealing killer. Do you think you're the only one on earth who can read people and find their weakness?"

The new and improved Cale was reverting back to the old Cale and ready to lose his temper. I left the room and made my way to the Sanctuary area on the sun deck. I didn't see another soul. The sky was filled with stars. I filled my lungs with salt air and closed my eyes. I leaned along the edge of the ship. One more deep breath followed as my body was once again calm. Then it happened. A cold sharp blade was pressed against my throat.

"Did you think you could destroy me when I reached the pinnacle, Novo? Sure the old men have no fight left in them. But I am neither old nor a man. So now, it is time for you to die."

Many have claimed their life passes in front of them when they think they are about to die. My only thought was dying knowing my wife was upset with me. I was at peace with everything else. I could feel Timmons tighten her grip around my chest and feel her alter the angle of the knife for a quick clean cut. Then a whoosh sound, a thud, and a body dropped to the deck.

I was trembling and afraid to turn around. I could feel a trickle of blood run across my neck. Then the confident voice of an old friend was heard.

"Rose never did like that bitch. Rose told you she would take care of things."

I turned to watch Rose drop a fire extinguisher from her grip and maneuver the limp body of Tasha Timmons to the top of the guard railing. I wanted to stop her. I knew what Rose was doing was wrong. But I have always been a human being before anything else, with few exceptions. The human emotions wanted Timmons out of my life for good. Moments later, she was. Rose tossed the knife overboard as well. We embraced. I gave her a kiss on the cheek.

Rose whispered in my ear. "Go back to that sassy wife of yours now, sugar. I don't think she likes Rose much." She ran her tongue along the blood that curved around my neck then gently bit the lower lobe of my ear. She pinched my backside. "Run along. Rose is done with you."

I searched the ship for the medical staff. I wanted to clean up any blood and if needed, find a band aid. The ship's nurse applied some mediated goo to ward off any infection and stuck on a band aid. She played twenty questions with me about how the wound happened, but I did my best to pretend I cut myself shaving.

I went back to the scene of the crime to make sure no one was the wiser. A lone person was standing on the spot where Timmons had gone overboard. I eased up next to her.

"It's a beautiful evening, isn't it, Cale?"

"Yes, it is. How are you?"

"I couldn't be better, thank you."

We stood breathing in the fresh salt air and gazing at the stars. I reflected on how many people had come and gone from my life, yet when I needed them, only a scant few good friends reappeared. I realized I should never take a true friend for granted, because even the deranged ones meant well.

I felt like the person standing next to me was a much better friend to me than I was to her. It was a huge failure on my part. I knew deep down I needed to get this person into a mental hospital. But I also knew it would kill her. It also crossed my mind that I had so few people who watched over me, one less might cut the number in half. I was torn apart over what was the right thing to do. I decided to look for the North Star and pray that Isabella would go back to Texas and find the same peace in her mind that I had in my heart for her. I felt I owed her that chance.

Isabella sighed. "After you left the library, I thought for hours about why a near stranger would offer me a free ticket for a cruise? That thought bothered me, Cale. Then I realized that maybe some people are meant to be together. I can't explain it, but in my mind I know we have met many times. Maybe we have traveled through time together? I really don't know. All I do know is that you and I have shared many good times and a few not so good."

I took her hand. "That's a beautiful thought, Isabella, and one I share. I am one who has always believed that sadness and euphoria are intertwined within the fabrics of our lives. Maybe we represent both emotions to one another. Maybe that's how we are joined in the universe."

Again she sighed. "That's pretty deep. But I was thinking you entered my life because you were supposed to help me finish my book. All that philosophical crap hurts my head." We smirked at each other. "I'm serious. If you were trying to write a book about a group of humans with a mission of robbing souls, how would you start it?" she asked.

I gave it a thought and said, "Scientists have done studies on what comprises a human body. They can account for over ninety-nine percent, but never one hundred. The part they can't find is the most important part, your soul. Take special care of the part few can see, touch or smell. If you don't, the few who can will steal it, and not feel guilty for doing so."

She giggled. "I'll think about it. But let's face it, you don't know crapola about stealing souls. At least I read a book on the subject. I'm going back to my room now, Cale. I want to be well rested for the show tomorrow with Dylan James and the band."

"There might be much more I need to learn about removing souls, but trust in this. You have an innocent soul, Isabella. I can see it. Good night."

She walked a few feet then turned around. "Rose is not

always so innocent, sugar. But she knows a fortunate soul when she sees one."

I went back to my cabin. Kalani was sitting on the side of the bed, sobbing. "I'm so sorry. You're right. Over all the years, never once have you ever questioned me about my work or my loyalty to you. I had no right to question yours. Will you forgive me? Besides, you know us pregnant women have raging hormones."

The new and improved Cale returned. "My beautiful wife, if there was ever a truth in this world, it is that you are the only woman I have ever loved. Wait, hold on. You're pregnant?"

"Yes, Cale. Seems you finished your honey-do list while we were home in California."

We spent the evening together enjoying a nice meal and a walk around the deck before being stopped by a cruise official. "We have reports that someone possibly fell overboard earlier. Did either of you see or hear anything?"

"No, sir. We were in our room before having dinner in the dining area. We just came out here," I said.

The officer thanked us and walked away. Kalani gave me a stare. "Why didn't you tell that man the truth?"

"Some secrets are better left at the bottom of the sea. Please don't ask me about my business."

I could tell she didn't like my answer by her wicked stare, but it was the only one she was going to get. We strolled along the deck a few more times before heading back to our cabin for a long rest.

The following afternoon, the main deck was filled with anticipation for what was being billed as the final performance of Dylan James and the Overture. I spoke with Dylan a couple of hours before he was due to perform. This wasn't a man ready to give his final performance, but the suggestion this would be their last concert did sell out all the tickets for the cruise.

As Kalani and I made our way to the performance area, she asked, "Why won't you return your grandfather's calls? He's calling and leaving me messages now. You do realize they voted on the new Council yesterday, right? You don't want to know if you are on the Council or not?"

"There will be plenty of time for that later. Let's enjoy the show."

As the band played on, I knew I had come full circle. Dylan was the first soul I had offered redemption and he took advantage of his opportunity. There was a new High Council in place. One that understood you can find a balance between work and family, plus restore the number of soul stealers. A Council willing to offer souls a second chance. The cast of characters I had met over the decades, raced through my mind as quickly as the songs being played on stage.

Now, as the performance winds down, and the audience is at a fever pitch, there can be only one encore. For me, there is little doubt, it will be a beautiful song.

Thank you to everyone who have taken the time to read my work. Every time I complete a project, I assume it will be the last one. But never say never.

The cast of characters who have survived past this book may one day force themselves into another story. However, for now, they are retired.

There is a new story kicking around in my head as this one ends. God willing, the new book will be out late in 2014 or early 2015. Until then, thank you for your kind and at times not so kind comments. It only inspires me to improve with each release. So please, do keep those reviews coming. You can leave your comments on my Goodreads, Amazon or Smashwords pages. If you prefer, drop me a line on Facebook or my web site. I respond to each one.

May you stop and see the beauty around you from time to time in order to keep Caeles Novo and his group of soul stealers from finding you.

Michael Cantwell, CCIM

ABOUT THE AUTHOR

Michael Cantwell, CCIM (1958-present) is an author and commercial real estate agent in Florida as well as a published photographer. He was born in Ft. Campbell KY, raised in Trenton, NJ. He attended Notre Dame High School and LaSalle University.

He now resides in Palm Beach County, Florida. He is married with three children and one dog. He loves music and is a Miami Marlins, Dolphins, Panthers and Heat fan. He also enjoys strolling Florida with his camera. He has served on many board of directors and volunteered many hours as a coach for baseball and basketball as well as for Junior Achievement in many schools around South Florida.

www.ksmmike.com

www.ingramcontent.com/pod-product-compliance
Lightning Source LLC
Chambersburg PA
CBHW070215260626
47160CB00002B/565